RETURN TO ME

RETURN TO ME

Julia Templeton

HEAT | NEW YORK

THE BERKLEY PUBLISHING GROUP
Published by the Penguin Group
Penguin Group (USA) Inc.
375 Hudson Street, New York, New York 10014, USA
Penguin Group (Canada), 90 Eglinton Avenue East, Suite 700, Toronto, Ontario M4P 2Y3, Canada
(a division of Pearson Penguin Canada Inc.)
Penguin Books Ltd., 80 Strand, London WC2R 0RL, England
Penguin Group Ireland, 25 St. Stephen's Green, Dublin 2, Ireland (a division of Penguin Books Ltd.)
Penguin Group (Australia), 250 Camberwell Road, Camberwell, Victoria 3124, Australia
(a division of Pearson Australia Group Pty. Ltd.)
Penguin Books India Pvt. Ltd., 11 Community Centre, Panchsheel Park, New Delhi—110 017, India
Penguin Group (NZ), 67 Apollo Drive, Rosedale, North Shore 0745, Auckland, New Zealand
(a division of Pearson New Zealand Ltd.)
Penguin Books (South Africa) (Pty.) Ltd., 24 Sturdee Avenue, Rosebank, Johannesburg 2196, South Africa

Penguin Books Ltd., Registered Offices: 80 Strand, London WC2R 0RL, England

This is an original publication of The Berkley Publishing Group.

Cover photo by Lisa Spindler Photography Inc./Veer.
Cover design by Lesley Worrell.

First edition: August 2007

Library of Congress Cataloging-in-Publication Data

Templeton, Julia.
Return to me / Julia Templeton.—1st ed.
p. cm.
"Heat trade paperback"—T.p. verso.
ISBN 978-0-425-21541-8 (pbk.)
I. Title.
PS3620.E467R48 2007
813'.6—dc22
2007013912

PRINTED IN THE UNITED STATES OF AMERICA

10 9 8 7 6 5 4 3 2 1

To Tracy Cooper-Posey, friend and mentor. You're an amazing writer and a wonderful friend. Thanks for all your support over the years!

ONE

The Battle of Bannockburn
June 24, 1314

Lying on the rain-soaked battlefield, Darius MacLeod looked up at the tall young man staring down at him with piercing green eyes. Dear God, was this the Angel of Death he'd heard folktales about as a lad? For some reason Darius had never imagined an angel to look so—human—or so finely dressed in expensive clothing.

"Who are ye?" Darius asked, the words coming out a ragged whisper, and with great effort as every inch of his body vibrated with pain.

The tall blond smiled softly, flashing straight white teeth, two of which were more prominent than the rest. Going down on his haunches, the man brushed the hair back from Darius's face with a gentle hand. "Fear not, my friend, I mean you no harm."

Uneasiness worked its way up Darius's spine as he stared at the man's face, noticing strange, faint purple lines that looked like tiny veins. His skin seemed oddly pale, and his green eyes seemed to glow from within.

The frozen ground enveloped Darius, piercing into his bones, making him shiver. Even his teeth chattered, and he could do nothing to stop it. Death had its hold on him.

"Are you in great pain?" the man asked, looking down at Darius's belly and the deep wound that would send him to an early grave.

"I can no longer feel my legs." Darius had been injured many times throughout the years, and had the scars to prove it. Such wounds could not be avoided in turbulent times of war, but he'd never before received such a punishing blow, and in such a deceitful way. The English solider had played dead, lying still among his fallen comrades—that is until Darius had walked past, on his way to camp to celebrate their victory.

The English soldier's blade sank into his belly, and Darius retaliated, slitting the man's throat.

Aye, he would die this night. Overwhelming sadness filled him, and he closed his eyes for a moment, remembering his beloved's face. Rose, with her long golden hair and beautiful green eyes. How delicate her features: so fragile, like the rest of her. Five months pregnant with their first child, she would have to raise the babe without him. Tears burned his eyes as he silently wept for the son or daughter he would never know. For the years he would never experience with the woman he loved more than life itself.

"Darius, my name is Remont," the man said, his thumb brushing along Darius's jaw. "I am a friend of your brother's."

Darius opened his eyes, trying hard to focus. "Where is he?"

The blond smiled reassuringly. "He is coming as we speak."

Thank God his brother lived.

"Listen to me, Darius. I can help you."

"Remont, no man can save me. My fate is sealed."

A deadly chill rushed along Darius's spine, and he clamped his teeth together as pain sliced through him. He was moments from death, could feel the life leaving him and the blood seeping from his body into the ground. "I do not want to die, Remont," he said, his eyelids growing heavier by the second.

"Darius, I can help you. I can save you."

"No man has the power to spare my life, Remont. Only God can choose my fate."

"I speak of another life, Darius. A life where you will never die. A life where you can stay as you are now—young, strong, and beautiful. Just think . . . you will never age and you will never die."

Darius would have laughed had he the strength. "Ye have the power to do this? To make me immortal?"

"Yes, I do."

"If only it were true. I would give anything to see the birth of my child and to hold my wife in my arms again."

"Darius, I can end your pain. A single word is all I need," Remont urged, his voice soft. "Say yes."

"Darius!"

Demetri appeared beyond Remont's shoulder, his gaze moving from Darius's to the wound. His stricken expression said more than words ever could.

Darius forced a smile, noting the blood that stained his brother's hands and arms. "Are ye hurt?"

"Nay. Who did this?"

Darius nodded to the Englishman who lay nearby, in the same place he had fallen. "Dead, just as I will soon be. Our parents are calling me home, brother."

A nerve in Demetri's jaw flinched. "Do not say that. Ye shall live."

Darius knew his twin better than he knew himself, and Demetri never gave up or accepted *no* for an answer. "Trust Remont, brother. He will help ye."

Demetri sat on the ground, resting Darius's head on his lap. Darius looked up at the familiar face and noticed something odd about his brother. Something he had noted about Remont's appearance. They both shared the same pale complexion, and, even more, his brother's eyes were odd, more brilliant than he recalled. "Let me die in peace, Demetri."

"I will not let ye die," Demetri said firmly, his pale face full of fury and fear. Darius and Demetri had never been apart in all their thirty years. Though Darius was younger than his brother by a few minutes, he had always taken on the paternal role to his more adventurous and daring twin brother. It had been that way since they'd lost their parents a decade before.

"Listen to me, brother. I'm dying," Darius said firmly. "Take care of Rose and the babe. Promise me this."

"Remont, change him." Demetri's voice held an edge Darius had never before heard.

And what in God's name did he mean *change him*?

Tears brimmed in his brother's fierce blue eyes. "Do not leave me, Darius. We have worked too hard and too long to see our country free from tyranny. Ye shall live to savor the freedom—"

"Tell Rose I love her." Darius winced as pain wracked his entire body. "Tell her to make a good life for our child."

"Ye will not die. I will not allow it." Demetri looked at Remont. "Do it now!"

Remont's brows furrowed. "I have not heard his consent."

"Ye have my consent," Demetri said through gritted teeth.

Remont nodded. "As you wish."

Darius felt his heart slowing, and his other organs followed suit. His vision dimmed, and Demetri and Remont blurred as a bright light filled his vision.

Demetri's voice faded as well, and a loud humming began to intensify. Oddly enough, a sense of peace washed over him, followed by images of his life—scene after scene, like pages in a book. He saw himself as he came from his mother's body, as an infant suckling at her breast, and as a toddler playing with his brother. On and on the visions flashed through all the stages of his life. He smiled as he relived the moment he first met Rose, the rush of excitement he'd felt the first time they kissed, the softness of her lips—

The memories faded as smooth lips touched his neck. He tried to open his eyes, but the lids were so heavy. A sudden, sharp pain made him curse. He had no strength to push his attacker off, and seconds later the desire to do so fled as strange sensations rushed through his body. The intense cold left Darius, replaced by liquid fire which coursed through his veins, starting at the top of his head and rushing to his feet.

"It is done," Remont said, sounding pleased.

"Thank ye, my friend," Demetri replied, his hand resting on Darius's forehead. "I shall never forget what ye have done for me this day."

A gentle hand smoothed the hair back from Darius's forehead. "Wake up, brother. Wake up."

Darius struggled to open his eyes. He tried to move, but even that small effort made him wince.

"Aye, ye shall be sore for a few days, but soon ye will be good as new. In fact, ye shall be better than new."

"Better than new?" he repeated, opening his eyes, squinting while trying to block the light from the candle his brother held.

"Sorry," Demetri said, blowing the light out and setting it aside.

Strangely, he could still see in the dark room, despite the fact that the only light had been extinguished. Why had a candle hurt his eyes so much? And where was he now?

"Ye have been sleeping for some time now," Demetri said, his voice soft. He looked tired, the dark circles beneath his eyes nearly purple.

"Apparently ye have not been. Ye look like hell, brother."

Demetri's lips curved. "I see ye still have a sense of humor."

"Why should I not? I have beat death."

He could not believe it was so. He had been so certain that death would claim him. Never had he seen someone live after such a substantial wound.

Yet he lived to tell the tale. And tell it he would. Indeed, he could scarcely wait to get home, to hold Rose in his arms, tell her how much he loved her.

A log popped, crackled. He glanced past his brother to the fire. "Why is that so loud?"

Indeed, it seemed like he could hear everything. The smallest of things, too. Dear God, was that servants speaking out in the hallway?

He could not make out every word, but he could most assuredly hear them.

"Where are we?" he asked, looking around the unfamiliar room filled with beautiful, elegant items. There was nothing familiar about this place, from its fine furnishings to the large tapestries hanging on the recently painted walls. The bed he rested in had been hand carved. A true piece of art in itself.

"Remont's home."

"Remont has a home in the highlands?"

"Yes, he lives close by."

Darius sat up, shocked that his wound did not pain him too much. Indeed, he could not even feel where the Englishman's blade had cut him.

Lifting the covers, he could not believe his eyes. "There is no wound." He pressed his hand against his pelvis, in the same place the deep gash had been. "Impossible."

He looked up at Demetri. "How can that be?"

Demetri smiled. "Ye are no longer human, Darius. Ye are like me. Like Remont."

Darius looked at his brother for a long moment, half expecting him to laugh, to tell him he jested, but he did neither.

"Then what am I, Demetri, if not human?"

Before his twin could respond Darius caught a movement in the far corner of the room. "It is me, Darius. Remont."

The blond-haired man stood from a chair in the corner, a kind smile on his handsome face. "How do you feel, Darius?" he asked, his voice hinting at an unfamiliar accent.

"I am well, although how, I do not know," Darius said, glancing at Demetri and then back to Remont.

Demetri put a hand on Darius's shoulder. "Ye are different, brother." He took a deep breath, released it. "Ye are now a vampire."

"A vampire?" Darius repeated, unable to keep the sarcasm from his voice. "There are no such things as vampires, Demetri. Vampires are creatures from folktales that are told to entertain and nothing else. Such creatures do not exist."

Remont folded his hands together, and Darius noted his slender fingers again and the long nails. "Ye are a vampire, Darius. As am I." He nodded to Demetri. "And your brother as well."

Darius's stomach clenched in a tight knot, reminding him of the wound that had been there when he lay dying on the fields at Bannockburn. He had died in his human life. He had. He'd received a death blow. He'd felt the blood leave his body.

"Soon you will be able to accept your new life," Remont said, placing a cool hand on Darius's shoulder.

A myriad of emotions rushed through Darius at Remont's touch, many that disturbed him.

Darius brushed Remont's hand away. "Ye say I am different, but I feel the same as I did before. How is it possible?"

"You died to your human life, Darius. You have the same body, but that is all that remains from that life. Your body now will never change, and you will experience things no human can."

"Never change?"

"That is right. You will never grow old, Darius. You will never age. Not even by a day." Remont's gaze slid from his, to his chest and even lower. "You will always be young and beautiful."

"What if I no longer wish to have this life? What if I wish to die?"

Remont looked down for a moment, but not before Darius could see the disappointment in his green eyes. When he glanced up again, all traces of disappointment were gone. "You will learn to embrace your new life. I did. Your brother did as well."

"Ye truly are a vampire as well?"

Demetri nodded.

And now the reasons behind his brother's recent changes came to light.

Remont placed a hand over Darius's. "Your brother and I will help you. Do not fear, soon the noises you hear will not be so loud. Your sight will also be much improved, and again, you will learn to adjust." His thumb brushed along Darius's in a soothing gesture.

Darius's first instinct was to pull away from the intimate caress, but he found he could not.

"There are things you must do in order to survive." Remont lifted his right arm, rolled up his sleeve, and proceeded to bite himself, breaking the skin with his sharp incisors.

"What are ye doing?" Darius asked, smelling Remont's blood, the scent like that of the sweetest perfume. His mouth watered and an unimaginable hunger made his stomach tighten.

Remont sat down on the bed beside Darius and extended his arm.

Darius looked from his brother, who nodded in encouragement, to the blond vampire before him. He *had* become this creature they spoke about. A mythical being that lived forever. The blood scent filled his nostrils and he nearly groaned as he reached for Remont's arm and brought it to his lips to drink.

The instant the blood touched his tongue Darius moaned in ecstasy, the taste exquisite. He closed his eyes, and exhilaration rushed through his veins, into every cell of his body.

Darius took his seat across the dinner table from Rose.

He had been home now for nearly a fortnight and the excitement of his miraculous recovery had dimmed with each day that passed.

Clan members dropped by to wish him well, and extended invitations to join them for dinner or just to visit. Darius always declined, preferring to stay home, except when he had to feed.

After all, he was no longer one of them. No longer human, but rather a beast that required blood to survive.

How horrified his parents would be to learn that both their sons had become creatures of the night.

Voices from the kitchen caught his attention. The servants were talking about him again. They feared him, and even now they argued amongst themselves about who would serve him dinner. Hearing the smallest of sounds from anywhere in the house had nearly driven Darius insane at first, but Remont had told him how to tune those background noises out.

"Did ye sleep well?" Rose asked, forcing a smile.

"I did, and ye?"

"Very well, thank ye," she said, her gaze shifting to the servant who stoked the fire.

The joy his wife had expressed when he'd come home just days after she learned he'd been wounded had soon turned to confusion and suspicion. Evening visits from his brother and Remont had only added to her concerns, especially since they left late at night to feed and returned shortly before dawn.

If only he had died on the battlefield before Remont had found him. Instead he had become a stranger to everyone he had known, save Demetri. A monster who would never again be the same.

Two servants entered and set plates of steaming duck and vegetables before them. The smell alone made Darius nearly gag, but he forced himself to eat. Rose picked at her food, glancing up at him every once in a while. He caught and held her gaze once, but she quickly looked away, keeping her head down. She had lost weight since his return, and he feared for their child. "Do ye not like the roast duck?"

How hypocritical he felt saying those words, especially since food had lost its taste. But always he ate, forcing down bite after bite when all he really desired was blood. Aye, his need had grown to an almost insatiable yearning. He craved it and could often think of little else.

"I am not hungry," she said, her voice barely above a whisper.

"But ye must eat for the babe's sake."

Rose set her fork down and finally held his gaze. Her throat convulsed as she swallowed hard. "Darius, the others say things about ye that are disturbing."

He sat back in his chair and steadied himself. "What things do they say?"

"They wonder why ye sleep all day and stay up all night. Why ye no longer meet with them in the village, but instead go off in the forests at night. They have seen ye out at night with your brother and Remont as well. What do ye do, Darius? Where do ye go?"

"To the pub some nights, but most of the time we go to Demetri's."

He had never before lied to his wife, or to anyone else for that matter. He had always lived his life as a man of honor. But that man had died on the battlefield, along with the life he had once known. He had been reborn as a creature of the night, a creature that required blood in order to survive.

Rose shifted in the chair, and his gaze slipped to her neck and the long vein that trailed down to her right breast. His mouth watered and he licked his lips as his gaze ripped back to her face.

She looked pale. "Darius, what has happened? Why do ye look so different?"

"I look different?"

She nodded. "Aye."

"In what way do I look different, Rose?"

"Ye are so pale and your eyes are strange. Like a wolf's."

He pushed his plate away with more force than necessary. Rose jumped, and what remained of his heart broke in that instant. His wife was terrified of him. "So what do ye think I am, Rose?"

She shook her head. "I do not know."

His heart pounded loudly in his chest. He had known this moment would come. Knew that he stood to lose everything he held dear. He could lie and hope to continue on as he had been, leaving with Remont and Demetri each night to feed. Returning to Rose, who would watch him with uncertainty that would soon grow to hate.

Or mayhap she already hated him.

Aye, he could lie or he could tell the truth. Just come out with it and hope she understood and didn't turn her back on him.

"Why do ye not go outside during the day anymore, Darius?"

He cleared his throat and sat up straight. "Something happened to me at Bannockburn that is difficult to explain."

She nodded. "Betsy said her husband saw ye run through by an English soldier. He was certain it had been a deathblow. The wound was immense, and yet ye bear no scar, Darius. How can that be?"

"Mayhap he saw another?"

"Nay, he swore it was ye, Darius. I thought perhaps it could have been Demetri, but ye told me yourself that he was not harmed."

Darius looked around the room where he had shared so many happy memories with this woman, who he had loved since the first day he saw her. Already his heart ached for all that he had lost, and now he could very well lose the one person he loved more than anyone else.

Unless she understood and accepted him as he was.

Please God, let her understand.

If only he could return to what he had been. What he wouldn't give for the simple pleasures of being human, of holding the woman he loved in his arms, telling her how much he loved her. How much he desired her.

But ye would be dead if ye were normal, he reminded himself. Any man would choose life over death—even if that life made him a monster that could never live in the light again.

"They say Demetri has changed as well."

His gut clenched. Strangely, Darius held no ill will toward his brother, who had given Remont permission to change him. No doubt he would have done the same had the tables been turned.

A life without Demetri would be unimaginable. Almost as unimaginable as living life without Rose.

"Darius, tell me that ye are well." Tears brimmed in her eyes, escaping down her cheeks unchecked.

"Promise me ye will hear me out, Rose."

"I promise."

"What ye heard is true. I was struck down at Bannockburn, and the wound was deep. A fatal blow."

Her brows furrowed. "Yet ye live and bear no scar . . ."

"Aye, my love." He ran a hand down his face and chose his words carefully. "As I lay dying, a man appeared. At first I thought he was the Angel of Death, but he was not an angel."

Her eyes widened. "Then what?"

"A vampire, Rose."

She stood so quickly the chair fell back and hit the floor with a resounding thud. "Darius, are ye a vampire?"

Darius nodded. "Aye."

"Such creatures cannot exist," she said, looking around wildly.

Darius wondered what she searched for. A weapon?

"I did not believe in such things either, Rose, but I have since learned the truth. Vampires *do* exist. They exist, and I *am* one. But do not fear me." He stood slowly. "I would never hurt ye."

She glanced at the door, and he read her thoughts. Felt her fear.

And revulsion.

His stomach knotted. God's breath, his wife detested and feared him.

"Rose, we can still be together."

"Of course," she said, a touch too quickly.

"I would never hurt you. Ye know that. Nor would I harm our child."

She flinched as though he'd struck her.

Mayhap Demetri had been right when he told him to forget Rose and leave Scotland with him and Remont. His twin had feared this very thing would happen.

She rushed for the door and opened it. He jumped, a skill Demetri had recently taught him—all he had to do was think of a place, and he could appear there . . . if it was within a reasonable distance. He landed at the door, blocking Rose's escape.

Rose screamed as she looked up at him and then back over her shoulder at the table. She crossed herself and took a step away. "Leave me be, Darius. Do not harm me. Do not hurt us," she said, placing a hand protectively over her rounded stomach.

He reached out to her, but she jumped back.

"I will not hurt ye, Rose. I swear I will not."

"I will not tell the others what ye told me, Darius. I swear it. I will do anything if ye let me and my baby live."

Me and my baby.

He moved toward her and she gasped, seeing he had not taken a step, but rather floated. "Ye are the devil."

"I am your husband, Rose."

"Nay, ye are *not* my husband."

His fingers encircled her wrist, and she tried to pull away. "The child in your womb is mine as well, Rose."

She jerked her hand out of his grasp and ran out of the dining room.

Trembling, he took a moment to catch his breath and wondered if he should let her go. Perhaps it was for—

Rose's scream reverberated throughout the room, ending abruptly a second later.

His breath caught in his throat, and he raced toward the landing, stopping short at the sight of his wife's twisted body, her beautiful green eyes staring up at him lifelessly.

"Oh my God!" a servant screamed as she came upon Rose's body. She looked up at Darius, accusation in her eyes.

"She fell."

"Of course," the servant replied.

Other servants congregated around Rose, but as Darius descended the stairs they fell back. God's breath, they all feared him—just as his wife had feared him.

A horrific pain ripped through his body, bringing him to his knees.

His wife was dead—along with their unborn child.

And he was responsible.

TWO

London
1818

"You are so beautiful, my dear."

In the dark interior of the elaborate carriage, the Viscount of Sutherland moved closer to Gabrielle. He deliberately sat on her gown, making any escape impossible.

"Thank you, my lord," Gabrielle murmured, fanning herself vigorously so as not to take the full impact of his rancid breath. She cursed her fate, and the uncle who had sold her in exchange for his mountain of gambling debts to a man old enough to be her grandfather.

"Your uncle said you have had a change of heart and are now most anxious to wed." He took a handkerchief from his pocket and wiped the sweat from his brow. "I cannot tell you how pleased I am to hear the news, especially since you originally declined my marriage proposal."

Little did Sutherland know her uncle had lied again. They'd had no such discussion, but she knew her uncle was positively desperate for money. Creditors had been knocking on the door of the townhouse since her arrival two months before. He'd had to dismiss his entire staff, save for one footman who served as butler, valet, footman, cook, and driver. No doubt the poor man's days were numbered as well. Gabrielle did her best to school her features, hoping the intense hatred she felt toward Sutherland would not show. "I am glad you are so pleased, my lord."

She felt no pity toward her uncle. He had made a mess of both their lives, selling her like chattel in order to save his own skin. Her mother, his sister, would be rolling over in her grave if she knew he had married her off to the horrible Lord Sutherland.

"In a fortnight you shall be Lady Sutherland. How does that sound, my pet?"

"A fortnight!" *Dear Lord, what happened to three months?* Even that was hasty, considering most engagements lasted a year. But at least three months would have given her the time she needed to plan her escape from this wretched man, and save money and other items needed for her journey. She had hoped to acquire enough to buy passage on a ship headed for Virginia. Surely in America she could disappear and not live in fear of Lord Sutherland or her uncle finding her.

She had to think fast in order to find a way to escape both of them. A difficult feat when her uncle kept her locked in her room day and night. Her punishment for having tried to escape the night she'd been told about the engagement.

Immediately after dinner that night, she had climbed out of her third-floor window and made her way down the rickety trellis. Misjudging the distance to the ground, she had twisted her ankle. By the time she had made it to the front entrance, her uncle and the footman had joined her, and taken her kicking and screaming back to her room.

From that day on she had become a prisoner in his home.

"Perhaps we shall journey to Venice for our honeymoon, my dearest. I spent an entire season in Italy after my first marriage and I had such a splendid time." He smacked his thin lips while patting his rotund belly. "And the cuisine was positively divine. There is nothing else like it, I tell you, Gabrielle."

She glanced at his huge stomach, and the straining buttons of his waistcoat. If need be, she could outrun him. And Lord knows she was ready to run.

"It sounds delightful," she murmured, wishing they would get to the ball so she could flee at the first given opportunity. The air in the carriage had grown stale and grew more so by the second.

"You shall love the canals, my dear. Such a lovely sight, and the art museums are astounding. There truly is not another place like it in the world," he said, placing his hand on her thigh.

She nearly came off the seat at the intimate caress. The blood roared in her ears as his thick fingers traced a path upward, terribly close to the vee of her thighs—a place where no man dared touch her before. Placing her gloved hand over his, she stilled his progress. His brows furrowed when she removed his hand from her leg, resting it back on the space between them. "My lord, you would ravish your intended in a carriage weeks before the wedding?" she asked, keeping her voice even. "And here I thought you a gentleman."

His eyes narrowed, and for a moment she saw true anger in the dark depths. No doubt his previous wives had witnessed the same. "How can you blame me when you are so beautiful?" he said with a shrug, his gaze shifting to the décolletage of her gown. *I suppose I shall have to content myself with the fact that in a fortnight you will be my wife and I will be able to do as I please, whenever I please, and however I please, and there will be no one who can stop me.*

It took her a moment to realize Sutherland had not said that last bit aloud, but instead she had read his mind. Gabrielle clasped her now trembling hands together and nearly wept with relief. She had spent the past two days reading her mother's book of spells, which had been passed down from one generation to another. She had reacquainted herself with chanting and meditating in the hopes her powers would return and help her find a way out of this mess she found herself in.

She had not used her "gifts" since her mother had died in her arms. When Gabrielle had been taken in by nuns from a nearby convent just days after her mother was buried, she had put the book away, and ignored the yearning to use her powers.

Her mother had come to her in dreams almost every night the first year after. Those dreams had stopped abruptly after the one-year anniversary of her mother's death along with the loss of her powers.

But now her gifts had come back, and she would not ignore them, especially if she could use them to get herself out of this mess.

She looked at Sutherland again, searched his thoughts, and was shocked by what she saw. The two of them were in a dark bedchamber, and the viscount was untying his robe while Gabrielle cowered on a bed, crying. His sinister laughter made the hair on her arms stand on end. One horrifying image followed another as Sutherland proceeded to rip her clothes from her body, his intentions obvious.

His hands slid around her neck and squeezed hard. Gabrielle was fighting him, but his huge hulking form made it nearly impossible.

Was this a premonition of things to come, or a sick, twisted fantasy?

Finally he released her, but with a warning. *I shall break that spirit and tame you, Gabrielle. One day soon you shall bend to my every whim.*

Sutherland brushed an imaginary string from Gabrielle's gown. She had to force herself not to jerk away. He caught her gaze and held it. "What is the matter, my dear? You look as though you have seen a ghost."

She forced a smile, imagining the force of his anger when she finally did escape him. And she *would* escape him, especially now that her powers had returned. Indeed, perhaps she would learn the spell for impotence. A man such as the viscount deserved to suffer such an affliction.

"Are you deaf, girl?" His brows knitted together, making his eyes almost nonexistent. "I asked, what is wrong with you?"

"Nothing at all."

She must leave tonight and never look back. With her luck her uncle would move the wedding date up yet again, and she could not take that chance.

They would reach the Vanderline ball shortly, and sometime during the evening she would make her way outside the manor's walls . . . and flee.

She would disappear into the night and hide where neither her uncle nor Sutherland would never find her.

If only she had money, she could leave London entirely, but unfortunately she had only the clothes on her back. She would have to stay in London for a little while, long enough to save enough money to leave. She remembered many times when she and her mother had to be resourceful in order to get to where they were going.

Suddenly more images flashed in her mind, interrupting her thoughts. She recognized herself standing next to Sutherland at the altar, and then it shifted once again to a darkened bedchamber. And he slapped her, over and over, taking great joy in her horror.

The blood in her veins froze as the pictures grew more violent by the second, until his hands encircled her neck and crushed the life from her. It seemed the more she struggled, the more excited he became. Her face changed to that of another woman, and Gabrielle realized with a start that he must be thinking about another of his wives. Had she met the very same fate? Would he kill her the very night he married her? Everyone would go on to say it was suicide—just like his other wives, or perhaps this time it would be an accident.

She shuddered.

"You're trembling, my dear." Sutherland moved to put his arm about her shoulders. She nodded the smallest bit, while thinking of a knife.

The viscount pulled back his hand as though it had caught fire. "Bloody hell, I was poked by something." He inspected his uninjured hand, and Gabrielle hid a smile.

Her powers had indeed returned in force.

While Sutherland cared for his seemingly injured hand, Gabrielle looked out the carriage window for the first time since leaving her uncle's townhouse a good quarter of an hour before.

Her stomach clenched. They should have been close to the Vanderline estate in the prominent Mayfair district, but instead, she noted the old buildings, with broken windows and shutters hanging askew. Prostitutes lined the sidewalks, yelling out lewd comments as they passed. What was he up to now? "My lord, where are we?"

Sutherland leaned forward and looked out the window. "I thought to take a detour."

"A detour. Whatever for, my lord?"

He shrugged. "Your uncle will be meeting us at the ball in a few hours, after he concludes a business matter. After the ball he will be escorting you home, so I hoped to take advantage of the time we had together to converse, and get to know each other better."

His beady eyes narrowed as he continued to watch her. He lied. He had prolonged the ride so he could ravish her in the carriage while she was without a chaperone. Damn her uncle for casting a blind eye to Sutherland's wicked ways.

Lifting her chin, she met his gaze boldly. "I have been so looking forward to the ball, my lord—especially since I have attended so few in my life." Though she hated to touch him, she reached out and squeezed his hand lightly. "We will have the rest of our lives to converse."

The carriage hit a pothole and shifted, Sutherland's heavy jowls jiggling with the movement. His thin lips pursed together, vanishing as he watched her closely.

Soon enough I shall fuck you until you cannot stand. I cannot wait to get my hands on you.

His crude thought flashed through her mind, and even more, the expression on his face changed, his lewd gaze shifting to the low bodice of her gown once more.

Before she said something she would come to regret, she rested a hand on her stomach. "My lord, I do not know if it is the carriage ride or the scone I ate before you arrived at my uncle's, but I fear I do not at all feel well. Could you please tell your man to make for the Vanderlines' estate?"

Rather than look concerned, he appeared irritated, the side of his mouth lifting in a smirk she yearned to wipe clean from his ugly face.

"The Vanderlines are known for their beautiful gardens," Sutherland said, straightening his cravat. "Perhaps I shall take you for a walk through the labyrinth upon our arrival?"

To get lost in a labyrinth with the man she hated most of all was the last thing she wanted. She managed a smile. "Perhaps. That is . . . if we manage to get to the ball at all."

With a heavy sigh, Sutherland rapped his cane on the carriage roof.

A footman leaned forward and popped his head in the window. "Yes, my lord?"

"Tell the driver to make haste to the Vanderline estate. Miss Fairmont is not feeling well."

The man's bewigged head bobbed. "Yes, my lord. Straight away."

A great yell and a slap of the reins followed.

Gabrielle smiled. "Thank you, my lord."

Sutherland mumbled something unintelligible.

The carriage lurched into a dangerously high speed, the wheels clattering and knocking against uneven cobbles. The view out the window blurred.

In the street, someone yelled, and the coach driver let out a loud curse. Metal squealed as the coachman hauled on the brake, but the forward motion of the carriage could not be halted.

They were traveling too fast.

Gabrielle held her breath as the carriage rocked and the horses whinnied, sounding frightened. She slid off the velvet seat, thrown forward by the sharp stop, but the viscount's weight on her dress pinned her down on one side. She threw out her arm against the window post, holding herself back.

The carriage slowed, and then, sickeningly, rose and fell on one side as the front wheel passed over something—then rose and fell a second time as the rear wheel climbed over the same object.

On the street, a woman screamed, and others cried out in dismay.

After a loud crash and a hard jolt, the carriage finally halted.

Sutherland swore and stuck his head out the window. "George, I swear I will feed you to the pigs! Why the devil did you stop?"

Gabrielle glanced out the window. People were hurrying to a place just behind the carriage.

Dread gripped her. They had hit something, or rather, *someone.*

While Sutherland yelled at the driver, she opened the door and stepped down onto the street. Gabrielle hurried over to the large crowd and nudged her way through the press of bodies. Stepping into the center of the circle she saw the boy who lay on the cobbles—his limbs cast all ways, his eyes closed, his face deathly pale.

Despite the filth and stains on the rags he wore, Gabrielle could clearly see two wide, wet bands across his middle.

Wheel marks.

"Dear God," she whispered aloud, pressing a hand to her racing heart. Gabrielle briefly considered appealing to Sutherland for assistance, but she could still hear him back at the carriage, berating the driver.

Careless of the fine silk she wore, she sat down beside the boy and cradled him in her lap. Gabrielle ran her fingers through the boy's dark curls. She didn't want to believe he was dead, nor could she accept that she was partly responsible for his death. Had she not pushed Sutherland to rush to the ball, the driver would not have plowed the boy down.

"You run 'im down," a woman yelled from a second-story window. "What the 'ell do you think your doin', racing through the streets like the devil is on your 'eels?"

"Shut up, Winnie!" a man's voice yelled back. "Don't ya see who you're talking to? Look at the carriage, woman!"

Through a hole in the crowd, Gabrielle glanced in Sutherland's direction and noticed he was occupied with the driver and footmen, who were trying to disentangle the carriage from a fruit stand.

He had no care for the boy. In fact, this would be a good time to slip away without being noticed, but she could not just leave this boy to die.

A prostitute hovering by her elbow said softly, "'E's dead, m'lady."

Gabrielle continued her gentle rocking. She noted his pallor, the blue lips. He was so young, perhaps not even ten. She closed her eyes and said a silent prayer.

"Prayer ain't going to 'elp 'im now," the prostitute added.

Though she knew the woman was probably right, she could not help grappling with the problem, seeking a solution. She could always use her gifts to help heal him. Her mother had cautioned her about casting spells in crowds, but the risk of being branded a witch was worth it in this case if she could save the boy.

Blocking out the commotion around her, Gabrielle let her mind sink into the melodic words of a chant she had read just last night. Once the words were spoken they could not be reversed, and it would take much of her strength. Releasing a breath, she began saying the words over and over again. As she continued whispering the chant, she felt the crowd begin to move away, afraid of her.

She heard Sutherland in the distance, yelling at her to get up and stop her mumbling, but she blocked his angry voice, focusing all her energy on the spell. The words rushed from her, coming quickly, her voice growing louder, and though she knew the danger she placed herself in, she could not stop it.

Just about the time she thought her efforts would fail her yet again, the boy moved. It was nothing more than a twitch, but it was enough, and a second later his eyelids fluttered.

"He stirs!" This from the prostitute, who put her hand on Gabrielle's shoulder in excitement.

The boy's eyes opened and he stared up at her like a startled doe. Gabrielle's heart leapt with joy. "How do you feel?"

"Who are you?" the boy asked, his voice hoarse.

She could not help the smile that came to her lips, or the laugh that followed. "My name is Gabrielle," she said, urging him to his feet, so she could stand. "What is your name?"

"Peter," he said, looking at the small crowd with wariness. It was obvious he had no recollection of the accident. Seeing the marks the wheels had left upon his chest, he touched the tattered shirt, first with a finger as though he could not quite believe it. Then he pressed his small hand flat against it, and glanced at the carriage, the large wheels, then back at her, his brows furrowed. "The carriage hit me," he said matter-of-factly.

The crowd drew back from him, and she could tell he did not understand their reaction.

She was nervous for him. People could be very unforgiving to those who were different.

"Yes, the carriage hit you, but you are unharmed." She ruffled his hair. "However, I cannot say the same for your shirt, Peter."

He smiled a toothless grin that made her heart lurch. "My da will not believe it when I tell him."

"Go along then. Back to your da and mum."

"I have no mum," he said, his voice sad.

"I have no mum either, Peter. She died two years ago."

"Do you have a da?" he asked, tilting his head to the side.

She shook her head. "No."

He frowned and then surprised her with a hug. It was the first time anyone had tried to comfort her since the death of her mother. Blinking back tears, she put him at arm's length. "You had best go, Peter. Your da will be worried about you."

"Thank you," he said again, and then walked away, past the people who jumped to get out of his way, and into the alley.

Gabrielle walked back to the carriage, noting the fury on Sutherland's face and the fear on the faces of those around them. When she was close enough for him to touch her, his thick fingers curled around her arm. He helped her into the carriage, all but shoving her into the seat.

Thankfully he took the seat opposite her, rather than sit beside her again. "I do not know what just happened back there, but you will deny any involvement, do you understand?"

Exhausted, she nodded and closed her eyes. Her head ached horribly. It had been ages since she'd tried a spell, and she had forgotten how spent they made her.

"Tell me you are not a witch, Gabrielle. Your uncle mentioned your mother was strange, and had a weird notion that she could heal people. Do you have the same illness?"

Illness?

She opened her eyes and looked at the viscount, who sat forward in the seat. His thumb brushed over the carved ivory handle of his cane, over and over, as though he yearned to use it on her.

What a sad, pitiful man he was. Abusing women so he could feel powerful.

What would he do if she were to tell him that she was indeed a witch just like her mother? Would he then call off the wedding? Or worse, would he move it up even closer? Mayhap even tomorrow?

"I am not a witch."

"Then how did you bring that boy back from the dead?" He brushed sweat from his forehead with his handkerchief and then put it back into his waistcoat pocket. "I would not have believed it had I not seen it with my own eyes."

She didn't know what was more terrifying—his tone or expression. "I did nothing but care for him. It must not have been his time to die."

"Rubbish! The wheels should have crushed him."

His beady black eyes narrowed as he watched her. She tried to read his thoughts, but it was no use. She was too spent from the spell.

"I am telling you the truth, my lord."

Thankfully he looked away, brushing the curtain aside, glancing out as though he expected someone to be following them.

"If anyone asks you what happened this night, you say nothing. If they ask if you were in this part of town, you deny it. You have ruined your gown, so we will stop by my sister's home that is not far from here."

"But what of the gown?"

“Her granddaughter is near your age, and I’m certain she has something adequate for you to wear.” He turned back to her. “I will have my drivers return to my estate, and we shall ride on to the ball with my sister.”

“Will she not think it odd?”

“She will say nothing. She is my sister.”

Be careful, Gabrielle. Her mother’s voice came strong and forceful.

Three

Darius looked out over the sea of people in the Vanderlines' ballroom with dismay. "I thought ye said it would be a small affair, Bernadette."

"A small affair?" Bernadette's throaty laughter rose to the high, painted ceilings of the cavernous ballroom. "Silly man. The Vanderlines' youngest daughter is coming out tonight. Nothing but the best will do: that means all of London will be attending."

"Is she pretty, this Vanderline daughter?" he asked with a wink.

Bernadette gave him a sharp glance. "Do not get any ideas, Darius. You are mine tonight—make no mistake about it." She smiled, but it didn't begin to reach her brown eyes. "Do not think I have not noticed the other women in the room watching you. I have, and I do not care for it. No, not one bit."

He had received his share of flattering looks since stepping into Lord Vanderline's mansion a half hour before. It had been so long since he'd last been to a social gathering that he felt sorely out of touch. "I believe those women ye speak of are actually looking at ye, my dear. Ye are so beautiful that they are sizing ye up as competition."

The words seemed to appease her. She tapped her fan against his chest playfully. "Flatterer."

"I only speak the truth, Bernadette." He leaned in, whispered in her ear, "All the men want ye in that lovely crimson gown that barely restrains those magnificent breasts of yours."

"Flatterer," she said, a wide smile on her full lips. "And I love your brogue, Darius. Sends shivers all the way up my spine," she said with a wiggle. "And everywhere else."

"I'm glad to hear it, lass."

Bernadette glanced over her shoulder at the small crowd that had gathered nearby, but not so close they could see beyond the strategically placed potted palm trees.

Three in all, they served as a wall of sorts, and now Bernadette made good use of that wall. Placing a hand on his cock, she whispered in his ear, "I want you now, Darius."

"Careful, darling. There are people nearby who might not understand why ye have your hand on my cock. Particularly your husband, who is in attendance tonight, is he not?"

She sighed heavily. "Yes, Harold is here. No doubt in the parlor losing the other half of his fortune."

"Even so, I do not think ye should open yerself up to gossip."

She chuckled again. "It's a bit too late for that. I fear everyone already knows our business. Half of them do not blame me for taking lovers, especially since Harold loves no one but his cards."

"I'm sure he cares for ye, Bernadette."

"Yes, he tells me he cares for me, but rarely shows it. Miserable man! Wish he would just die already."

Darius intentionally stared at the impressive emerald nestled between her ample breasts. One of Harold's many gifts to keep his beautiful wife happy since he failed to satisfy her in the bedroom, and everywhere else for that matter.

How sad that people married for money and not for love. A curse of being rich, he supposed. Fortunately he had been able to choose his own bride, and choose her well he did.

So well he had not found one who could compare in all these five centuries.

Perhaps that in itself was why he only took married women to his bed. They were eager to please and more experienced in the art of lovemaking. Plus, they expected no commitment. Only mutual satisfaction.

Aye, they were the safest lovers of all. Always appreciative, and not overly possessive, though he did have to end a few liaisons when the women became too demanding or attached.

Lord knows he did not need another wife.

Suddenly Rose's face appeared. His dear, sweet Rose. Even now, five hundred years after her death, he missed her desperately. Still mourned for what could have been. Mourned for the child he never had.

"Penny for your thoughts," Bernadette said, lifting his chin with her fingers. "You were a million miles away just then."

Someone coughed, and she dropped her hand back to her side. Thankfully, it was only a footman and not another guest.

"I was thinking how very much I abhor these events, and how I would much prefer to see ye lying on a bed of satin." His gaze shifted from the stunning emerald resting between her breasts, to the white silky mounds nearly bursting from their confines, to her long, slender neck. If you looked close enough you could see the faintest hint of where he had bit her. He always tried to get near the hairline, and he always drank further back on the neck; oftentimes, not even the victims themselves could see the wounds.

Last night he had fed from Bernadette. She had no idea, of course, that he actually drank her blood. Instead, she thought it merely a game, one that she had enjoyed immensely.

He did not drink enough to harm her, only to let her enjoy the aphrodisiac feeling his kind experienced during sex. It magnified everything—especially the climax.

Bernadette had cried out, her sex throbbing around his cock as he drank deeply while still experiencing tremors from his own climax.

"I do wish your brother and his friend would not have chosen tonight to meet up with you." Her ruby red lips turned down at the corners. "I want to have you all to myself this evening."

"I told ye that I will do everything in my power to break away for an hour this evening, lass. However, I cannot promise ye that."

Her eyes lit up. "Just an hour?"

He grinned. "Or perhaps two."

She clapped her hands together. "Perhaps your brother will not show up at all," she said, a touch too hopeful.

He was not about to tell her that Demetri would arrive just as he promised. If his twin said he would be somewhere at a certain time, then that was that. He would be there. Demetri always kept his word. "Perhaps," he replied, feeling a strange rush.

"When will you come to me, do you think?"

Darius checked his pocket watch for the tenth time in as many minutes. It was not like Demetri to be late, especially to an event such as this. Perhaps he had already arrived and was feeding.

His brother had always thrived on mingling with the bluebloods of society. He'd said they tasted sweeter than the less fortunate men and women who lived in the slums.

After Rose's death and the death of their child, Darius had rejected blood, wanting to die instead of living. But the hunger had quite literally taken hold of him, and he fed, mostly on the unsavory beings who lived in every city and every town. They lived their wretched lives making others miserable.

Darius learned that he did not mind feeding on those types. Indeed, if anything he was doing a service to decent, honorable people living in those same cities and towns.

"I'm afraid you will not come to me once he arrives," she said, caressing his cock once more. "Let's slip into one of the rooms on the first floor, Darius," Bernadette whispered in his ear, motioning toward the hallway. "No one will know we are missing. I wore nothing beneath my gown. It will make it easier and faster. Come, Darius. Please."

"Wicked woman," he said with a grin, half tempted to take her up on the offer. "I can't, lass."

She sighed loudly. "Well, I must find my husband before people begin noticing I'm not at his side. Save a dance for me?"

He winked. "Of course."

Darius made his way further into the room, amazed at the amount of people squeezed into one room.

He did not miss this. The senseless chatter, everyone sizing each other up. Smiling when inside they were trying to find something wrong in each and every person. He missed the days of old. Days when men had honor.

Suddenly, a ripple of exhilaration rushed through his entire body, from his head to his toes. He smiled to himself. His brother had finally arrived.

The two of them had always shared a sixth sense, even as children, but that sense had become even stronger after both were made into vampires. Another one of their dark gifts.

Darius looked toward the top of the elegant staircase to find his twin there, dressed in severe black. Hands on his narrow hips, Demetri looked directly at him, a wide smile on his lips.

His twin's long hair was held back by a black ribbon that only served to draw more attention to his sharp cheekbones and light blue eyes. The only difference between the two of them was the fine scar above Demetri's right eye from where he had fallen as a boy and cut his brow. The hair there had never grown back, and it had turned out to be one of the few ways others could tell them apart.

To his brother's immediate right stood Remont. As light as Demetri was dark, their maker wore buff-colored breeches, a gold coat made of fine silk, and a snowy white shirt with an elegantly tied cravat and large diamond stickpin. One would never guess Remont had been just nine and ten, and a messenger in the Austrian court of King Leopold, when his maker had taken one look at him and made him into a vampire.

He rarely spoke of that day, only to say he had loved his life before receiving the dark gift.

Darius had little doubt that was the reason Remont had asked him over and over again if he wanted his help. Had Demetri not pushed him, he probably would not have gone through with it.

Every so often when in Remont's presence, Darius could remember the feel of his maker's lips on his neck. The touch of his cool, slender hands on him. The taste of his blood that had been like the most intoxicating elixir.

Having become a vampire, Darius had learned there was a beauty that both sexes could appreciate, and his brother appreciated their maker very much. In fact, the two had been lovers since the first months after Remont had made them.

Not to Darius's surprise, especially since he had been thinking of him, Remont's haunting green gaze locked with his. The tall blond grinned, flashing white teeth and not at all hiding his fangs from the crowd below.

And the women in the room stirred, their desire a palpable thing as the two handsome men—one so dark, the other so light—made their way through the crowd.

Darius listened to the comments and smiled, knowing his brother enjoyed being the center of attention.

Remont reached up and brushed an imaginary piece of lint from Demetri's shoulder, his hand lingering far longer than necessary.

The crowd parted like the Red Sea and Darius met them halfway. Demetri embraced Darius tightly. "How good it is to see ye, brother. It seems the highland air has done you good. You even have a bit of color to your pale cheeks, or does that have something to do with the redhead you were occupied with when we entered? What is her name—"

"Bernadette, I believe," Remont finished for him.

Darius laughed under his breath. "How is it that ye have been living in Venice all these years, and yet ye would know a member of the English aristocracy by her Christian name?"

Remont smirked. "You forget that I know everything." He failed to keep the sarcasm from his voice.

Demetri snorted. "We've been in town for a month now, brother. Bernadette's reputation is well known."

Darius shook his head. "Ye have not changed."

"I hope not," Demetri said, flashing a devilish smile.

"Come, greet me with the same enthusiasm with which you embraced your brother, Darius. I have missed you, my friend."

Darius released his brother and embraced Remont, not at all surprised that the same rush of emotion raced through him yet again. "And I've missed you as well."

"How is it that ye have been able to put up with my brother for all these centuries?" Darius asked, motioning to nearby chairs.

A strange expression flashed over Remont's face before he covered it with a boyish grin. "I manage, though at times he pushes my patience."

Demetri laughed under his breath. "The same could be said of you, love."

Darius had never been able to see inside his maker's thoughts. Remont, being one of the older vampires, could shield his thoughts not just from humans but from his own kind as well. Yet for a moment his expression had spoken volumes, and made Darius wonder if perhaps all was not well between his brother and their maker. "I was pleased to receive your letter."

"I had hoped you would be."

"You have almost lost your brogue, I see."

"Aye, I have." Unlike Darius, Demetri had little brogue left to his voice, no doubt from centuries of living with Remont in Italy.

Demetri grabbed two glasses from a servant's tray. "Thank you, my dear," he said with a wink, his gaze lingering on the woman's impressive cleavage.

The servant's gaze kept shifting back and forth between the three of them. Her thoughts were risqué, as she fantasized about the four of them on a large bed of scarlet-colored silk with all of the men pleasuring her at once.

It was obvious Demetri had seen the vision as well, because he leaned forward and whispered in the woman's ear, "Have you ever had three men at the same time, lass?"

Her eyes widened, and she shook her head so vigorously, she almost upset the tray. "No, not yet," she said breathlessly.

Demetri's gaze slid up and down her body, his lips pursed together. "Tonight might be the night you experience paradise."

Her chest rose and fell heavily. "Oh, I do hope so," she said with a wicked smile before she disappeared into the crowd.

Demetri laughed under his breath and turned with a sly grin. "I'm enjoying myself already, but I can tell you are anxious to know why I summoned you here."

Darius nodded.

"Well, I missed you for one."

"And secondly?"

A group of young women walked by, three of whom giggled, while the bolder of them nodded and said, "Good evening" as her gaze wandered slowly over them.

Demetri and Darius both nodded and replied in unison, "Good evening."

When they were out of hearing range, Demetri continued. "I asked you to meet us here tonight because I want you to meet a young woman who will be attending this evening."

"Who is she?"

Demetri smiled softly. "Her name is Gabrielle Fairmont, very young, and you shall love this—she is fresh out of the convent. I was fortunate enough to see her at the opera a few nights ago, and I think she is perfect for you."

Darius laughed under his breath. "What gave ye the impression I was in the market for a lover?"

"I would not laugh so fast, brother. You wait and see. Anyway, as I was saying, this lovely young woman is set to marry Vincent Lemory, the sixth Viscount of Sutherland."

"Sutherland?" Darius repeated. Though he lived in the Scottish highlands, he still read the London newspapers, even if the news was history by the time they reached his home. "Isn't he the lord who is rumored to have killed a wife or two?"

"Actually, it was four," Demetri replied. "Gabrielle is a rare beauty, and far too young to marry someone as old and depraved as Sutherland."

"Then why does she?" Darius asked. "If she was living in a convent, then I'm assuming she was either there because she wished it, or because she had no one else to care for her."

"And the latter is exactly the case. Her mother died two years ago and no family stepped forward to take her in . . . until recently when suddenly the half brother decided to visit his long-lost niece. His visit apparently came after a long night of gambling, in which he lost the title to the only real estate he had left, a rundown townhouse in dire need of repairs. So he visited the convent, and immediately upon leaving the meeting he went straight to a friend's house."

"Let me guess, Lord Sutherland is his friend?"

Demetri nodded. "Yes, he's old, widowed, and one of the wealthiest men in London. Plus, he does not expect or need a dowry. He agreed to the marriage without even seeing Gabrielle."

The footman at the top of the stairs cleared his throat loudly. "Lord Sutherland and Miss Gabrielle Fairmont."

Demetri's eyes twinkled. "Ah, perfect timing. Turn around, brother and see for yourself why I asked you to meet me here tonight."

Intrigued, Darius turned and saw the old viscount at the top of the stairs. The man's jowls mingled with his intricately tied cravat, and his thin lips curved into a greasy smile as he turned to the young woman at his side.

Darius's breath caught in his throat. "Rose," he whispered, unable to believe his eyes.

Demetri's hand rested on Darius's shoulder as he leaned in. "Amazing, is it not? I could scarcely believe it when I first set eyes on her. Such a striking resemblance."

Darius's throat was too tight to reply. In fact, he could scarcely breathe.

Dressed in an exquisite short-sleeved gown of light green taffeta that fit a bit too snug across her full breasts and a tad too loose at her slim waist, Gabrielle Fairmont was truly a vision to behold. Her pale hair had been adorned in a high coiffure with an assortment of tiny pale flowers and a string of small, cream-colored pearls. She was without question the most attractive woman in the room, and yet he sensed from her flushed cheeks and shy smile that she had no idea how truly astoundingly beautiful she was.

"I wanted you to see her with your own eyes, brother. I knew telling you in a letter would not do her justice."

"I cannot believe the resemblance," Darius said, wondering if this woman could be his Rose reincarnated. After all, if vampires existed, then why couldn't a person be born again in the same body? If that were the case, and this Gabrielle was his Rose, would she remember him?

Dear God let it be.

"I do not know if Gabrielle is your Rose, Darius, but I will do what I can to help you capture her heart if that is what you desire. I am completely at your disposal."

"As am I," Remont added.

Darius glanced at them and nodded. "Thank ye, thank ye both."

Demetri grinned wolfishly. "Does that mean you want her?"

"Aye, I want her," Darius said, a million different emotions racing through him, most of all excitement and an exhilaration he thought never to feel again.

"Then you shall have her," Demetri said with resolve.

And though he told himself that he would not search her thoughts, he did exactly that. He could not help himself.

She was nervous, as anyone could tell by looking at her. Even more, she did not want to be here. In fact, she yearned to be anywhere else. That thought alone made him smile. His Rose had been the same way, preferring solitude to larger crowds.

Darius felt the blood course through his veins, thick and hot. Memory upon memory flashed in his mind, and he had to remind himself again that this woman was *not* his wife, just as Demetri said. "But she is to marry Lord Sutherland."

Remont laughed under his breath. "Even I can tell she hates him. I think you could persuade her quite easily to leave the current circumstance she finds herself in. Indeed, read her thoughts for even a minute and you will know the truth for yourself, my friend."

"You've read her thoughts already?" Demetri asked, shaking his head.

Remont shrugged. "I could not help myself. And do not try to tell me you have not done the same. Even Darius has."

Darius watched Gabrielle intently, and though it took effort to calm his mind, he finally settled enough to read her thoughts again. He felt her anxiousness. She disliked being here in this large group of people who all stared at her like an animal in a cage. She hated the man at her side and yearned to escape him. Suddenly, an image hit him, hard and fast.

Darius could see the dark interior of a carriage, and plush, velvet seats. He saw Gabrielle, but she wasn't wearing the gown she now wore, even though her hair looked to be adorned the same way. Could it have been from earlier tonight? Anxiety and fear rushed through him—at the same time the viscount touched her, his hand on her leg.

Darius's hands tightened into fists at his sides as the vision changed, and now they were in a dark bedchamber. Gabrielle tried to get away from Sutherland and his pawing, but the man would not relent. The image broke away for an instant, and then he saw her again struggling beneath the viscount, who was choking the life from her.

Rage rushed through him. Had this happened already or was he seeing the future?

Darius broke the thought before he did something he would regret. He didn't need to see anymore. And although he didn't know Gabrielle Fairmont, he would move heaven and hell to get her away from the madman.

"She comes this way," Demetri said, nudging Darius forward. "Get her attention, and I shall keep Sutherland occupied."

The closer Gabrielle Fairmont came, the more he could not get over the resemblance to his Rose . . . which had him wondering if perhaps this wasn't his second chance at happiness.

The chatter of London's elite, mixing with the music of the twenty-piece orchestra, made Gabrielle's heart accelerate. Dear Lord her corset was too tight. She could scarcely draw a breath, and it did not help that every eye in the room was fixed upon her and Lord Sutherland. She heard them talking about her.

To make matters worse, the further they drew out into the crowd, the tighter the viscount's hold on her became, his fingers biting into her skin. It was as though he knew she wanted to bolt, to leave and never look back.

Little did he know she *would* escape, especially since she'd heard his conversation with his sister. "*Be ready with the carriage tomorrow morning, sister*," he had said, his voice urgent. "*We travel to Gretna Green at sunrise*."

Even Sutherland's sister had seemed surprised by the news, stammering and stuttering that quick marriages in the small Scottish border town were the things of scandals, but after a firm tongue-lashing from the viscount, she had agreed.

"Straighten your shoulders," Sutherland urged, pulling her out of her musings. "And for God's sake, smile. This is not a bloody funeral. I want everyone to know how delighted you are to be my bride."

"Yes, my lord," she said, forcing a smile she didn't feel. The room was enormous and filled with roughly five hundred bodies. At least it would make disappearing easier than had it been a small, intimate party. Unfortunately, saving the boy had drained her immensely, and she needed all the strength she could bolster to escape.

"Do you know how many women would love to trade places with you, my dear?" Sutherland murmured.

And I would trade places with any one of them right now if given the chance, you murderous pig.

Without replying, she scanned the room, noting four sets of double doors on the far side of the ballroom. Two of them were wide open to allow cool air to circulate in the room. Foliage blocked some of the garden from view. Excitement rippled along her spine. All she had to do was slip out one of those doors unnoticed . . .

As they approached the manor, she had noted a stone retaining wall surrounding the property. There were also several trees, which shouldn't cause her trouble. She had climbed many a tree in her youth . . . but not in an ill-fitting gown, of course.

"The poor dear thing," an older woman said as they approached, a sympathetic expression on her face as she stared. "She will probably be dead by this time next year. What a pity."

Sutherland pierced the bold woman with a scathing look, his hold on Gabrielle tightening.

"He would be a fool to kill her so quickly. Look at that face," the woman's friend said. "She's a beauty."

"But he *is* a fool, darling. She will probably die on her wedding night, if not before. The beast!"

Sutherland turned abruptly, his icy gaze shifting over the woman, who flipped open her fan and started waving it vigorously. The slight tremor of her hand gave away her false bravado.

To maintain her sanity, Gabrielle tuned out all the voices and focused on what she must do to get away from Sutherland.

Above on the balcony a large orchestra played, and below them guests danced, while others mingled. In an adjoining room men and women gambled.

"I would like to introduce you to a good friend of mine," Sutherland said, escorting her through the crowd that grew thicker by the second. Her hand slipped from his elbow as a small group of young women separated her from the viscount.

Gabrielle took advantage of the separation and turned away, running straight into a man's chest.

"Forgive me, lass," a deep, strangely familiar voice said, while strong hands steadied her.

"It is I who am sorry," she murmured, looking up into piercing blue eyes. She opened her mouth to say something else, but all thought slipped away. Dear God, the man was staggeringly beautiful. Her heart rate accelerated, and her breath caught in her throat.

"Forgive me, lass," he said again, his voice bearing the slightest hint of a Scottish burr, a pleasant sound that matched an equally pleasant face.

Not just pleasant, but gorgeous. Such strong features—high cheekbones, full lips, square chin. Light blue eyes framed by long, thick lashes, and silky dark hair that fell in soft waves to his immense shoulders. Oddly, she saw a flash of a vision of a medieval warrior, who was without question the man standing before her now. But instead of the expensive black suit and silver waistcoat he wore tonight, he wore snug brown leather breeches, a linen tunic, and a plaid sash. His hair was worn long as it was now, but with two braids on either side of his face.

"Have we met before?" she asked, and the man smiled boyishly. That smile had her heart skipping a beat. He turned to his companions, and Gabrielle noted the man's twin—who grinned widely at his brother—and a tall, equally gorgeous blond. Indeed, the three men shared a secret smile before he turned back to her.

"Perhaps—a long time ago."

His words intrigued her, and she yearned to find out exactly what he meant, but reality came in the way of Sutherland's firm voice. "Gabrielle!"

The handsome men turned to Sutherland, their smiles losing their luster.

"Who are you?" Sutherland asked the men rudely, as he reached for Gabrielle's hand. She tried to use her powers to send a similar shock, like she had earlier, but this time it didn't work. No doubt she had overused her powers when saving the boy. To her dismay, Sutherland grabbed her hand and pulled her closer.

The Scot glanced at Sutherland and gave a curt nod. "I am Darius MacLeod, and this is my brother Demetri and our friend Remont."

Darius MacLeod. Even his name sounded familiar, but where had she heard it before? She had never been to Scotland, though she had longed to, particularly the highlands.

Demetri asked Sutherland a question, while Darius bent down and picked up her fan, which she hadn't realized she'd dropped. His gloved hand brushed up against hers as he handed her the fan, and she saw a vision of an old manor house made of dark gray stone, sitting in a large heather-strewn valley between two immense hills. The grass-covered hills were so tall, almost disappearing into the thick clouds.

Was she seeing Darius's home?

"A pleasure to meet you all," Sutherland said brusquely. "Please forgive us. I have promised to introduce my *fiancée* to friends. Come, my dear."

Gabrielle saw Darius's face change when Sutherland mentioned the word *fiancée*. "It was nice to meet you, Mr. MacLeod," she blurted, wishing she could marry a man like him instead.

"Call me Darius, Gabrielle," he said loud enough for her alone.

"Lord Sutherland, perhaps later you would like to join us in a game of cards?" Demetri asked, pulling out a pocket watch. "In an hour or so?"

Sutherland's gaze shifted from one man to the other, no doubt taking in the fine fit of their impeccably tailored clothing. He nodded. "I look forward to it."

As they walked away, Gabrielle could feel Darius's ice blue gaze linger on her. She dared a glance behind her to find him still watching, and the sides of his mouth lifted in a soft smile. Her heart hammered as she grinned foolishly back at him. Lucky was the woman who won that man's heart. His brother clapped him on the back and grinned widely as he whispered something in his ear.

What did they talk about, those two sinfully handsome brothers who had all the women staring at them and their beautiful friend? She could scarcely blame them. Even God must have wept when he made them.

Strangely, as she looked at the men, she felt a sense of déjà vu. Why was Darius so familiar to her, this man who she surely would have recognized had she seen him before?

Who could forget a face like that? And what of his response to her question about meeting him before: *Perhaps—a long time ago.*

Sutherland stopped and introduced her to a group of his friends. After they exchanged pleasantries, he became involved in a conversation about business. Bored, Gabrielle scanned the ballroom for the handsome MacLeod brothers and their companion.

She found them soon enough—across the room talking to a group of giggling, young women. Jealousy rushed through Gabrielle when Darius flashed his white teeth in a smile as a woman leaned into him, placing a delicate hand on his shoulder.

Silly woman! You have no business being jealous over a man you do not even know.

None of them compare to you, Gabrielle.

Her breath caught in her throat, and she dared a glance at the Scot again. To her shock Darius MacLeod looked straight at her and smiled softly, before turning his attention back to the other woman.

She felt him watch her from the corner of his eye, and suddenly, without warning an image slammed into her thoughts, blocking out everything else.

Both Gabrielle and Darius lay naked on a large, canopied bed. The only light came from the fire blazing in a nearby hearth. She trembled as she lay back on the silky blankets, and he covered her with his large, hard body. His lips were soft as he kissed her gently, his tongue tracing the seam of her lips, urging her to open.

Her hands moved up his back, over his strong, broad shoulders, and back down again. Though his skin was smooth, the muscle and sinew beneath were rock hard. She grabbed his high, firm buttocks, her nails biting into the skin, and he smiled against her lips.

His mouth left hers, and he kissed her chin, her neck, her chest, the swell of her breasts, and then he kissed her already sensitive nipple. She wove her fingers through his hair, keeping him anchored there. She sighed as he sucked lightly, and then flicked his tongue over the tight nub over and over again. Her nails dug into his scalp, but he didn't complain. She arched her back a little, giving him better access.

His thick cock felt like steel against her leg, and she shifted, aching for him to fill her. Glancing down, she watched him pleasure her, his long lashes fanning against high cheekbones, his long, pointed tongue, making love to her with such skill.

A long-fingered hand splayed against Gabrielle's belly and she held her breath. A second later that breath came out in a rush as Darius touched her woman's mound, his fingers sliding over her wet, hot slit, circling her weeping entrance. The blood rushed to that part of her body, and she lifted her hips, aching for more.

He kissed her, his tongue mating with hers frantically before he pulled away to whisper, "Ye are so hot, Gabrielle." He slipped a finger inside her and she gasped. "And so tight. I cannot wait to feel your slick heat surround me."

His wicked words sent shivers along her spine, and his finger inside her felt wonderful. Feeling bold, she replied, "And I cannot wait to have you inside me."

His white teeth flashed, and then he bent his head, playing homage to her breasts once more, kissing one, while touching the other. Indeed, he had a delicious way of using his teeth with just the right pressure, and his fingers rolled around the nipple just so, then pulled.

His thumb brushed over the tiny button at the top of her sex, a place she'd discovered by accident quite recently. With the pad of his thumb he stroked around it over and over again, in a delicious rhythm that had her arching her hips. He slipped another finger into her slick channel, and she bit her bottom lip to keep from crying out.

Her insides tightened, and she climbed toward a delicious pinnacle that had her heart racing and the blood in her veins boiling.

"Do you not agree, Gabrielle?"

Gabrielle looked at the woman who watched her with a quizzical expression. *Oh dear.* "I . . . Sorry?"

"You looked a million miles away."

If she only knew . . .

"Forgive me, I thought I saw someone I once knew, but I'm mistaken."

"That's quite all right, my dear. I know this must be overwhelming." She winked. "And on the eve of your wedding."

Gabrielle's stomach tightened.

"Vincent told us he cannot wait another moment to make you his bride," she said with a wink. "Don't worry. Our lips are sealed."

She wanted to go back to the vision, where she was making love to Darius MacLeod, instead of the reality and hell that her life had become.

Gabrielle took the opportunity to sneak a glance at Darius but he was not where he'd been only moments before, nor was Demetri or Remont.

Disappointed, she looked about, almost frantically. Surely he hadn't left already?

The woman's lips curved into a smile. "Oh my goodness, if only I were forty years younger."

Gabrielle followed the woman's gaze to find Darius walking toward them, his brother and Remont right behind him.

Her heart missed a beat as the image came back to her in all its glory. Oh the things she'd imagined him doing to her with that lovely full-lipped mouth and those long-fingered hands.

"I know you are to be married, but any woman, married or no, would give their right hand to have just one night with the three of them." She tapped Gabrielle's hand with her fan. "Truth be told, I'd be elated to have just one."

So would I.

"Though any one of the three would make for a satisfying night, to be sure." The woman's gaze was positively wanton as she stared boldly at the approaching twins and their handsome friend.

Gabrielle's heart soared when Darius stopped before her and bowed formally. "Miss Fairmont, may I have this dance?"

Before Sutherland could stop her, she nodded and took the arm Darius offered. "I tried to get your attention earlier, but it looked as though ye were a million miles away."

Was he a mind reader? Dear Lord, could he read her wicked thoughts? "I'm guilty of daydreaming."

"And was it a good daydream?" he asked, his voice low and seductive.

She met his stare boldly. "Yes. Yes, it was."

He grinned devilishly, and her heart gave another tug. In fact, it was odd how safe and familiar she felt around him . . . as though she'd known him for ages, which was strange . . . because she rarely felt safe around anyone, particularly those of the opposite sex.

They took their place among the other dancers, and Gabrielle tried not to stare at him, but she couldn't help herself, especially after her wicked fantasy.

Again she wondered why she couldn't marry someone like Darius MacLeod instead of Sutherland.

I want ye, Gabrielle. All those images, or daydreams as you call them, are real. That is what we will experience together and more. Paradise. If you will just trust me.

Her stomach turned, and thankfully the music started and the dance began.

Come away with me, Gabrielle. Far away from London and Sutherland.

Good gracious, what was happening to her? She was hearing and seeing things that couldn't be real. Was she going crazy, or perhaps hearing what she wanted to hear, and seeing what she wanted to see?

Her mother had always said she had an overactive imagination.

She shook her head and focused on the dance steps. From the corner of her eye she could see Sutherland talking to Remont and Demetri.

She glanced up at Darius and he smiled.

Mind, body, and soul, I shall have ye again. Return to me, Gabrielle. Return to me, my love.

FOUR

Darius's heart raced faster than it had in centuries. He could not believe the similarities between Gabrielle and Rose. How could two women look so alike, and yet live five hundred years apart?

Extraordinary.

For centuries he had yearned for just one more minute with Rose. Just to stare into her eyes and memorize every feature. And now that wish had come true, for he stood face-to-face with a woman who could easily be his wife's twin.

Aye, but a woman who was betrothed to another.

To a man she clearly detested.

Thank goodness Demetri and Remont had managed to divert Sutherland's attention long enough for Darius to ask her to dance. In fact, the two did their best to block the dance floor from the old man's vision, but he doubted they would be able to hold the old murderer off for long. Especially after the way Sutherland had held onto Gabrielle as though she'd bolt at any moment.

"Are ye enjoying yourself tonight?" he asked, unable to keep from staring at her.

"Yes, I am. And are you enjoying yourself?"

"Aye, I am. In fact, it's going to be an unforgettable night."

She lifted a tawny brow. "Unforgettable? Now you've intrigued me."

"Have I?" he asked, his voice lower and huskier than intended. She must have noticed, too, because a blush bloomed on her cheeks, making her even lovelier. "It is unforgettable because I met ye here tonight."

"What a lovely thing to say," she said, a soft smile on her full lips.

Sutherland sidestepped Demetri and Remont and walked toward the dance floor. He would not interrupt the dance, but he was ready to reclaim his fianceé, and chances were, he would make Gabrielle refuse Darius for the rest of the evening.

"Do ye wish to marry him?"

She missed a step but recovered quickly. "No. I—I have no choice. My uncle had gambling debts, and Sutherland paid him handsomely for my hand." She lowered her voice. "I hate both of them. Even my uncle. Does that surprise you?"

"No, not at all. I would despise whoever forced me to marry against my will."

"And what about you?" she asked, glancing at his hand. "Are you married?"

"No."

"You have not found the right woman?"

"Actually, my wife died."

Her eyes widened, and he could see her surprise and remorse. "Forgive me. I didn't know. I did not mean—"

"It was a long time ago," he said, reaching up and brushing aside a wayward curl from her cheek.

She started for a moment, and even missed a step.

"You remind me of her."

She grinned. "Do I? In what way?"

Where did he start? "In many ways. She was beautiful, like ye. And had blonde hair and green eyes."

"Was she Scottish?"

He nodded. "She was."

"I've often dreamed of Scotland."

"Ye have?"

"Yes."

"Perhaps ye will have occasion to go there one day."

"Perhaps," she said, leaning into him.

Gabrielle pulled back just in time. Dear Lord, she'd almost kissed Darius MacLeod in a room of over five hundred people, her fiancé included.

How she wished she could take Darius by the hand, leave this place, and go somewhere quiet where they could be alone, just the two of them.

"Who does she think she is?"

The question brought Gabrielle back to the present, and to a group of women, slightly older than herself. Six in all, they watched Gabrielle and Darius intently, snickering and giggling behind expensive fans.

A couple of them shook their heads, no doubt thinking the worst of Gabrielle, who danced with a handsome stranger over her fiancé, even if that man was a suspected wife killer.

The ton. Amazing how wealth and prestige could make an entire social class turn a blind eye to murder. And four of them at that.

Gabrielle flashed the group a winning grin, and their eyes widened. Darius's deep laughter made her smile. Thank goodness she had met him this evening. He had truly been her saving grace on what had been an exceedingly dark day.

However, the women's reaction did remind her that she'd had a different agenda tonight, especially since her uncle would be arriving at any time. In a perfect world she could marry a man like Darius MacLeod and dance and laugh and make love with him to her heart's content.

But such was not her fate. She must forget about the Scot and the ice blue gaze that promised wicked delights.

Besides—did men like Darius MacLeod really marry, or would he want just one night with her? Her mother had said men were untrustworthy, devious creatures, and Gabrielle's own experiences had proven that theory true.

But Gabrielle had never been attracted to someone the way she was attracted to Darius MacLeod. The intensity of the attraction both scared and excited her, and the intimate visions had made her blood boil. The flesh between her thighs still tingled as she remembered the delicious feel of him pleasuring her. What she wouldn't give to have him fill and inflame her, and pleasure her beyond reason.

Who knows, if she was forced to marry Sutherland, perhaps she could take a lover like Darius MacLeod?

The side of Darius's mouth lifted in a cocky smile. *I have no intention of sharing ye with any man. Mark my words, Gabrielle. Ye will be mine, and mine alone.*

Her insides twisted. He had not said a word, and yet she had heard his response as though he'd whispered the words in her ear. Good gracious, he could read her mind!

Perhaps there was a reason she was hearing and seeing things since meeting him. They'd had an immediate connection, one that went beyond simple attraction. What if he was like her—a witch, or rather a warlock, the male version of a witch? Aside from her mother, Gabrielle had never before met another person with similar gifts. Exhilaration rushed up her spine.

Guard your heart, my dear.

Gabrielle's breath lodged in her throat. It was her mother's voice. *The man you dance with is a creature of the night. A vampire to be feared.*

She nearly tripped, but caught herself at the last moment. Darius gave her a questioning look and she quickly looked away. *Vampire?* How could that be?

Look into his soul, Gabrielle. Look hard and you will see a dark mark there. The mark that proves he's a monster, damned for all eternity. You are weak now, especially after having saved the child. But when you are rested, you will see him in his true form. He is a creature, a bloodsucker, that will bring you nothing but misery.

Not human? True, he could read her thoughts, but that did not mean he was a creature of the night. Any warlock could do the same.

What of the explicit thoughts? Had he put them in her mind to seduce her into believing he wanted her, when what he really wanted was to drink her blood?

Trust me, daughter. He is not like us. He is a vampire.

With the last of her mental energy, Gabrielle tried to block out all the voices around her, including her mother's. She was so tired, so drained, and the little hope and happiness she'd felt while in Darius's presence had quickly disappeared with her mother's accusations.

Cruel, cruel world.

The music stopped and Gabrielle nodded to Darius. "Thank you. It was a pleasure meeting you."

He nodded formally, and she turned and started walking away. She didn't see or hear Sutherland, and for that she was grateful. She wanted to clear her head, forget about everything except getting as far away from this place as possible.

The music had started up for another dance, but ended abruptly. Everyone's attention turned to the far end of the ballroom where they had entered earlier in the evening. Gabrielle kept walking, but glanced over her shoulder. Her heart jolted when she saw Peter, the little boy she had brought back to life. He still wore the same raggedy shirt with the wheel marks across them. At his side stood a man, who had to be his father, as the resemblance between them was unmistakable.

Gabrielle did not have to guess why they were here.

Run Gabrielle! Her mother's voice rang in her ears. *If they catch you, you will be charged with practicing witchcraft.*

She saw Sutherland rushing toward the boy and his father. No wonder he had not been at her side the moment the dance with Darius had ended. He had seen Peter and known why he and his father were here. To accuse her openly of witchcraft, or perhaps he would demand money for his silence?

For the first time she was actually grateful for the old man's intervention, and even better, it gave her time to escape while everyone's attention was diverted.

The boy looked terrified when his father pulled out a knife, but Sutherland kept moving forward, hitting the man square in the chin.

The crowd moved forward and Gabrielle got caught up in the swell. She heard Darius mentally call out to her, but she ducked through the hard press of bodies, and into the nearest hallway she could find.

Slipping into a room, she shut the door behind her. It was dark and nearly impossible to see even her hand in front of her face.

At first all she could hear was the pounding of her heart, but a second later she heard a strange, deep-throated moan.

What in the world?

Gabrielle squinted into the darkness and saw the couple cast in moonlight. They were on the opposite side of the large room. The woman's gown had been shoved above her hips, and she bent over the settee in a very unladylike position, her bottom pushed high in the air. The man's pants were bunched about his knees, and he held onto the woman's hips as he thrust against her again and again.

There was no question what the two were about as moans and groans filled the air.

Good gracious, of all the rooms she *would* have to pick this one. Could things get any worse?

Now she would have to wait the couple out before she could flee, since they were just inches from the window. The same window she would slip out of the minute they finished doing their business.

Gabrielle hunkered down behind a chair, hoping they would be quick about it. What if Sutherland came looking for her and found her here? Or Darius? Vampire or human, it was not smart thinking about Darius just now, especially as the sounds of the lovers vibrated in her ears.

"I'm going to come," the man said through gritted teeth.

Come? Gabrielle craned her neck to see a bit better and almost wished she hadn't as heat warmed her belly, sweeping lower to her nether region.

"Not yet, my love," the woman replied, lifting her hips to meet each one of her lover's thrusts. "Touch me."

Touch her where? Gabrielle squinted, looking intently now. The man slid his hand in front of the woman, and began touching her there, in the same spot Darius had touched her in the daydream.

Gabrielle's own clit pulsed, aching to be touched. As the man grunted and the woman moaned, she grew more uncomfortable by the second. Her heart pounded against her breastbone as the man's thrusts increased. Gabrielle shifted, and licked lips that had suddenly gone dry.

Just then the woman's muffled cries rang out. The man finished seconds later with an impressive growl that had his lover laughing wickedly. He held onto the woman's hips firmly as he ground against her. Finally, with a contented sigh he withdrew and quickly buttoned his pants. "Lovely, Bess. Just lovely."

The woman's teeth flashed in the moonlight. "You are not so bad yourself, Jasper."

"We'd best get back. My wife will be suspicious if I don't return soon. I told her I was having a cigar and brandy with Lord Atherly."

Gabrielle opened her mouth in disgust. *Men! What devious creatures.*

"Go first and I shall follow later," Bess said, righting her skirts. "I am just going to freshen up a bit."

Jasper kissed her noisily. "I shall see you on Tuesday then?"

"I am not certain Frederick will be away, my dear. I shall send my man around if I can meet you at the hotel."

"Very well, love. Until then." With a soft pat to her bottom, Jasper left the room.

Gabrielle could not believe her ears. Was anyone in this town faithful to their spouse?

The strumpet hummed gaily, walking to the gold-framed mirror which hung above the fireplace. She patted her dark hair, straightened her necklace, and smiled at her reflection. She looked quite pleased with herself.

Gabrielle almost gasped as she recognized the woman as the wife of a friend of Sutherland's whom she'd been introduced to upon entering the ballroom. Recalling that Bess's husband had been older than Sutherland and rude as well, Gabrielle decided not to pass judgment.

Apparently satisfied with her appearance, Bess crossed the room, peeked out the door, and walked out, shutting it behind her.

"Shocking, isn't it?"

Her breath lodged in her throat when Darius stepped out from a dark corner.

"Were you here the entire time?" she asked, fearing his answer.

"I came in shortly after you did. I saw you enter, and well, I could not resist."

"I only stayed in the room because I feared they would alert some one as to my whereabouts."

"You do not need to explain anything to me."

Gabrielle could feel her cheeks turn hot. Thankful for the dark room, she moved toward the door, but he stopped her with a hand to her wrist. *He's a vampire.* Her mother's words came back to her, reminding her that the handsome man before her was a dangerous creature of the night.

"It is not safe for you to go out there right now. Sutherland is searching the hallways as we speak."

Once again, he brushed a wayward curl off her face. "You have lovely hair, Gabrielle. So pale. I have rarely seen anything like it."

Vampire or no, she enjoyed being touched by this man. She thought of the couple who had just made love here, and wondered what it would feel like to have Darius MacLeod's long, hard manhood inside of her.

His hands moved to either side of her face and he lowered his head, his lips inches from hers.

Part of her wondered if she should push him away, and yet she could not bring herself to do anything . . . or say anything for that matter.

He kissed her, his lips soft and gentle.

Having never kissed a man before, she had nothing to compare it to . . . but she enjoyed it.

Very much so.

His tongue brushed against the seam of her lips, urging her to open.

A million warning bells were going off in her head, but she ignored them all, including her mother's warning. Her entire life Gabrielle had listened to what others told her to do, be it right or wrong. Just once she wanted to experience this, because she didn't know if she would get another chance.

She wasn't sure how her hands had gotten there, but they rested on his narrow hips, before traveling up, over his broad shoulders.

He stepped in closer, to where their bodies touched, and she nearly gasped when she felt the obvious ridge of his sex against her.

How large he was. So thick. Impressive.

His hands moved down her body, too. One hand cupped her breast. Her breath hitched, but she didn't push him away. Instead she allowed herself to feel. His fingers pushed aside the material and played with her nipple, rolling it between forefinger and thumb.

How different it felt than her own hand. She had always thought herself wanton when she had touched herself. Perhaps she was the only young woman who had read her mother's books that talked of love and the things that happened between a man and woman.

Or perhaps other women did read such books, but they did not feel compelled to experiment. She could not help it. Her body had needed release, so she had done what she could about it and found the experience not at all disappointing, though she had felt guilty about it, thinking perhaps it was only something witches did.

But now even that would not be enough. No, she would very much like to make love to Darius MacLeod one day.

How she would love to have him touch her there.

Suddenly, the door opened abruptly, and the woman who had just been in the room making love to a man other than her husband looked at them with wide eyes. "I apologize. I must have the wrong room."

Darius moved in front of Gabrielle, and she fixed her bodice. "We just stepped in a moment ago."

"Oh, I see," the woman said, peeking around Darius to Gabrielle, who had put herself to rights and returned the smile. "I left something here earlier." She walked past them to the settee. Not finding what she looked for, she then went down on the floor. "Ah, there it is," she said, pulling a fan from beneath the settee. "Can't imagine how it got down there."

Gabrielle forced herself to keep a straight face.

"Sorry to have interrupted you," the woman said.

Darius followed the woman to the door. “Actually we were just leaving ourselves.”

“Sorry to interrupt,” Bess said again before slipping out the door.

“Would you mind checking on Lord Sutherland for me?” Gabrielle asked Darius, an idea forming in her mind.

“Of course.”

“I’ll be back in the ballroom shortly. I just need to take a moment to . . .”

“I understand. I’ll see ye in the ballroom shortly.”

“I hope so. If I do not get the chance to tell you later, I want you to know I had a wonderful night. I enjoyed our dance.”

He smiled, and her heart jolted. How handsome he was. So virile and masculine. She desired him so much it was unsettling. Especially knowing she could never be with him.

Life was so unfair.

“I shall tell Sutherland ye will be along shortly. I’m sure he will be relieved to hear the news.”

“I’m sure he will. Thank you again, Darius.”

“Certainly,” he said, lifting her hand, kissing it softly before walking away.

She watched his retreat, enjoying the way the black jacket fit across his broad shoulders and fell perfectly against his lean waist. And his pants were cut just right for his strong thighs. With a sigh, Gabrielle locked the door, raced to the window, and threw it open.

Hopefully this attempt would work better than the one at her uncle’s house. Thank goodness there were fewer obstacles beneath the window. No trellis, and even better, there was a tree.

Gabrielle slipped out the window. Unfortunately, the tree was a bit farther away from the ledge than it looked from inside the room.

Standing on said ledge, she took a deep breath and jumped, making a rather unladylike landing on the thick branch.

Looking down, she figured she had two choices, and hearing a voice from nearby, she let go and dropped to the ground, wincing as she turned her ankle.

She raced for a hedge, and just in time, too, as a young couple walked by, right under the tree she'd been hanging from.

Catching her breath, she looked toward the large, stone wall that surrounded the estate. Checking to be sure the way was clear, Gabrielle made a run for it.

She scratched her arm quite badly on a tree branch, but aside from that she had no trouble. Climbing up another sturdy tree, she made her way out on a branch, and then swung herself onto the wall. Straddling the wall, she gathered her skirts in one hand, and was ready to jump down onto the sidewalk when she heard voices coming from the street side of the wall. An old couple walked by at a snail's pace. Gabrielle's heart pounded in her chest, and despite the cool evening, sweat beaded on her forehead as she waited impatiently for them to pass.

Glancing once more at the Vanderline manor, she wondered if she and Darius MacLeod would cross paths once again. *Darius MacLeod, the vampire.*

The old couple's footsteps faded, and Gabrielle looked down at the sidewalk. Throwing both legs over the side of the wall, she twisted her body and tried to drop slowly.

Her gloved hands slipped and she swallowed a scream as she landed on her rump on the wet sidewalk.

Scrambling to her feet, she winced at seeing how soiled her gown had become.

Looking in both directions, she immediately crossed the street and walked at a brisk pace. She removed her wet, dirty gloves and tossed them in the brush.

Now what was she going to do?

She had no money, and no clothes, save for the ill-fitting dress that would provide little shelter from the elements. Already the chill made her shiver.

Hearing a carriage approach she jumped into the brush and crouched down, her heart pumping like mad against her breastbone. She had no doubt Sutherland would start searching for her immediately upon discovering that she was missing. Where could she go in London with no money and no friends?

Remembering the dance she'd shared with Darius MacLeod made tears burn her eyes. It was just her luck that the man she had had such an incredible moment with would end up being a vampire.

Gabrielle, trust me.

Gabrielle's breath caught in her throat. The voice belonged to Darius MacLeod. Could he have followed her? She turned around but no one was there.

Did he speak to her in her mind or was he nearby?

Her heart accelerated. How badly she wanted to trust him, to ask for his help, but she did not know who to trust now. She had never felt so alone in her life. And if her mother kept warning her about the vampire, then she needed to heed that council and keep her distance.

She blocked Darius out, but she couldn't block out the memory of kissing him, the taste of his lips, the feel of his strong shoulders against her palms.

Her cheeks burned knowing he had been in the chamber while the woman and her lover had been having sex.

Had watching excited him as well?

It had to have.

She had felt the hard ridge of his sex when he'd kissed her. Just for a moment, right before the woman had interrupted them.

He had been large. Much larger than the woman's lover had been. She brushed her thighs together, surprised at how aroused she had become by the single thought of Darius MacLeod's manhood.

The sound of his voice rippled within her, reminding her of the touch of his hand on hers. And the way he smiled, his lovely lips curving into a wolfish grin. Her nipples pebbled beneath her gown. What had caused him to become a creature of the night? Her mother had said oftentimes vampires did not choose their lifestyle.

Perhaps it was not so different than witches.

At least witches could choose to use their gifts, where vampires had to drink blood in order to survive. She wasn't sure she could do the same.

And what of the men with him? Gabrielle recalled his twin and Remont. She had sensed the blond's power when she had looked into his strange eyes. He was so intense.

Regardless, Darius MacLeod was a vampire and thereby dangerous, and she must heed her mother's warning. She could trust no one from this moment forward.

FIVE

Darius watched Sutherland walk the length of the ballroom for the tenth time in as many minutes. For the past half hour he had been combing the lower level of Lord Vanderline's impressive home.

Rumors were already circulating that Sutherland's fiancée might be the witch in question. After all, when asked what the witch looked like, the boy had said a beautiful angel with light blonde hair.

Not many in the room would fit that description . . . save for Sutherland's fiancée, who had mysteriously disappeared about the same time. The only thing that didn't make sense was the boy said the woman had worn a blue gown. Much like the one Darius saw in the vision.

But Sutherland would not be put off. He denied the rumors as fanciful, took the man outside, and when they came back in, the man apologized, saying he had been mistaken.

Amazing how money could wipe one's memory clean.

Remont took a step out on the verandah, and told Darius to follow. "Did you know she brought the boy back to life?"

"No, what did ye hear?"

"Apparently Sutherland's carriage ran the child down. Gabrielle got out of the carriage, took the child in her arms, and chanted in a mysterious language and minutes later the child awakes, alive and well."

"That is impossible."

"I tell you, it is true, Darius. She might very well be a witch."

Demetri lit a cigar and exhaled. "And are witches dangerous to vampires in any way?"

"Not that I know of."

"So why are you warning him?" Demetri asked, leaning against the door.

"Just be wary. Witches are dangerous creatures. Witches who can heal are extremely powerful."

"But there is nothing that says I cannot take a witch as my lover, correct?"

Demetri's lips quirked. "You are taken with her, aren't you?" He laughed. "I knew it."

"I want her, and now that Sutherland is no longer scouring the hallways, it is safe to find her and bring her back to the townhouse."

"Where is she?"

Demetri clapped him on the back. "We'll find her, brother. Do not worry. Remont, you search one wing, and I'll search the other. Darius, perhaps you should scour the surroundings."

Darius nodded. "I shall meet ye both at the front entrance in a quarter of an hour."

"All right, we'll see you then."

It would have been simple to jump rather than walk away, but he did not need to draw any suspicion tonight. Everyone was on pins and needles, believing they had a witch running rampant in the ballroom.

If he were to disappear all of the sudden, it would send off another shock wave, and that would not be good.

Darius followed a servant down the long hallway to where he had found Gabrielle earlier. He smiled, remembering the look on her face when she had caught the lovers.

She had been so intent watching them, she had no idea he had slipped in unnoticed.

Her heart had pounded out of her chest and he could feel the heat in her body rise.

Much as his had.

She would be a wonderful lover. Sensual, aware of her body in a way few virgins were. Aye, she had touched herself before, brought herself to orgasm a time or two.

A sexual being that wanted desperately to experience everything that could happen between a woman and a man.

He was jerked from his thoughts when a scream penetrated the night.

"Vampire!" came the bloodcurdling cry.

Gasps and screams came from the ballroom.

Darius's breath caught in his throat. It had come from the top floor . . . where his brother would be searching.

His brother had a ravenous hunger—one that apparently could not wait until after the ball. "Damn it, Demetri!"

Darius jumped to the third floor and ran into Remont, who had obviously heard the scream as well.

Another scream sounded from a nearby room, and a second later the door opened and Demetri walked out, calm as could be, wiping blood from his mouth with a sinister smile.

"For God's sake, Demetri! Could it not wait until after you completed your search?" Remont said, disgusted.

Demetri shrugged. "I could not help myself. You know how I like the plump ones."

Remont looked furious, especially when the sounds of multiple footfalls could be heard rushing up the staircase. "You've given us no choice but to leave." He glanced at Darius. "Fear not, my friend. We shall find her."

SIX

"You look cold, love."

Gabrielle stopped short, surprised to find a woman smoking a pipe in the back doorway of a townhouse that had seen better days. At least sixty in age, she wore a soiled apron over a threadbare dress, and her stockings were rolled down to her ankles; stained slippers covered her feet. She looked Gabrielle up and down, her brows furrowed. Exhaling a stream of smoke, she asked, "Are you lost, dear?"

"Yes, I—I suppose you could say that."

The woman chewed on the pipe, her eyes narrowing. "By the looks of your dress, and the fancy bits in your hair, I'm gonna guess ye are runnin' from someone, or ye had too much to drink this night and have lost your way."

"Do you live here?" Gabrielle asked, avoiding the question.

"Aye, I do," the woman replied, brushing off a drop of rain that had fallen on her cheek. "Would ye like to come in, love?"

"Yes," Gabrielle said, so relieved she wanted to hug the woman.

Gabrielle followed the woman into a warm room where a fire blazed. The furnishings consisted of two chairs and a worn-out settee. Two makeshift tables were made from wooden crates. "It's not much to look at, but it's home."

"It's lovely," Gabrielle said, meaning it. The woman had made the most of what she had, and the room, though tiny, was warm and comforting with personal effects placed here and there, a chipped vase with wildflowers in the middle of the table.

Gabrielle savored the warmth, reaching out to the flames.

"My room is downstairs, just through that door there. I used to sleep upstairs, but I can't get up and down the stairs like I used to. There's a small room in the loft there," she said, pointing to the steep staircase. "Nothing but a cot, a chair, and a small vanity, but you are welcome to it, for as long as you need it."

Gabrielle could not believe her good fortune. She reached out and touched the woman's wrinkled hand. "Thank you for your kindness."

The woman walked into the small room; the sound of drawers opening and closing followed. A second later she walked out with an old chemise. "Here ye are. This will keep you warm and dry tonight. I 'ave to go to market in the mornin'. You can join me and we can look for something for ye to wear."

"No," Gabrielle blurted. "I—um should stay here."

"Very well and my name is Bev."

"Thank you, Bev. I shall never forget your kindness."

"What's your name, love?"

"Oh, sorry. My name is . . . Sally."

The side of Bev's mouth lifted. "Very well then, Sally. You'll be takin' the upstairs room. It's not much. Just a place to lay that pretty head of yours."

"I'm grateful, Bev."

"Well, it's late, and you'd best get out of those wet clothes or you'll catch your death. I'll fix ye up a bowl of rabbit stew in the meantime."

"Do not go to any trouble."

"It's no trouble, Sally. I've been alone for many years. Plus," she said with a wink, "I like takin' care of people."

Walking up the steep stairs to her attic room, Gabrielle felt a sense of freedom for the first time since her mother's death. She had escaped Sutherland, and for now she had a roof over her head.

Darius stared at the picture of Rose in oils. It had been painted the night of their engagement, and it went everywhere with him.

He brushed his thumb over the lovely face. He was coming to see that Gabrielle did look a lot like Rose, but there were also small differences. Rose's nose was a little broader at the tip than Gabrielle's was, and her eyes a darker shade of green. Her hair was also more golden, where Gabrielle's was a paler blonde, but those differences were all slight. Anyone else might not spot them.

Moving to his bed, Darius removed his boots and socks, then his shirt. He took off his pants and drawers and slipped beneath the sheets, pulling the black bed curtains shut, leaving him in darkness.

He closed his eyes, remembering Gabrielle as they danced. The look in her eyes as she stared at him. She had known him, maybe even remembered him. Had it not been for the commotion from the boy and his father, he might be with her right now. He had seen her stricken expression, and watched along with the other guests as Sutherland pushed them out.

His Gabrielle was a witch. No wonder she had been able to read his thoughts so clearly.

He wondered what other powers she possessed. Had she used those powers to escape the ball? One moment she'd been there, the next she was gone.

After all these centuries, all these endless months, he was convinced he had found his wife again.

Only to lose her.

But he would find her again.

He had to find her again.

He concentrated on her face and sent the same message he'd been chanting over and over since meeting her. *Come to me, Gabrielle. I will not harm ye. Let me take care of ye. Let me show ye everything a woman and man can be together.*

In his thoughts he kissed her softly, just as he had earlier tonight, and she responded eagerly. Her arms moved up his back, and she trembled, much as he did. She was a virgin, untouched and waiting to be discovered.

He would be her first and, God willing, her last.

Let me touch you, Gabrielle. Make your body soar to unimaginable heights. If she was this witch who could read his mind, then mayhap she could feel this . . .

In his mind she was there with him, in his bed, naked and in his arms. *He deepened the kiss, his tongue sliding over the seam of her lips, seeking entry.*

She trembled from her head to her toes. "Let me love ye," he whispered in her ear, while cupping one of her perfectly shaped breasts, the nipple pressing against his palm. Her sighs and moans sounded like music to his ears.

Bending his head, he took a nipple into his mouth and drew on it slowly. Her fingers wove through his hair, holding him there.

Oh, but he longed to taste her life's blood, to feel it rush though his body. Even though his fangs grew imagining it, he knew he would never bite her. No, he could never harm her. Instead he would protect her, keep her safe from anyone who would try to hurt her or use her in any way.

She relaxed beneath him, and he used his thighs to part her legs, just enough so he could touch her there. His fingers brushed over the soft curls that covered her sex, slipping between the silky, slick folds. His thumb brushed her clit, and circled around it. Her quick intake of breath told him she was surprised, but liked it. His finger slid into her, and he heard her gasp once more.

Do ye like that, Gabrielle?

Yes.

Do ye want more?

Yes.

He added another finger, and her head rolled from one side of the pillow to the other.

Her stomach clenched as he kissed the underside of her breast, and then her navel. Gabrielle's inner muscles tightened around his fingers. He gritted his teeth. She was so hot, so wet, so ripe for the taking.

And on the brink of orgasm.

His cock was so hard, a tiny bit of precum rested on the slit of the purple head. He ached to slip inside her molten core, but not yet.

He moved lower, and lifted her buttocks so he could taste her. Her musky scent invaded his nostrils and he smiled as he licked her slit.

She moaned low in her throat, a satisfied groan that made him harder. Her fingers fisted in his hair. His tongue flicked over her clit, the sensitive nub hard as he continued to suck. He slid his finger inside her just as she came, her nails digging into his scalp.

He crawled up her body, and looked down into her flushed face.

His fingers wrapped around his cock at the base.

She licked her full lips and looked down at his rigid length. Her eyes widened.

"Do not worry, Gabrielle. It will only hurt this once."

He glanced down at her wet core, at the pink folds that beckoned him.

"Sir, are you asleep? Your brother is here."

Darius opened his eyes and cursed both his valet and brother.

His cock was so hard, he trembled with the need to climax. "I'll be right down," he said, wrapping his fist around his engorged length. He closed his eyes and envisioned Gabrielle as she'd been in his dream. He slid his hand up and down, faster and faster, his balls lifting against his body as he came with a moan.

SEVEN

Darius walked across the room, untying his cravat, his blue eyes bright with an inner fire that both scared and titillated Gabrielle.

She sat up against the headboard, drawing the blanket up to her chin. "What are you doing here?"

"I'm giving ye what you want, lass. What ye have been yearning for since I saw ye again."

"Again?" she said, the word sounding huskier than normal. "What do you mean?"

"We are connected. Do ye not remember me, Gabrielle?"

"You are familiar, I cannot deny that."

He nodded, looking pleased. "Aye, I should be familiar, lass. I was your husband."

"My husband? I have never been married."

His shirt came off next, and then he started on the buttons of his pants. "Not in this life, lass. We were married a long time ago. Do ye not remember it? Taking our vows at St. Mary's cathedral in the highlands?"

"You talk in riddles, Darius. I do not remember this cathedral, nor have I been to Scotland. I have never known you before the Vanderline ball."

"And yet ye see images in your mind of a place that is familiar. A place with tall hills, heather-filled valleys, and a manor house."

She gasped. "Yes, I've seen this place."

Gabrielle's gaze fell to Darius's wide chest and down the muscled planes of his abdomen where a thin strip of hair traveled from his navel and disappeared beneath the band of his pants.

Excitement pulsed through her, making the blood in her veins hot. She swallowed with expectation.

"I remember when I returned to the village after being away for several months. Ye were at the market, selling flowers with your mum, and ye had on a light-colored kirtle and a ringlet of heather in your hair. Ye always wore that ring of heather on market days, and by God, ye were beautiful. I wanted ye so desperately." His lips curved in a soft smile. "I still do. Relax, Gabrielle. See what I see. Feel what I feel. Be there now."

Gabrielle imagined the large, heather-strewn hills and the now familiar lush valley from her earlier visions. She glanced down at her bare feet, and the simple gown, or kirtle, that fell to her ankles, the color a soft blue. She touched her head and felt the crown of heather.

Could it be?

"Rose!"

She turned to find a young man wearing soft leather braies that hung low on narrow hips. A sleeveless black tunic, belted at the waist, showed well-muscled arms. Dark hair fell past broad shoulders, two braids on either side of his handsome face.

"Darius!" she yelled, running toward him, heather and grass caressing her ankles.

He laughed, his smile warm and welcoming as he opened his arms to her.

She flew into his strong embrace, her arms wrapping around his neck, holding him tight. "Darius, ye are finally home!" Gabrielle inhaled the soft, masculine scent. His hair felt like silk against her face. "I have missed ye so much. I can hardly believe it is ye."

"It is I, lass. It is I. The English took one look at us, turned tail, and ran, all the way back to England."

An overwhelming sense of relief flowed through Gabrielle. "Are ye home to stay then?"

"For a little while."

Disappointment washed over her. "How long this time?"

He set her back on her feet, cupped her face between his hands. "Long enough to marry ye."

Her heart skipped a beat. "What?"

"Marry me, Rose. Make me the happiest man in all of Scotland."

She stared into his beautiful blue eyes and knew he was serious. Joy, the likes of which she'd never before known washed over her in waves. "Aye, I shall marry ye."

Gabrielle swallowed past the lump in her throat, the memory fading as she opened her eyes. "I remember. I was your Rose."

He stood at the edge of the bed now, looking at her with those amazing light blue eyes. Her heart pounded hard against her ribs, expectation making her wet her lips.

He did the same.

Her gaze shifted to his body once more, and she saw white marks here and there, all over his chest and arms. Scars from the past.

He'd been a warrior in that life. A soldier, and she had been his wife. Before he'd been made into a vampire.

Her heart skipped a beat when he pushed the pants from his lean hips, taking his drawers with it.

The statue David did not compare to Darius MacLeod in all his naked glory. Especially in the nether region.

Her insides burned, her nipples stabbing at the material of her chemise. The flesh between her thighs grew wet as she looked at all of him.

"You are—" she stammered, unable to find words to describe that part of him.

He laughed lightly. "I want ye, Gabrielle. Do ye want me?"

"Yes," she said, meaning it. In fact, she let the blanket drop and reached out for him.

Darius's gaze shifted to her breasts, over her stomach, and further, to stare at her mons. "Ye are even more beautiful than I remember."

He lay down beside her, holding her, his body molding to hers. How perfectly they fit together.

His tongue brushed along the seam of her lips, urging her to open. The feel of his tongue stroking against hers was nothing short of heaven, and she was aware of everything about him. How hard his body was compared to hers, the feel of a powerful thigh as it nudged between hers.

Then he rolled so she lay beneath him.

His cock, hard, like stone, rested against her belly. She felt it throb against her, and knew she was moments away from becoming a woman.

Darius's woman.

His lips left hers, drawing a path down her neck and shoulders, to the swell of her breasts where he lightly kissed her.

She felt the cool air on her breasts, and a second later his mouth covered a nipple, drawing on it. Her breath left her in a rush, and her hands cradled his head, anchoring him there.

"Don't stop."

He used his teeth with restraint, his tongue laving, licking her, making her moan and shift beneath him. She arched her hips, aching for him in every way.

"Darius," she breathed.

He looked up at her, his blue eyes even lighter than before. "Aye love?"

"Make love to me."

His gaze searched hers. "There will be no going back."

"I don't want to go back."

"Open your legs wider," he urged, using his knees to spread them.

But rather than lay on her, he kissed her belly, his tongue swooping into her navel, swirling, before moving down. He placed a kiss on her mons, and then he moved lower and licked her heated slit.

She felt on fire as his tongue worked magic, moving over the tiny, sensitive nub. He flicked it over and over again with his tongue until she was moaning and arching beneath him.

He slipped a finger inside her, and she bit down on her lip to keep from groaning aloud.

"So tight," he said, flicking his tongue over her small bud again, "and so wet." He slipped another finger in, moving it in and out with the other.

She tightened around his fingers, and he sucked hard on her tiny button.

She climaxed hard, her tight sheath pulling his fingers in deeper, coating them with her juices.

When the last spasms rocked her body, she opened her eyes to find Darius above her, his eyes soft yet intent.

"Are ye sure?"

"Yes," she said, her hands moving over his back, loving the play of muscle there.

He reached between their bodies and guided his hard cock inside her, just so the plum-sized head stretched her.

She winced, and he stopped, his blue eyes filled with concern. "Did I hurt ye?"

"It hurts a little."

"Do ye want me to stop?"

"No."

She could see the relief in his eyes, and then he thrust quickly and she cried out, biting his shoulder.

"Shh," he said against her neck. "I will not move, to give your body time to get used to the feel of me inside ye."

She nodded, shifting her hips a little. How strange it felt to be stuffed completely by his long, thick cock. It hurt, but the sensation was not entirely unpleasant.

After a few moments he withdrew, leaving just the head of his cock kissing her opening, and then thrust again, but slowly.

This time she felt a fluttering within. A wonderful ache that had her lifting her hips.

"Are ye all right, Gabrielle?" he asked, and she nodded.

He smiled then, resting his head against her forehead as he thrust inside her again and again with more urgency.

He withdrew all the way, and she lifted her hips, not wanting the pleasure to end.

Once again, he entered her, easing the head of his cock into her. Her hands cupped his buttocks, and she pulled him toward her, wanting more of him.

He bent his head and took a nipple into his mouth, the dual sensations making her heart skip a beat. How wonderful it felt, like being lifted higher and higher on a silky cloud.

Her hands moved up his muscled back, splaying over his shoulders, her nails grazing the olive skin. He must have liked it, for he groaned as one hand moved back downward and cupped a buttock. Once again she squeezed him as she opened wider for him.

His strokes increased, faster and faster, and with it came a need so intense, so devastatingly exhilarating, she could hear her heart pounding in her ears.

The climax was so strong, she cried out in bliss. She heard his pleased masculine moan, and she clung to his shoulders, her inner muscles throbbing around him.

Darius kissed her passionately as he thrust a few more times, and met his own release with a wonderful groan that vibrated his entire being.

He collapsed beside her, and pulled her against him. His heart raced and his chest rose and fell with great effort.

"Sally, time to wake up, love. It is half past six."

Who was Sally, and why was someone interrupting such a wonderfully erotic dream?

"Sally, get up, girl." Incessant knocking followed this last request.

Opening her eyes, Gabrielle glanced around the room.

Damn! She most certainly wasn't at Darius MacLeod's home, nor was she at her room in her uncle's townhouse.

"Sally!" the woman's voice said from the other side of the door, and everything came back to her in a rush.

She had escaped Sutherland and her uncle.

"Time to get up, girl. And I have items to get at market. I wanted to double-check your size, since the good Lord knows you need a dress or two."

"I'll be right down," Gabrielle said, glancing down at the borrowed chemise. .

Her nipples were still hard and sensitive. The erotic dream came back to her in all its wicked glory, and she couldn't help the grin that came to her lips.

Darius MacLeod had done things to her in her dreams that she had not even known were possible.

It made sense that she would dream of him since she'd read his mind last night and seen erotic images then. Had he sent those images or dreams last night? Did he have the same dream? If so, did he wake up aching, just as she ached?

"Sally!"

Gabrielle groaned and noticed the robe hanging on a nail. She put it on and belted it. It was a few sizes too big, so she lifted the hem as she carefully made her way downstairs. She hated the fact that she had lied to Bev about her identity, especially since she clearly could not afford to buy Gabrielle a dress, let alone two.

Somehow she would help Bev out, and pay her back for not just the dresses, but for the room and food. Indeed, the older woman had been far kinder than her own uncle had been.

Gabrielle walked into the small living area where Bev was busy draping Gabrielle's underclothes over one of the chairs before the fire.

"You did not need to wash my garments, Bev. I could have done so myself."

Bev scratched her gray head. "You are my guest, dear. I was washin' me own, so it didn't do no harm to add your underclothes to the barrel. The dress is ruined, I'm afraid."

Gabrielle resisted the urge to hug the woman. "How kind of you," she said instead, and rested a hand on Bev's shoulder. "I shall return the kindness you have shown me one day soon, I swear it."

"Think nothin' of it, love. I'm glad to have your company." Bev smiled warmly, clearly flustered. "The dress ye wore was a bit of an odd fit for ye, so I want to be sure to get ye one that fits all your bits."

Bits meaning breasts. "I certainly never called them *bits* before."

Bev's own breasts heaved as she laughed. Gabrielle stayed still while the older woman walked about her with a piece of string. "All right, dear. I'll do my best to find something lovely, though I can't promise silks and lace."

"Anything is fine, Bev," she said, meaning it. A plain dress would draw less attention, and that's exactly what she needed. "And again, thank you for your kindness."

"Think nothing of it. I just wish you could come with me. A bit of fresh air could do ye good. You are so pale."

The last thing she wanted to do was be seen by anyone in London. Sutherland and her uncle would be combing the streets by now. Being seen by even one of Bev's neighbors could put her in danger, and Bev as well. "Perhaps next time."

"Oh, I do hope so." Bev started for the door and stopped short of it. "I made a pot of tea. It's sitting on the stove. Just help yerself, and I'll be back shortly."

The door closed behind Bev, and Gabrielle made herself a cup of tea and glanced out the window. Children played in the streets, their clothes a bit thready and some with holes. However, they seemed content, laughing as they kicked a ball about. A woman close to Gabrielle's age swept the sidewalk. Suddenly, she turned and looked at Gabrielle, her eyes narrowing as she continued to stare.

Gabrielle backed away from the window. She needed to be careful and stay out of sight. One day she could tell Bev the truth about her circumstances, but not now. She knew word would start circulating, and she had no idea what the boy's father had said at the ball. For all she knew the entire city could be on the lookout for a blonde witch.

Good gracious she had made a mess of things.

Hopefully Sutherland and her uncle would not think to look for her here, in this neighborhood.

Looking about the small room she knew she could easily be content in such surroundings. Her time at the convent had proven to her that material things meant very little. Instead it was the people in one's life who made the difference. If a person found love, had a roof over their head, food in their belly, and clothing to wear, what else was needed?

And what of Darius MacLeod? Would he feel the same? The visions she'd had of him, and the fine clothes he'd worn, made her believe he was a man of means. Not titled, but rich.

Could he live in a place such as this and still be content?

Being a vampire, he could probably live just about anywhere. She shook her head. Why was it she seemed to always forget that one important detail about Darius MacLeod?

He was a vampire, which meant he was dangerous, and her life was complicated enough.

She recalled the vivid dream she'd had and the visions of his past. Or perhaps *their* past. What had he called her in that dream? "Rose," she said the name aloud, as though it would trigger a memory. She did recall the manor house, the same hills and valleys of what had to be Scotland. And there was no denying she felt comfortable with this man . . . who was supposed to be a vampire. Everything she had ever heard about the dark creatures did not match up with what she knew of Darius MacLeod.

But what do you really know of him?

Aside from the fact that they shared a strange connection and he could speak to her in her thoughts. Would he know she heard him, or could everyone hear vampires?

And what of Rose? Why did Gabrielle see herself, or rather this other woman, and Darius together in another time? Had Darius been a vampire back then?

She took a sip of tea and winced when it burned her tongue. Of course Gabrielle would never know the answers to those questions because she would probably never see him again.

Unless she went looking for him, but that would be too dangerous. He'd be staying in a fine hotel, or if he was as wealthy as she assumed he was, he could own or rent luxurious rooms or a townhouse in one of London's most affluent neighborhoods. Yet even in her dreams he had asked her to trust him.

He would be a nice ally to have.

But should she trust him?

She had trusted her uncle and look what had happened. She had gone from the confines of a convent to the prison of an arranged marriage.

For the time being she was safe from Sutherland, and Bev seemed genuinely happy to have her as a guest.

No, she must stay here, out of sight, and not trust anyone, including the handsome Scot. She would try as best she could to make money as fast as possible and flee London. Go wherever she wished, as far away from London, her uncle, and Sutherland as possible.

EIGHT

Sitting in the very back of the smoke-filled tavern, Darius took another drink from the tall glass. He drank rarely, usually only at balls or social occasions.

But he could not help drinking now. He hoped the whisky would help wipe away all memories of Gabrielle Fairmont.

He knew Demetri had meant only good by bringing him here and showing him the woman who so resembled his dead wife.

But Gabrielle had fled, and no matter how much he called out to her, she did not respond.

That meant she didn't want to be found. Not by Sutherland, her uncle, or him.

Very sobering.

He had searched the streets, inquiring about a young woman, but most everyone merely smiled, saying there were a good many women of that same description.

Desperate, he had a good friend check all the outgoing ships to see if a young lady traveling alone had booked passage, but no one matching Gabrielle's description had.

Perhaps she had discovered he was a vampire. Memories of Rose's death flashed through his mind, and he swallowed the last of his drink.

Unfortunately no amount of alcohol would take away the pain in his heart.

Not even Remont's or Demetri's constant companionship could pull him from his dreary mood. Nor the taste of blood for that matter.

Feeding only reminded him of the differences between himself and Gabrielle. She was mortal, just as Rose had been. And though she had powers of her own, she at least lived a normal life span, and could be part of society without preying on it.

Gabrielle would no doubt be as repulsed by Darius as Rose had been.

"Have they caught the witch yet?"

Darius sat up straighter at the question being asked by one of the men playing poker at a nearby table.

"Not yet, though I understand some high-fallutin' gent has put up one hell of a reward for whoever captures her."

"How much?"

"I don't know for certain, but me brother said it would be enough to buy me a whore for a month."

The man next to him guffawed, and Darius counted to ten.

"A rare beauty, I hear, though I doubt she's a witch," one of them said with a snicker.

Another of the men sat forward in his chair. "I hear she brought the boy back from the dead. Could a mere woman do that?"

"Perhaps she was just lucky."

"That could be, too."

The answer was Gabrielle Fairmont was indeed a witch. A healer who could read minds, which meant she was not so very different from himself. And as he feared, Sutherland was pulling out all the stops to get her back.

"Perhaps she left on a boat and is far away."

One of the men scoffed at that. "With no money?"

He nudged his partner. "She's a woman, gents. All she need do is spread those lovely thighs of hers and any captain would take her where she wished."

Darius stared at the man, who lifted a glass of ale to his lips. He took a long drink, then his eyes widened as he choked. The men around him laughed at first, but as the man dropped the glass, and the contents flew up, soaking each of them, the humor faded as curses filled the air.

Darius ignored them as a tavern wench approached him, a saucy smile on her thin lips. "Another drink, love?"

He nodded. "Aye."

"Should I just bring the bottle then?"

"I think this will be my last, but thank ye, lass."

She winked. "Well, be careful when you leave. Try to stay east of Hawthorne Ridge."

"Why is that?"

"Have you not heard?" she asked, excitement in her voice. "We have ourselves a highwayman, it seems."

"A highwayman?" he repeated, unable to keep the sarcasm from his voice. He had read about thieves who preyed on the rich and powerful, robbing the well-to-do of their money and jewels on dark roads far outside the city.

"Indeed, it is true. I hear the highwayman himself is very gallant and polite, and from what I understand, has quite a way with the ladies."

"Does he, indeed?"

The wench placed beefy hands on her ample hips. "Yes, and he kisses their hands seconds before he takes their rings, bracelets, and baubles. His lips are soft, I hear. And he is also quite striking."

"He does not wear a mask?"

"He does, but it covers just his mouth. He has lovely eyes, I hear. Light green."

Light green eyes. Much like someone else he knew.

"Apparently the Dowager Countess of Castile has become quite smitten with him. Rumor has it she has been up and down this stretch of road a good dozen times in the hopes of seeing him again."

Darius laughed. "The countess must have an armory of jewels to keep the highwayman busy."

"Indeed, she does. Though I doubt she wears her best, knowing full well the highwayman will take them." The wench laughed gaily, making Darius smile. "I imagine it has given her some excitement in her old age."

"We could all use a bit of excitement in our old age," Darius murmured, his gaze shifting to the woman's generous breasts that nearly swelled from their small confines.

"Strange thing is I hear the highwayman is said to be quite small in stature. Not much taller than myself," she said, "and slender. It's a wonder no one has been able to stop him."

"Perhaps the lad has a large pistol?"

"Or perhaps he has a partner in crime," she said with a wink. "Someone lurking in the shadows to come to his rescue in case things go badly."

"That could very well be the case, and I appreciate you letting me know of the danger. But I might just travel the road out of curiosity."

She slapped him playfully on the arm. "I secretly hope he continues to haunt this same stretch of road. It has been great for business. We have been bursting at the seams since word has circulated."

"I would not count on it continuing much longer, if he knows what is good for him. Luck only lasts for so long."

"Indeed, it does. Well, I had best get your whisky, love."

The door opened, letting a brisk wind inside. Darius smiled, seeing his brother and Remont. It was comforting having them both with him. He had grown melancholy in the past few days as his hopes of finding Gabrielle had diminished.

Remont, dressed in a frock coat made of fine silk and buff-colored breeches, ran his hands up and down his arms. "It is so cold. I can't get the damn chill out of my bones."

Demetri smirked. "I know a way I can help with that."

Remont merely smiled and sat down next to Darius.

"Have you had any luck finding Rose?" Demetri asked.

"You mean Gabrielle," Remont injected.

"Sorry. Of course, I meant Gabrielle."

The wench came over with Darius's drink. "Here you go," she said, a wide smile on her face. "And what can I get for you two gents?" Her gaze skipped over them, and settled on Remont. "A bit young, aren't you?"

"I'm older than I look, love," he said, with a smoldering smile that had the woman blushing.

They were all used to similar reactions from the opposite sex, but Remont was always a favorite—of both sexes.

"We would each like a glass of your finest red wine," Demetri said, putting a firm hand on Remont's knee. A full second later he moved it further up his thigh and in clear view of the wench.

The woman's eyes widened. "Oh. Your twins?"

Demetri nodded. "Ever *serviced* twins before?"

Darius kicked his brother beneath the table.

"No, but I would service you, your brother, and your friend as well any day of the week. No charge."

"No charge?" Remont smiled tightly. "Tempting, but we shall have to pass, love. We have business to attend to."

Demetri whispered something in Remont's ear that made his lips quirk.

The tavern door flew open, nearly hitting the barmaid. A wide-eyed man looked out of breath. "The highwayman has struck again! He held up our carriage not a mile from here."

"Highwayman?" Remont lifted a brow. "Did I hear him correctly?"

"Indeed, you did," Darius replied. "The tavern maid was just telling me that a *gentleman* highwayman has been haunting this stretch of road."

"Gentleman highwayman?" Remont repeated, laughing. "Only the English would romanticize a highwayman."

"Yes, apparently this particular robber has impeccable manners and charms the women he steals from."

Demetri tapped his long fingernails on the table. "Perhaps we might have ourselves a bit of fun tonight after all."

"We should just leave the poor lad alone. He apparently needs the money, or he would not take such a chance," Remont remarked.

"Our driver just left," Demetri said, tossing back the rest of Darius's whisky. "Come, before he gets away."

Within minutes Darius found himself shoved into Remont's carriage.

Remont, who sat beside Demetri, released a heavy sigh as he stared out the window. "Why the hell do I always let you talk me into something I do not want to do?"

"Because you love me," Demetri said matter-of-factly.

Remont looked at Demetri's hand, which had crept higher still. "You always think sex will make everything better."

"Doesn't it?" Demetri asked, turning to Darius. "What do you think, Darius?"

"Sex is nothing without love," he said absently, realizing how much he meant it, and how much he yearned for Gabrielle Fairmont. He needed her in his life to feel whole again.

"Stand and deliver!" Gabrielle yelled, her heart pounding so loud it was a roar in her ears.

A gust of wind nearly knocked the hat from her head. At least the kerchief covering her lower face had not blown up.

The carriage driver looked at her as though she'd grown another head. "Bloody 'ell, I hope you're stronger than you look, lad, 'cuz I ain't givin you a shilling." He lifted the reins, ready to use them, when she produced another pistol from the band of her breeches and cocked it.

"Drop those reins and open that door or I shall blow a hole clean through your head!" She gave a mental shudder, finding it hard to believe she had sunk so low in such a short period of time.

But she'd had no choice. She needed money, and she clearly was not going to make money working with Bev at the market selling flowers.

The driver sighed loudly and moved slowly, climbing down from his perch, huffing and puffing the entire way.

Bloody hell.

She heard the passengers in the carriage whisper amongst themselves—anxious and scared. Gabrielle felt a pang of remorse when she heard a woman crying.

She couldn't very well tell them she meant no harm and would never use the gun, unless her life was in real danger. In fact, she had limited experience with firearms. Bev kept one of the pistols hidden in a kitchen drawer, and the other under a plank in the attic room where Gabrielle slept.

She had raided Bev's closet for clothes. Her husband, who'd left her a year ago for another woman, had been a man of small stature, thank goodness. Pulling the coat tighter about her, she leveled her gun on the driver.

The carriage shifted as he finally jumped off, onto the hard ground. He slipped on the mud, compliments of the rain, landing firmly on his backside. "Damn it all!" he muttered, struggling to get up.

Gabrielle's first instinct was to help him, but she stopped herself short of doing so. "Get up, man! Hurry!" she said gruffly, shifting on her feet as he managed to stand and open the door.

She had robbed a carriage just a quarter of an hour before. Unfortunately the couple had had little in the way of riches on them, and aside from taking the man's gold ring, she let them go, the woman wailing all the way.

Though Gabrielle took a chance by holding up two carriages in one night, she could not go home with so little. Perhaps after tonight she would have enough to leave London. "Step out of the carriage now!"

The driver pulled the steps down, and a pretty brunette appeared at the doorway.

Gabrielle nearly groaned aloud. The woman's gaudy satin dress marked her as a whore. Another woman, this one a voluptuous redhead, followed, her dress barely reaching to her knees. She sobbed as she clung to the brunette. "Do not kill us, kind sir." She hiccupped, and proceeded to cover her mouth with a trembling hand.

The woman might have taken up acting. She was quite good at it, though she might work a bit at actually producing tears to match the wail.

A man stepped down next, the entire carriage rocking under his weight. He was massive, standing at least two heads taller than the girls and quite thick around the middle.

He placed a hand in his waistcoat.

"Do not move, sir!" Gabrielle shouted.

His pudgy hand fell to his side. "I merely wanted a handkerchief to wipe the sweat from my brow," he said, his voice reflecting his anger. His fleshy lips pursed as he gawked at her. "Perhaps I can borrow the one you use to disguise your face?"

"I think not," Gabrielle replied. For once she might actually enjoy robbing someone. "I would like all of you to first empty your pockets. Slowly. One hand at a time. We shall start with you," Gabrielle said, pointing to the man.

He sighed heavily, his jowls wobbling as he took his sweet time emptying each pocket, which proved to be a chore for him since he kept cursing every few seconds.

Gabrielle tossed her velvet bag between them. "I want all your rings, all your necklaces, and all your earrings please. Place the items in the bag."

"At least you are polite," the man said, doing as asked, and encouraging the women to do the same. The brunette moved slowly, staring at Gabrielle with a coy smile as she took off each piece of jewelry, which hopefully wasn't just paste and glass.

The redhead sobbed as she pulled the rings from her gloved fingers. "I cannot believe this is happening to us."

Once finished, the man tossed the bag back at Gabrielle. "Can we leave now, sir?"

"I want the ring," Gabrielle said, looking at the brunette, who tried to hide a lovely ruby ring by covering it with the other hand.

"I worked too hard for this ring."

"I'm sure you did, but I will have it now or put a bullet in your head. The choice is yours."

"Bloody hell, Renona, I shall buy you another," the fat man said, clearly exasperated.

The brunette kissed his cheek and proceeded to pry the ring off her finger, tossing it toward Gabrielle, but it landed short. "How about buying me two rings, love?" Renona said to her fat lover, who merely shook his head.

"And me too?" the redhead asked, brushing fake tears from her face as she looked at her lover with a hopeful smile.

In the distance Gabrielle heard the sound of a carriage coming. "I have what I need, now please go." Snatching up the bag and the ring, she stuffed both into her jacket and bowed. "You may go now. Godspeed!"

She rushed into the trees, untied the horse, and mounted it. She had borrowed the mare from the livery, two blocks from Bev's. At first the poor animal had reared up in fear of Gabrielle, but she had spoken softly to it, all the while chanting beneath her breath. The horse had been docile ever sense, and a faithful companion.

Perhaps she would even take the mare with her north, if she had enough money to buy her.

She did not know if it had been the dreams that haunted her each night that had planted the thought of Scotland in her mind, but she was drawn to the northern country.

She *could* live in Scotland and live a simple existence. A remote house where she could grow her own vegetables, perhaps buy livestock. A simple, solitary life. If Bev could do it, then so could she. Or perhaps a lovely manor house that sat between two large hills in the highlands.

Do not fool yourself, Gabrielle. You want Darius MacLeod, and that's why you desire to live in Scotland.

Why was it the handsome highlander always entered her mind when she thought of the future? The dreams she'd had each night, of him making love to her, played over and over. Every night, never changing, burning into her memory, to the point that it was almost all she could think about throughout the long day.

Perhaps one day she would know what it was to make love to a man like Darius MacLeod in real life. To feel his hands on her body and his thick length filling her completely.

Sadly, the dream ended when she opened her eyes, and always she awoke feeling sad and empty, her body pulsing with a need that could not be extinguished. There could never be anything between her and Darius MacLeod. After all, he was a creature of the night.

A vampire. A creature to be feared.

But then again, she was a witch. They burned and hung her kind. Witches were ostracized for being different, which was not so very far from what a vampire must go through.

She had never been so confused in all her life.

Her horse stopped so abruptly she had little time to hold onto the reins. She patted the sack of jewels and money, tucked into her coat pocket to be sure she wouldn't lose it.

The carriage came along at a solid clip.

It was close. Should she take the chance and hold up a third carriage, or would that be too greedy?

If she managed to rob this third coach, and her take was substantial, then perhaps she could leave London by morning, and even have a big chunk left over to give Bev for all her help.

She could leave and never worry about Sutherland or her uncle again.

Or Darius MacLeod.

NINE

The road was bumpy and not at all pleasant to travel on, Darius decided as he was once again thrust against the back of the black velvet seat of Remont's impressive carriage.

His brother and their maker did not seem to mind the ride. Not that they had paid him any mind. In fact Demetri's hand still had not moved from Remont's thigh.

"Perhaps this wasn't a good idea," Darius said, looking at the passing landscape that consisted of road and tree after endless tree. He could see quite well in the dark, and noted the creatures looking back at him as they passed.

No wonder the highwayman had chosen this bit of road.

Demetri moved his hand back to his own lap. "Come, Darius. Don't you want to have a little fun?"

Darius shrugged.

Remont sat up abruptly, putting his hand up as he cocked his head. "Do you hear that?"

"What?" Demetri asked, his brows furrowing.

Remont's eyes lit up. "Ah, I think the infamous highwayman is about to pay us a visit."

Demetri rubbed his hands together. "Oh, this shall be great fun."

"Do not harm him," Darius said sternly, and received a scowl from both Remont and Demetri.

The driver pulled on the reins hard, forcing them to brace themselves.

"Stand and deliver!"

Demetri grinned like a boy on Christmas morning. "This is fantastic!"

"For God's sake, how old is the lad?" Remont asked, looking out the window. "Twelve?"

"Not much younger than you, love," Demetri replied with a devilish smile.

"Fuck you."

"Gladly."

The carriage shifted as the driver climbed down, and met Darius at the doorway. The poor man's face was pale in the moonlight as he looked at Remont. "Sorry, sir. I could not help but stop."

"That is quite all right," Remont said, stepping down and giving the man an encouraging pat on the back.

Demetri followed and shut the carriage door behind him.

"Oh dear God," Darius thought he heard the highwayman say, though it was muffled by the dark kerchief covering his face.

The lad wore light-colored breeches that barely disguised long, slender legs. He wore a jacket that looked a good three sizes too big, and a hat so large it nearly covered his eyes.

Remont's gaze shifted over the boy. "Not bad."

Demetri lifted a brow but stayed uncharacteristically quiet.

"Your money or your life," the lad said in a gruff voice, removing another pistol from the band of his breeches.

Demetri laughed under his breath, but stopped when Darius elbowed him.

"What if we have no money?" Demetri asked, his gaze sliding over the lad slowly. "What else might we give you?"

"You *have* money." The highwayman's voice cracked.

"Not really," Remont said, crossing his arms. "I left it behind at the hotel. Would you like to come back to our hotel room?"

The lad shifted on his feet. "Certainly you have money on your person. I do not believe the three of you would be out on such a night with no coin. After all, look at your clothing."

Darius noticed the pistols quaked in the boy's hand.

"Our clothing?" Demetri asked, already stripping off his jacket, and quickly moving to the buttons on his pants. "I assume you want them?"

Darius shook his head. "Brother, the lad means that we are dressed so finely, he therefore does not believe us when we say we have no money."

Demetri shrugged back into his jacket and buttoned his pants. "What if we have no riches to give you?"

"Then I shall have to kill you."

Demetri's lips curved in a sinister smile. "Not if we kill you first."

Darius looked at Demetri, who took a step closer to the boy.

The lad cocked the gun. "Do not come one step closer."

"Do you think we fear you?" Remont asked, his voice silky soft.

Horses' hooves sounded in the distance, and all three heard it at the same time. As did the lad apparently, since he ran for his horse.

But Darius was quicker. He grabbed the boy by the jacket, turned him around, and pushed his back up against a tree trunk.

"Bloody hell, Darius," Demetri said behind him. "Seems you have a bit of fire left in you, after all."

The lad fought him, but Darius tightened his grip. "Shh, Gabrielle."

Her light green eyes narrowed. "How did you know?"

Exhilaration rushed along his spine the moment he'd stepped out of the carriage. It had taken just one look into those green eyes to know he'd found his woman again.

"Be still." He leaned back, glanced at his brother and Remont. "Leave now. I shall be fine."

Remont smiled knowingly and took Demetri by the hand. Apparently his brother was the only one of them who had not guessed the lad was Gabrielle.

Darius pulled the kerchief down past her chin. "Gabrielle, trust me," he whispered.

She stared at his lips. "I cannot. I have to leave, Darius. The other carriage could have made it to town by now and I could be arrested at any moment. I cannot stay here and wait. I must return."

"Return where?" He lifted her chin with his fingers, urging her to tell him the truth. "Trust me, Gabrielle. I swear to ye I will not harm ye. But ye must trust me."

She glanced at the retreating carriage that disappeared around the bend. Remont and Demetri would deter anyone coming to capture

Gabrielle. The problem now was getting them away from there. He could try to use his powers and jump to another location, but while it was a nice trick when in close confines, great distances could not be covered, especially when jumping with a mortal. At least, he had never tried such a feat, and the one of them who could do it had just left in the carriage. Remont, since he was an elder, could travel longer distances than he or Demetri put together.

Which meant he hoped luck was on their side.

Gabrielle looked up at him, her green eyes frightened. "I trust you, Darius. Just get us out of here."

Unable to help himself, he kissed her, softly at first, but then with all the anger, fear, and excitement he'd been feeling since meeting her at the Vanderline ball.

Even more surprising was the fact she readily accepted his kiss, and her arms wrapped around his neck. The blood in his veins sang as he kissed her, hard, long, his heart pounding unsteadily.

Suddenly the horse raced past them, and Gabrielle tore away from Darius, ready to cry out, but he stopped her. "Shh, we can do nothing about it now. Let it go. Perhaps it will deter the men who are coming."

"But she has been so docile until now."

"I have that effect on horses," he said, sincerely sorry.

"I see," she said, and he knew she knew the truth of what he was.

"Look over there!" someone yelled, the voice coming from nearby.

Damn, he had hoped for more time.

He put a finger to his lips and started for the trees, being sure to watch their step.

There were so many twigs, leaves, and broken branches on the ground that he feared making too much noise. They would have to stay put until the threat passed.

Resting his back against a tree trunk, he pulled her into his arms and covered her with his cloak.

She sank into him, resting her cheek against his chest. How perfectly she fit his body. Just like Rose had.

"Stay alert, gentlemen! The lad can't be too far off given his horse is here."

She looked up at him, fear shining in her amazing eyes. *It's all right, love. No one will hurt ye. I won't allow it.*

She nodded. *I trust you.*

He had waited five hundred years to hear those words.

"Spread out into the woods, men! Let's get this thief once and for all!"

There are so many of them. Gabrielle's nails dug into his sides. *We will never escape!*

Do not move. Someone is coming our way. No matter what happens, I want ye to stay here, right by this tree and do not, under any circumstances, move. Understand?

She nodded.

The men fanned out into the woods, and unfortunately, one was heading right for them. Darius put Gabrielle from him, and crept slowly toward the man coming toward them on horseback.

Darius was at a definite advantage, as he could see so well in the dark. The man had a rifle resting on his lap, and as he approached, Darius stepped out in front of him, reached up, and pulled him from the horse.

The man let out a startled yelp.

Darius held the stocky man by the throat and hoisted him up, pushing his back against a tree. The man's gun fell into the brush as he looked down at Darius with a horrified expression.

"I won't—" he gasped, wetting himself. "What are you?"

"Shhhh," Darius said, lifting his free hand to his lips. "Quiet."

"Kenneth, is that you?" came a nearby voice.

The man's eyes widened. "Hel—"

Darius bit the man's neck and began to drink. As always when feeding, his body thrilled at the metallic taste of the blood that re-energized him and gave him strength.

"Kenneth, is that you?"

Someone came closer. Darius dropped the man he was feeding from and turned around to find a young man looking at him with wide, frightened eyes. He glanced from Darius, to the body of his friend that lay at his feet.

"Do not kill me," the man said, nearly in tears as he took a step back. "I won't say anything, I swear it!"

Gabrielle was going to be sick.

She couldn't believe her eyes. Darius had held a man who outweighed him by five stone up against a tree trunk, leaving the man's feet dangling. Even worse, he had sucked the life from him right in front of her.

She had been paralyzed, unable to move. Even when the boy came toward them. He'd seen Gabrielle first, his eyes narrowing as they looked her up and down. Her hair had come loose of its tight knot, and without the kerchief to cover her lower face, he had to know her true sex.

She'd read his lascivious thoughts immediately. Seen his wicked intentions, and then he'd looked at Darius and his now dead friend.

Gabrielle screwed her eyes shut, not wanting to see another life drained.

If she'd had doubts before, now she knew Darius MacLeod was indeed a vampire. A bloodsucker. A creature of the night.

She swallowed hard.

Was she in danger now, too? Should she run for her life?

How could she when the woods were thick with men who wanted to see her hanged?

Gabrielle took a step backward, and then another and another. Suddenly a hand clamped over her mouth and she was pulled up against someone taller and larger than herself. "Shh, I am not going to harm you."

Beside her a man stepped out, and Gabrielle recognized Darius's twin. He put a finger to his lips, and Gabrielle nodded. The man, who must be his blond companion, released her a moment later.

Three vampires.

It looked as though she wasn't going anywhere.

Gabrielle pointed in the direction Darius had gone. Demetri nodded and moved forward, a dagger in hand.

They weren't fooling around.

A small commotion followed, but Darius and Demetri surfaced not even a minute later.

Gabrielle's heart gave a happy jolt at seeing that Darius was unharmed, aside from a long scratch on his neck.

Darius looked concerned, and she wondered if he'd read her mind. She must remember to block him, because he could read her thoughts as easily as she could read his.

"We have no time to lose," Remont said, heading back through the trees. "The carriage is down the road a half mile. The two of you jump. I'll follow behind with Gabrielle."

"Thank ye, Remont," Darius said, brushing a hand through his dark hair. "I thought about ye the instant the horse ran off."

"I did, too, my friend." Remont took Gabrielle's hand. "Now you must go. We shall be right behind you."

"Come, brother," Demetri said, pulling Darius with him. Darius stared at Gabrielle for a long moment, and with a reassuring smile, the two brothers vanished into thin air.

There one second and gone the next.

Remont smiled at Gabrielle. "We will do the same in a moment. You will be safe and no harm will come to you."

He was exceptionally beautiful, this young man standing before her. Even more so than she remembered. He could not be much older than herself. Tall, blond, and with eyes that seemed otherworldly, he would make any woman's heart accelerate.

"You are all vampires then?"

"Yes."

"I saw Darius bite those men."

"He saved you, did he not?"

She nodded. "Yes, and they will die."

"He fed from those men, Gabrielle. Just because he fed from them, doesn't mean they will die."

"You can choose whether or not to kill someone?"

"Yes."

Voices came closer, and Remont glanced past her shoulder. "My friend is a good man, Gabrielle. He will not hurt you, nor will I."

"And what of Darius's twin?"

Remont laughed under his breath. "Demetri has a temper, to be sure, but he will not harm you. You have nothing to fear from any of us. You have my word."

Perhaps it was the man's trusting green eyes, or maybe the soft smile that put her at ease. Whatever the case, Gabrielle felt safe in his company.

Had Darius, his brother, and Remont not come along when they had, she could be raped, or even dead by now.

"I shall have to embrace you in order to jump. Hold me tight in return and close your eyes." He opened his arms, and she went into them.

She was surprised she felt no fear, but instead the same comfort she had experienced with Darius.

"You're trembling, Gabrielle," Remont said, humor in his voice. "Trust me, I won't bite."

She smiled against his chest and closed her eyes.

TEN

Gabrielle awoke with a start.

Sitting up in bed, she looked around the elegant chamber and knew she was no longer at Bev's. Nor was she at her uncle's, thank God. Glancing down, she sighed with relief seeing she still wore the borrowed pants and shirt.

She lay in a large, comfortable bed with soft sheets and an impressive headboard and footboard. A dresser of rich mahogany and a matching wardrobe with glass knobs took up one wall. Directly across from the bed, a fire burned in the hearth, the mantle made of white marble etched with roses and vines. A cheval mirror and a vanity, complete with brush, comb, and toiletries, took up another wall. Heavy shutters covered the windows, giving her no idea of the time of day.

She shifted and winced. A few days in the saddle and every muscle ached. Hopefully nothing bad had come of the horse that had been her companion during her short run at being a highwayman.

Somewhere in the house, a clock tolled. Gabrielle counted eight rings. Did that mean it was eight in the morning or eight at night? Even more important—where was she?

Was this Darius's home, or perhaps Remont's or Demetri's? Was she still in London? Unfortunately, she remembered nothing after Remont had told her to hold onto him and close her eyes.

Though she could not remember how she got here, she did remember everything up to that moment. The somewhat successful robberies. That was until Darius, Demetri, and Remont stepped from an elegant carriage. She could not believe her luck. What were the chances that on a long stretch of road, the one person she could not stop thinking about would come rushing back into her life?

How ironic that the very man her mother had warned her about was the same man who had saved her life. If he had not come along, she might very well be dead by now. If not shot, then hanged by an angry crowd. Or perhaps burned at the stake, since she was not just a highwayman, but a witch as well.

Witch. Highwayman. The list just kept on growing. Could her life get any more complicated?

And how was Darius able to see beyond her highwayman disguise? He'd known it was her all the time and had played along until he realized she was in danger.

But even then, he had surprised her and taken a moment to kiss her. His touch had seemed frantic, like he had been waiting to do so for a long time. Truth be told, that touch had been heavenly.

She smiled, touching her lips, reliving the moment. For as long as she lived, she would never forget that kiss. How gentle his lips had been on hers. At least at first. Then the kiss had changed, becoming more primal, with an intensity that had her aching for more.

Much more.

As strange as it sounded, especially knowing he was a vampire, she felt safe with Darius. Safer than she'd ever felt with her uncle.

Where was Darius now?

As much as she wanted to leave the chamber to search for him, she was wary, and afraid of what she would find. After all, didn't vampires sleep in coffins, most often in a crypt? Where would they keep a coffin in a place such as this? Down in a dark cellar, or perhaps in a room just like this one—with heavy shutters on the windows to keep out the light?

A door opened and closed somewhere in the house. The hair on the back of her neck stood on end.

Getting out of bed, she crossed the room and pressed an ear against the door. She heard several masculine voices, one with a Scottish brogue, but she couldn't make out any words.

Catching her reflection in a cheval mirror, Gabrielle winced and took a few minutes to brush out her hair using her fingers. She also straightened her clothing, and pinched color into her cheeks and lips.

If this is how she looked last night, it's a wonder Darius bothered to rescue her from her assailants.

Remembering the robbery and the jewels, she went to the jacket that had been tossed over the back of a chair, and removed the velvet bag.

Sitting on the plush rug, she emptied the bag's contents, and her heart gave a leap. She did far better this time out. Indeed, one of the prostitutes' rings might be the real thing. "How like a man to shower his whore with real jewels, while the wife gets paste and glass," she said to herself, setting the ring aside and picking up another.

Hopefully she could find a pawnshop nearby where she could get enough money to buy a few dresses, some underclothes, and repay Bev for all she'd done. The poor woman was probably tearing her hair out wondering what had happened to Gabrielle. Perhaps she could write a letter to Bev and ask Darius or a servant to deliver it.

A soft knock sounded at the door, and Gabrielle didn't have time to stand when it opened a second later. "Sorry, I thought you would still be asleep." Darius looked ready to leave. "I'll come back later."

"No, I want you to stay." Ignoring the sudden increase of her heart rate, she came to her feet. "I was just seeing what I had—" She could not say the word *stolen*. In fact, she could still hardly believe she had done such a thing.

His gaze shifted to the stolen jewels at her feet, and she could feel her cheeks turn hotter by the second. What must he think of her?

"Do not be embarrassed, Gabrielle," he said, shutting the door behind him. He walked toward her, and went down on his haunches, picking up one of the rings. "This is lovely."

Speaking of lovely, he had lovely hands. Strong, long fingers. Hands that could bring pleasure. A taste of which she had sampled last night. "Ye did what ye must in order to survive, lass. There is no crime in that."

"You are lying in order to make me feel better."

He grinned, exposing a deep dimple in his left cheek she had not noticed before. "Did ye sleep well?"

"Very well, thank you." She began to pick up the rings and other items, putting them back into the bag, aware that he stared at her.

She glanced up and caught his gaze. How serious he looked. He placed the ring he held into the bag, his fingers brushing against hers as he did so. How odd that such a casual touch sent a shiver of awareness through her body. "I want to thank you," she blurted, trying to forget the erotic images that danced through her mind.

"Thank me?" he asked, his gaze shifting over her face, as though he wanted to memorize each feature.

"For last night. For protecting me. For coming along when you did."

"I didn't mean to scare ye in the woods, Gabrielle. I did what I had to do."

She could not believe he had such a frightening side to him. To lift a grown man who outweighed him by so much, the way Darius had, took immense strength. And she didn't want to think about the vicious way he'd bit the man's neck. "You don't have to explain."

He reached out and touched her cheek, a long finger brushing along her jaw. "I know I've said this before, and I shall say it again and for as long as ye need to hear it. I will never hurt ye, Gabrielle. Ever. I care for ye, and I will kill any man who means ye harm. I mean it . . . with all my heart."

She stared into his ice blue eyes. Eyes that had turned fierce last night, like a wolf's. There was nothing fierce about them now. Instead, she saw a vulnerability there that surprised her. "I know you mean it, Darius. Thank you." She looked at his full lips and could not help herself. Leaning forward, she gave him a soft, gentle kiss.

His hands cupped her face, and he deepened the kiss, his tongue sweeping past her lips. Her tongue brushed against a fang and she nearly pulled back, but he held her fast and softened the kiss.

Trust me, Gabby. Trust me.

The only person to call her Gabby had been her mother. She had not heard the endearment for so long, it brought tears to her eyes to hear it once more. And to hear it from his lips felt right.

Even though her mother warned her Darius was a vampire, she still trusted him. After all, he had put his life, and the life of his brother and friend, in jeopardy to save her, and she had no one else to trust.

He smiled against her lips, and she guessed he must have heard her thoughts. Just in case he hadn't, she whispered, "I trust you, Darius."

"Thank ye, lass. Those words mean more to me than ye will ever know." He pulled her into his arms, holding her tightly to him.

She could hear his heart pound, and it sounded so much slower than her own. Perhaps it sounded that way because hers felt like it might beat right out of her chest.

From the corner of her eye, she caught her, or rather *their* reflection in the cheval mirror. Her heart leapt because she could see Darius clearly, and she had always believed vampires could not cast a reflection. However, now that she looked a bit closer, see noticed a black mark ran through his chest. The mark didn't touch her at all. That must have been what her mother meant when she'd said if she looked hard enough she'd see a mark across his soul. Looking away from the disturbing sight, she asked him, "What will we do now?"

"We shall wait a few days and go about our normal business. Ye will have to stay here, Gabrielle, and it is imperative ye stay out of sight."

She nodded. "Where will we go when we do leave?"

His lips curved. "We're going to my home in the highlands of Scotland. It's a lovely place I think ye shall enjoy. No one will bother us there. Ye will have no need to hide, as ye do here."

Gabrielle thought of the manor house she'd been seeing in her dreams since the night they met. "Darius, I want you to know how sorry I am to have involved you in all of this. You can always—"

He put a finger to her lips, silencing her. "I became involved the moment I saw ye. I want to help ye, and there is no way I'm letting ye go now that I've finally found ye again."

"I will only cause trouble for you. Sutherland is a dangerous man, and my uncle is quite terrifying when he's desperate, and he will be quite desperate since Sutherland gave him a good deal of money. If I disappear, then Sutherland will want the money back, and my uncle has no means to repay it."

"I am not afraid of anyone, and *your* uncle made a deal with the devil. He deserves everything that comes his way, Gabby. He had no right to sell ye to Sutherland, and that's what he has done. He sold ye."

"Yes, he did. Sutherland is a horrible man, and I could not marry him. I left the night of the Vanderline ball because I had overheard a conversation he'd had with his sister. He planned to take me to Gretna Green and marry me the very next day. He knew I didn't want to marry him, and perhaps he knew I'd tried to escape my uncle's townhouse already."

Darius's jaw clenched. "Ye were wise in leaving, Gabrielle. I wish ye had told me all of this then, because I would have helped ye then and there, and ye would not have had to endure this by yerself."

She dropped her gaze, unable to tell him the real reason she hadn't asked him for help. He would probably think her crazy if he knew her dead mother spoke to her from the grave and that she'd informed Gabrielle that Darius was a vampire. "They say Sutherland killed his previous wives. Do you think it's true?"

"Aye, I do, and in time he would have done the same to ye. Gabrielle, believe me when I say the man will get what is coming to him. He will die for what he has done."

She could not believe how safe she felt, especially after all the uncertainty of the past few weeks. She wanted to ask him where he slept and if he would be nearby, but couldn't bring herself to.

His white shirt had been unbuttoned partially, showing part of his strong, wide chest. In the erotic visions of the past weeks she remembered him looking much the same, aside from his manner of dress. Now he wore snug navy breeches that clung to his long, muscled legs, knee-high Hessians, and the shirt that contrasted fiercely with his dark hair that curled at the ends. "So as we'll be here for a while yet, what kind of things do you do for enjoyment?" she asked, stunned by the husky quality of her voice.

He stood and held out his hand to her, helping her up. "I draw, paint, read, take walks, and ride horses when I'm at home."

"You paint? What kind of things do you paint?"

"Ye are surprised that I paint," he said with a light laugh that made her smile. "It has been some time since I have done so, and to answer your question, I prefer painting landscapes, though I've drawn a portrait or two."

"Perhaps one day you will paint my portrait?"

He nodded. "I would like that very much."

His gaze became so intense she walked across the room to the window. "May I?"

He nodded. She opened the shutters and looked down at the street below. The streetlamps had been lit, and the road filled with carriages. "I slept all day?"

"We both slept all day."

She could feel his gaze on her, and then heard him walk toward her. Her hand that rested on the windowsill trembled.

He walked up behind her, reached up, and closed the shutter. "Ye must be careful, Gabrielle. There are people looking for ye."

He stood so close, she could feel the heat from his body. She swallowed past the sudden lump in her throat. "Do you have anything else I could wear besides this?" she asked, looking down at the borrowed clothes.

"I'm certain I can find something." He moved away from her and she instantly felt his absence. "I'll send my man out to purchase some items in the morning. For now one of my shirts might have to suffice. Will that be all right?"

She turned. "Of course."

"By the way, how did ye ever get away from Vanderline Manor?"

"I climbed the back wall."

He laughed as though he didn't quite believe her.

She straightened her shoulders. "You think I'm lying?"

His smile faded a little. "No, I just can't envision ye climbing that wall in a ball gown."

"It was not exactly easy."

"I imagine not." He ran a hand through his thick, dark hair, and she wanted very much to do the same. What a handsome man he was. So handsome, she could stare at him for hours.

"Well, let me see what I can find for ye. I'll be right back."

He closed the door behind him and she returned to the window, opened the shutter, and looked out. A couple walked hand-in-hand, chatting away, while an older gentleman crossed the street and walked past a young man. Gabrielle's pulse skittered. That same young man leaned against a tree, and appeared to be looking at the townhouse. Good gracious, he seemed to be looking straight at her. Perhaps he waited for someone—or perhaps he watched her.

She stepped back, out of sight, and closed the shutters. Darius walked into the room with a shirt draped over his arm. He hung it over the footboard. "So ye never said if ye enjoyed being a highwayman."

She wondered if she should mention the man across the road and decided against it. "I do not recommend it to anyone. One's imagination begins to wander when alone in the woods at night, particularly on a long, lonely stretch of road."

"I can imagine," he said, resting his hip against the footboard. Damn, but he was gorgeous.

She cleared her throat and walked to the fire and stared into the flames. "When the first carriage came along, I was actually quite relieved. In fact I felt calm. I suppose because I needed the money and knew stealing it from the rich was the only viable option for me."

"Were ye living in the woods then?"

"No, a lady named Bev took me in the night of the Vanderline ball. While I stayed with her, I would only venture out at night. You know as well as I do that there are only a few things a woman can do at night to make money, and selling my body was not an option."

"Thank goodness for that," Darius said, and she looked at him, half expecting a smile on his lips, but there was no humor there. Just a possessioness that oddly pleased her.

"Speaking of Bev, she has to wonder what happened to me. I borrowed her husband's clothing and pistols without her knowledge. I do not want her thinking I took advantage of her and stole from her. She was really good to me, and she deserves something for her trouble."

His lips curved in a soft smile. "Ye have a good heart, Gabrielle. We'll be sure to get word to her, and perhaps a gift or two to show our appreciation. Consider it done." He pushed away from the bed and crossed the room. He reached out, and cupped her cheeks.

Excitement rippled along her spine, and she lifted her chin. "Thank you for all that you've done for me, Darius."

He brushed his thumb over her lips, and her breath left her in a rush. "Ye are welcome, lass."

Without warning he kissed her, and there was nothing passive about it. Indeed, she brushed her tongue along the seam of his lips, just as he had done to her earlier. She could sense his surprise. Did he think her too bold?

His tongue mingled with hers as strong arms wrapped around her waist, holding her tight.

Her arms slid around his narrow waist. How she loved the feel of his hard body against hers. As the kiss deepened, her hands moved lower, to the high curve of his buttocks.

His cock swelled against her belly, long and thick, making the flesh between her thighs tingle. Even her nipples ached to be touched.

"I want to make love to ye, Gabrielle," he whispered against her mouth.

"I want you, too."

He smiled then, and lifted her in his arms, kissing her as he walked around the bed and lay her down on the soft sheets. His hands made busy unbuttoning her shirt, which he did with skill. A moment later the shirt was off and he was making fast work of her pants, pulling them from her and leaving her naked to his all-consuming gaze. He stood back for a moment and just stared.

How nervous she was, her entire body trembling, but she did not try to hide herself from him, even though she wanted to.

"Beautiful," he said, putting her fears to rest. His eyes had turned dark and the lids heavy. He gave off a sensual heat that made her heart skip a beat.

Her mouth went dry when he didn't bother with the buttons on his shirt, but rather yanked it up and over his head and tossed it aside. He unbuttoned his pants and slid them over his hips, along with his drawers, exposing his huge cock.

She might need a drink, she thought to herself, as she stared at the impressive cock that might prove to be too large to fit inside her.

How perfectly formed he was, his body all muscle and sinew under lovely olive skin. The body of a warrior. She wanted to know every inch of that body intimately.

He snapped his fingers and two candles flickered and flamed. She gasped.

"Impressed?" he asked with a cocky smile.

"Yes," she whispered, looking at his thick length. "But not just by the candles."

"Ye know just what to say, don't ye lass?"

"I don't know. I have never done this before."

His smile softened. "I am honored to be the first."

"I'm glad you are my first."

He kissed her lips, her nose, her eyelids, her forehead, and her lips again.

And I shall be the last.

Never in her life had she been so aware of another person. The pounding of his heart against her own. The touch of his silky hair as he leaned over her. The hard ridge of his cock that felt velvety soft as well.

His kiss intensified, growing more ravenous. One hand slid up her side, and covered a breast before his fingers circled around the nipple. Blood rushed to her groin, and there seemed to be an invisible string that ran from her aching breasts to the sensitive flesh between her legs. The tiny button at the top of her sex twitched and she shifted, arching her hips against him, needing that contact.

He removed his hand just a moment and flexed his hips against hers, hard enough to give her the contact she craved. She gasped as her channel tightened and began to pulse. This was even better than her dreams. Gabrielle swallowed a moan, shocked at the strong climax and sensations rippling through her.

Darius's fingers slid over her dewy folds, and her hardened clit. His pressure increased while he lowered his head and took a nipple into his mouth.

Weaving her fingers through his silky dark hair, she pulled him closer as he sucked, laved, and used his teeth in a way that had her heart pounding nearly out of her chest.

Darius could not remember ever being so hard. When Gabrielle had reached climax so quickly, it had taken all his willpower not to slide his hard cock into her wet heat.

His mouth left her breast, kissing a path downward over her trembling stomach, to the soft downy hair that covered her mons. He parted her lips and licked her.

Her hands fisted in his hair, and she cried out, her legs instinctively clamping against his shoulders.

He laughed softly, a purely primal sound that had her stomach tightening. He continued to lick her slit from back to front, his tongue circling her hard little button before he did it all over again. "Oh my

God," she breathed, her hands moving to his shoulders, her nails biting into his skin.

Reaching beneath her, he cupped her bottom, bringing her closer to his mouth. He inhaled her scent, and thrust his tongue into her sheath.

She nearly came off the bed.

He slowly licked her, taking his time, wanting her to savor the sensations. Her head rocked from side to side, and she reached up to hold onto the headboard, nearly knocking the candle over in her haste.

She didn't notice the impending danger as her fingers curled around the thick wooden rail.

Gabrielle could scarcely breathe as Darius's tongue worked its magic. No wonder women took lovers, because she could not imagine doing this with any husband, unless that husband happened to be Darius MacLeod.

His lips curved and he looked up at her. The heavy-lidded, devilish gaze made her heart pound in triple time. She watched as his long tongue lifted, swirled, and entered her weeping sheath, making her cry out as she reached for the second climax in as many minutes.

Darius slid a finger inside her molten core and gritted his teeth as the tight inner muscles squeezed around him.

"Darius," she said on a moan.

He knew what she needed, and he was only too happy to oblige. Crawling slowly back up her body, he kissed a path from belly to breast, from chest to throat.

What he wouldn't give to sink his teeth into that creamy flesh. Indeed, he could smell the blood rushing through her, heating her veins.

But instead of biting her, he kissed her hard, and was pleased when she did not recoil from the taste of herself on his lips.

He smiled inwardly.

How uninhibited she was already.

His cock rested at her entrance, and she spread her thighs wider, ready to recieve him. He could wait no longer.

Slowly, he slid inside her hot sheath, closing his eyes as she enveloped him like a glove.

She shifted a little beneath him and he knew she must hurt, that her tissues were stretching to accommodate him.

"It will hurt only for a moment, lass."

She nodded, and he kissed her at the same time he thrust.

Gasping against his lips, Gabrielle felt her entire body tense. She could hear her heart pounding hard against her breastbone, could feel him swelling inside her. "Try to relax, lass."

She tried to relax all her muscles, especially the ones squeezing his thick cock. Seconds later he began to move, sliding in and almost out, before doing the same motion over and over again.

Instinctively she moved with him, lifting her hips to meet each thrust. He kissed her neck, his tongue outlining her ear, swooping along the inside ridge.

She moaned.

With each thrust her stomach tightened, and she felt like she was being lifted on a soft, puffy cloud. Higher and higher, closer to climax with each thrust.

Darius held off an orgasm. He arched his hips, going as deep as he could, while putting pressure on the tiny button that gave a woman so much pleasure.

She ground against him, crying out his name as she climaxed, her honeyed walls clamping around his cock, over and over again.

Sweat beaded his brow, but he waited until the final tremors wracked her body before he moved again. It took less than a handful of thrusts to reach orgasm.

ELEVEN

Remont stood beside Demetri in the parlor of Lord Gresham's rented home on the outskirts of London. They had attended the small soiree in the hopes of finding information pertaining to Gabrielle's uncle and the pig of a man she was engaged to. Apparently Lord Sutherland had put up a generous reward for any information about Gabrielle's disappearance, and was leaving no stone unturned.

The room had become positively stifling with a combination of too many bodies and too much perfume. Remont wondered why humans always felt it necessary to cover bad body odor with enough cologne or perfume to choke a horse. Why did they not just bathe?

Probably out of sheer laziness.

Demetri shifted on his feet and leaned toward Remont. "There, to the right of the potted palms. Beside the fat man with the bad suit."

Remont looked in the corner where four round tables sat, surrounded by men of differing ages and social class. "You just described a dozen or more men, darling."

Demetri's lips quirked. "The cheap, green suit."

"Ah," Remont said, eyeing the man in the thready green suit who glanced nervously about the room.

No wonder Gilbert Fairmont was nervous. Rumor had it the Viscount of Sutherland had given him a generous amount of money for Gabrielle's hand. And if the rumors were correct, said uncle had already spent every shilling. A problem since his niece had up and run.

A young man strolled into the room and walked directly to Gilbert. He kneeled down beside Gabrielle's uncle and whispered in the older man's ear.

Fairmont nodded, and the boy looked about the room, his gaze lingering over Remont and Demetri before returning his attention to the older gentleman. Gilbert slipped a coin into the lad's hand, who in turn left as quickly as he'd appeared.

"What do you suppose that was about?" Demetri whispered.

"I do not know, but perhaps I shall find out. Keep an eye on Fairmont," Remont replied, following the boy out the door.

Once out of the room, Remont jumped, meeting the young man in the hallway.

The startled boy glanced back over his shoulder.

"Is something wrong?" Remont asked, picking a nonexistent string from the boy's shoulder. He couldn't be but seventeen, perhaps a bit older.

The boy shifted on his feet. "I—I thought I just saw you in there," he said, pointing in the direction of the parlor.

Remont smiled. "You noticed me then."

"I did not say that," he blurted, then bit his bottom lip as though he'd said too much already. "It's just that ye look familiar."

"Can I walk with you?" Remont asked, already starting down the long hallway that led to the front entrance. Thank goodness all the servants appeared to be in the parlor with the other guests.

The boy nodded, but he looked increasingly wary.

Remont read his thoughts easily enough and could see all the despicable things he had done in his short life. A boy with no soul, who had been serving as Fairmont's eyes and ears, looking for Gabrielle in the hopes of receiving a handsome reward. It didn't matter to the boy that the young lady he hunted would likely end up dead, murdered by her fiancé.

Then Remont recognized Darius's townhouse in the boy's thoughts. His heart missed a beat when he saw a flash of Gabrielle glancing out a second-story window.

Damn it! The boy knew Gabrielle was with Darius at his townhouse—and Gilbert Fairmont did now as well. Sutherland would too, unless Remont waylaid the boy.

Resting a hand on the lad's shoulder, Remont pulled him into the nearest room, shut the door, and pushed him up against a wall.

"What are you doing?" the young man asked, looking frightened and yet excited at the same time.

Remont had not yet fed tonight, and his fangs extended.

"What do you want?" the boy asked again.

Remont smiled softly. "I want to have a little taste."

"Taste?" the lad repeated, his gaze shifting to Remont's mouth. The young man released a sigh, and his breath reeked of stale tobacco and ale.

To Remont's surprise the lad's insignificant yet hard cock brushed against his thigh.

Remont reached out, cupped the boy's jaw. The lad leaned in, but at the last minute Remont turned his head—and pressed his lips to his neck, over the pulse that beat in triple time.

The young man groaned and arched his hips.

Remont bit down hard on his neck, his incisors breaking the lad's skin. He seemed not to mind, for he moaned and his hands came to rest on Remont's hips.

As his mouth filled with the young man's blood, Remont closed his eyes and savored the taste and the exhilaration that rushed through his blood and heated his veins.

He had to be careful and not drink too much of the boy's blood. Remont could easily make him into a vampire, but he always chose who he turned carefully. Like Demetri and Darius. They had been exactly what a vampire should be—powerful warriors, masculine, loyal, full of pride.

The opposite of what this devious boy was, and would always be. Tonight the lad had served his purpose, and tomorrow he would wake extremely weak, like he had consumed a few too many glasses of wine—but alive and still human, and with no memory of what happened here tonight.

As the boy slid to the ground, Remont pulled a handkerchief from his waistcoat pocket and wiped the blood from his lips.

The door opened, and Remont turned to find Demetri standing there, arms crossed over his impressive chest. As always, the sight of his lover made his blood stir. Dressed in a navy suit, knee-high Hessians, and a stark white shirt, Demetri's dark beauty could make a grown man weep.

Demetri glanced at the young man on the floor, and lifted a dark brow. "Did you get what you wanted?"

Remont picked up on the double entendre instantly. Demetri had rarely been the jealous type, but every once in a while he showed that side with such a comment.

Remont shrugged and stepped over the boy. "He served his purpose quite well."

"He desired you." Demetri's voice held a definite edge. "I could tell by the way his gaze lingered on you earlier."

Remont pushed the handkerchief back in his pocket. "You noticed all this in a stare that lasted two seconds? Extraordinary!"

Demetri's eyes narrowed. "You must have noticed him if you knew the stare lasted two seconds."

"Just as you did, darling."

Demetri flashed a devilish smile. "Touché."

Remont touched his lover's face, kissed him softly. "Come, we have done our job."

"What did he tell you?"

"He told me little, but I did read his thoughts. Unfortunately, the lad has been watching Darius's house. Even more he saw Gabrielle glancing out a window."

Demetri's looked alarmed. "Damn it. Are you sure?"

Remont nodded. "Yes, which means we have to let Darius know."

"You go. I'll be along shortly." Demetri reached out, touched Remont's cheek. "I have a friend who asked me to drop by."

Remont straightened. "Who?"

"The Earl of Whitcomb's mistress."

"She is in attendance tonight?" Remont managed to keep his voice even.

"She is."

Remont had seen the brunette eyeing them the moment they entered the soiree. "And Lord Whitcomb?"

Demetri grinned. "Him too, which makes the deception all the sweeter."

Remont's heart sank. Why did he allow this blue-eyed devil to get the best of him? Here he had thought Demetri would be anxious to return to his twin's townhouse to relay the news to Darius and plan their upcoming departure. Instead he was more concerned with fucking Lord Whitcomb's mistress. "You desire her?" he asked, managing to sound calm when he felt anything but.

"Yes." Demetri's dark brows nearly lifted to his hairline. "Creamy white skin, black eyes, and silky rich brown hair. Very exotic looking, don't you think?"

"I did not think you cared for brunettes."

Demetri shrugged. "I like anything that is beautiful." He leaned in, nipped Remont's ear. "That is why I like you so very much."

Like? Remont's heart sank even deeper.

"Far be it from me to stand in your way." Remont started for the door. "I shall tell your brother what I have learned. Since he has asked us to stay with him, I already told our driver to pick up our bags from the hotel."

"You always take care of me," Demetri said, following him to the door and giving him a kiss, a soft peck on the lips.

Remont brushed his thumb over the pocket watch in his pants pocket, and specifically over the inscription, which read, *To Remont—yours forever, D.*

Demetri had given it to him three Christmases ago, and he never went anywhere without it. Unfortunately, Demetri would never completely belong to Remont. He could never be faithful to one person.

Just walk away from him. Leave him to this life and walk away.

Remont closed his eyes for a brief moment. If only he could walk away. If only he was strong enough to tell Demetri to leave once and for all.

Remont wondered what would have happened had he not stopped at that Scottish loch a summer evening over five hundred years ago. If he and Geoff had not parted ways in London.

Remont had not seen his old lover since Charles II's reign, and that had been a quick conversation during the intermission of an opera.

Geoff had been a loyal lover, but Remont had not loved him the way he loved Demetri.

He feared he would never love anyone like he loved Demetri, meaning he would spend eternity in a living hell of his own making.

TWELVE

Darius lay on his side, staring at Gabrielle, who slept soundly. She had barely moved throughout the day, after they had fallen asleep in each other's arms. He had been able to sleep a few hours, but now he wanted to stare, to take in everything about her when she was unaware. He had yearned to see her for so long now, and his heart swelled with love for this woman who had come rushing back into his life.

Her eyelids fluttered, and her breathing quickened. He went up on his elbow, unsure if he should wake her from what appeared to be a disturbing dream.

"No, leave me alone!"

He put a hand on her shoulder, his thumb brushing along her collarbone, hoping to soothe her. "Shh, lass."

"I will not go back with you, my lord! You cannot make me. I would rather die."

"Gabrielle," he whispered softly. "You are dreaming, lass."

She awoke with a start, her light eyes staring at him without blinking. He snapped his fingers and lit a candle so she could see, and not be afraid.

"It's alright. Ye are with me, and ye are safe. Ye were just having a nightmare."

Gabrielles heart slowed down a little. *Thank God it had been a dream.*

"Can I get ye anything?"

"It was so real, Darius. Sutherland had found me, and then tried to kill me."

He pulled her close, kissing her forehead. "Sutherland will not harm ye, lass. I won't let him."

She reached up, cupped his jaw, and kissed him gently, happy and relieved to be with him. "Thank you for keeping me safe." Snuggling closer to Darius, Gabrielle rested her head on his shoulder.

"He has a lot of influence and power. Much more than you know, Darius."

He pulled back a little, enough to look into her eyes. "Do ye doubt me, lass?"

She touched his handsome face once more. "I don't doubt you. It's just that I don't trust Sutherland, and I know him. He uses people to get what he wants." How desirable Darius was with his long, dark hair all ruffled.

Sutherland was forgotten as the blood in her veins warmed, swooping low into her belly, making her hot and moist between her thighs.

He reached out, cupped her jaw, brushed his thumb across her bottom lip. "I want ye to stay with me, Gabrielle. I'll take care of ye."

"I hate that I am putting you at risk."

"Ye are not putting me at risk, Gabrielle."

"But what of your brother and Remont?"

He laughed under his breath. "They enjoy the game much more than ye know," he said, leaning in, kissing her.

Tired of talking, she accepted his kiss and even went so far as to deepen it.

He moaned, a wonderful sound that made her bold.

She ran her hands up and down his back, feeling the muscles move beneath her fingers. Right at the base of his spine she felt the puckered edge of a scar and ran a finger over it.

In a flash she saw Darius as a boy, running in the trees, and in the distance a wild boar rushing after him. Gabrielle could even feel the pounding of his heart, the fear rushing through him as he slipped and fell, and the pain he experienced as the boar's tusk ran through his back.

Seconds later Demetri appeared in the image, his sword bloodied, no doubt from skewering the boar. He pulled his brother up and over his shoulder, and rushed for the manor.

Her heart skipped a beat because it was the manor Gabrielle had seen in an earlier vision.

He pulled away, his eyes searching hers. "Ye remember, don't ye?"

"I keep seeing things that are familiar. Just now I saw a manor, the same manor from previous visions."

She could see the hope in his eyes. The excitement.

THIRTEEN

Darius had dreamt of such a moment, and now he could hardly believe that his wife had returned to him. That Gabrielle was Rose.

He kept waking up throughout the night, looking at her, making sure she was still there . . . as though she would vanish in thin air.

How grateful he felt to know they had years together.

But she is not immortal, like you. She will only live a normal life span, if she's fortunate.

Five hundred years ago he had gone through the same thing, ending in tragedy.

Not this time. He would not think beyond this minute, beyond today and perhaps tomorrow. He wanted only to keep her safe and get her out of London before Sutherland or her uncle harmed her.

To think that her uncle and Sutherland had taken such advantage of her made Darius beyond furious. He knew he would meet

Sutherland face-to-face one day—blade to blade—and he looked forward to that time.

But now he wanted only to put Gabrielle at ease. To enjoy their time together, get to know each other again.

Her hand brushed up and down his back, making the hair on his arms stand on end.

His cock stirred. Last night he'd watched the pleasure on her face, could see the wonder in her eyes as he brought her to orgasm time and time again.

Her hand slipped from his hip, down beside his aching cock. He was already as hard as stone.

She moaned, and moved her leg against his erection.

It's not like he had brought her here believing they would do more than sleep. He only wanted to keep her safe, keep her by his side so Sutherland or her uncle would not get to her.

Or the constable or anyone else for that matter. He still could not believe this young woman of such small stature had held up carriages at gunpoint. What must have been running through her mind when she was alone on that long, dark deserted road waiting for someone to come along? He smiled to himself. Her bravery amazed him, as much as her will to survive and find happiness. Here was a woman who would not accept her fate, and she was willing to do whatever she had to in order to do that.

His Gabrielle.

And though Gabrielle shared many similar traits with Rose, his wife would never have found herself on a long stretch of road in the dead of night in order to steal from the rich. Indeed, his wife had been terrified of the dark. So much so that he'd had to make sure a lit candle illuminated the room.

Gabrielle sighed and closed her eyes, the thick lashes lying against pale skin. She'd had dark circles beneath those lovely green eyes. No doubt she had spent many a sleepless night since escaping Sutherland.

Darius remembered her threat of "stand and deliver." He also recalled looking down the barrel of her pistols, and wondered if she would have actually used one if pushed.

She moaned, turned a little, wedging her leg further between his thighs. "Are you not tired?" she asked, opening her eyes.

Brushing back the hair from her forehead, he smiled. "Aye, I could use more sleep."

"Do you require less sleep than a normal—um, I mean less than . . . "

"Than a human?"

"Yes."

"No, I require the same."

She lifted her head. "Really?"

"Why are ye so surprised?" he asked, his heart skipping at the soft grin on her luscious lips.

"I don't know. I just thought that you would need less sleep if you were not human."

He hated being reminded that he was not human and that he would live forever. When around his own kind it never bothered him, but being with her now only reminded him that they were not the same.

That she would die one day, just as Rose had died. And he would have to suffer her loss yet again.

She surprised him by kissing him, her tongue slipping into his mouth, sweeping across his. Indeed, she seemed most urgent in her need.

She smiled against his lips as her hand reached for his cock, her fingers encircling the immense girth.

His brows lifted.

"I want to taste you. Just as you tasted me."

His throat convulsed as he swallowed hard.

Her gaze slid from his, down over his chest and stomach, and then to his cock that reared up between them.

She licked her lips, bent her head, and tasted him.

He closed his eyes, released the breath he hadn't realized he'd been holding. Her inexperience excited him, and as her hot mouth covered the head of his cock, he reached for her, his fingers weaving through her soft, shiny hair.

Sweet Jesus. He gritted his teeth as she licked and sucked his rigid length, her teeth lightly grazing him.

She found a rhythm that worked just as her hand wrapped around the base of his cock. Her hair fell across his thighs, heightening his pleasure.

He would come any second if she did not stop. She cupped his balls with her free hand.

"Enough," he said, pushing her just beyond range of his erection. Gabrielle scarcely heard his ragged whisper. Confused, she looked up at him.

His eyes were so dark and heavy-lidded, and she realized with a start that what she was seeing was a man in the throes of passion. A man on the verge of climax. Of giving up his semen, just as he had last night.

She glanced at the plum-sized head of his cock that had now turned a deep red. The hard length arched toward his navel, the veins prominent.

An ache had grown between her thighs, making her wet and so hot. She squeezed her legs together, but it didn't help. "Did I hurt you?"

His lips curved into a wicked smile she would never forget for as long as she lived. "Nay, lass. You did it perfectly. I stopped you because I didn't know if you were ready for what would have happened."

His answer perplexed her a little, but she didn't question it. Last night he had brought her unbridled pleasure over and over again.

And that is why she had wanted to return that pleasure. Apparently she had given him that, but her body still ached for more.

"I want you," she said, and he rolled onto her, covering her with his hard body. Gabrielle shifted, the sensation of having his weight atop her still so new. But it felt right, and her heart raced with anticipation.

His erection probed at her opening, and he reached between their bodies. The kiss deepened, and as the head of his cock slipped into her, she gasped against his mouth, still sore from last night.

Her channel stretched to accommodate his size, and she relaxed as he entered her with a firm stroke.

Her body tightened a bit with each thrust, his hips moving in controlled strokes. It felt incredible having him buried deep inside her. She opened her legs wider, relaxing as his hips ground against her.

She felt her body reach for climax. He bent his head and licked one of her nipples, the other hand moving over her other breast, cupping it, and then playing with the nipple. He pulled at it and pinched it lightly. She groaned at the exquisite ache, the invisible thread that seemed linked from her breasts to her sheath, now stuffed full of his thick, long cock.

His teeth lightly pulled at a nipple and it pushed her over the edge, her inner muscles squeezing him as she climaxed with a low moan.

Darius felt Gabrielle's walls grip him, the throbbing heat and her sweet sighs bringing him that much closer to completion.

He kissed her neck, his canines ready to pierce the skin there, but he stopped himself just in time.

He could not drink from her. He would deny himself that much. As the last glimmering waves of her climax rocked her body she opened her eyes slowly, a satisfied smile on her luscious, full lips.

Oh, but he was not done with her yet.

Pulling out of her hot, tight core, he positioned a pillow beneath her and urged her onto her belly, her arms out to her sides. He could see her confusion as she glanced back at him. "Trust me," he said, slipping a finger into her soaking wet slit.

She moaned, and shifted her hips, thrusting her heart-shaped buttocks up in the air.

His cock reared against his belly.

He slipped another finger inside her heat, and she gasped, her heartbeat accelerating.

Hc trembled with need.

He bent forward and licked her from her swollen folds, over her back passage, and to the indentation at her lower back. He kissed a path up her spine, to the back of her neck. How he yearned to drink from her. The craving tested his willpower in a way he never imagined.

Working his fingers in and out of her until the juices flowed freely again, he smelled her musky scent and knew he could not hold off much longer.

Placing his hands on her hips he entered her slowly.

She gasped, her fingers clutching at the sheets.

He released a satisfied groan as her inner walls hugged him snugly. "So tight," he said, making sure to be gentle.

Thankfully she could accommodate him, even in this position, taking every inch of him until his sac touched her lips.

Gabrielle breathed heavily into the pillow. She could not believe how full she was. He stretched her, and though it hurt, it also aroused her. He reached around, his fingers finding her hidden button.

She gasped as he played with the tiny bundle of nerves, flicking it, pressing it, circling it over and over.

Then he began to move.

Slow, controlled strokes.

She had always known there were many ways to make love. Already in the space of a few hours she had learned more than she ever imagined. Her body had known exquisite bliss, and now as Darius moved in and out of her in long, even thrusts, she felt herself reaching for that pinnacle yet again.

His fingers grew bolder on her button, and she cried out as she came, her inner muscles squeezing his thick length over and over again.

She pressed her hand over his, keeping his fingers there, afraid he would stop.

But he didn't and continued until he brought her to completion again. His strokes increased, and soon the bed was moving beneath them, the headboard hitting the wall.

Even though the hand that had been on her sex was now holding her hips steady, the pillow beneath her caused friction and she pressed her hips into it, at the same time as Darius thrust deep within her.

She came again, moaning with ecstasy into the pillow.

He held her hips tight, nearly bringing her off the bed as he let out a low groan.

Her heartbeat was a roar in her ears as he fell on the bed beside her, his arm around her, pulling her near.

She trembled, every inch of her satisfied in a way she could have only dreamed.

No wonder women wandered from their marriage beds to find lovers who would satisfy them where a husband might never be able to.

"And don't ye forget it, lass."

She looked at him. "You read my mind!" she said, trying to sound outraged, but failing.

As he grinned boyishly her insides twisted. She had never been so happy in all her life. So content. So wonderfully satisfied.

She never wanted to leave this bed or leave this man.

FOURTEEN

Remont stood on the wet sidewalk, across the street from the opulent apartment in this most prestigious of neighborhoods in London.

Truth be told, he had grown tired of the city not long after arriving. English society had always set his teeth on edge. Always everyone trying to outshine the other. Now he could scarcely wait until they left for Scotland.

Knowing Darius as he did, his friend would want to leave the city the moment he heard the news about Gabrielle's uncle, and he could not blame him. Gabrielle's life depended on it.

After leaving the soiree Remont had returned to the townhouse to tell Darius what he'd found out about Gabrielle's uncle.

However, Darius had been in his chamber, and Remont had no desire to disturb him. After all, he had only just been reunited with his wife after a five-hundred-year separation. Lord knows they could use the time to get reacquainted. And why ruin the night for all of them?

Remont could not be happier for his dear friend. Darius deserved all the happiness in the world. To watch him go through Rose's death had been horrific. Everyone deserved to have a soul mate, he convinced himself, even though he knew that he would never know the kind of love Darius and Rose had shared, and were going to share again.

Not as long as he continued to love Demetri.

Case in point, he stood outside Lord Whitcomb's mistress's humble dwelling waiting for his lover to surface. How tempted Remont had been to send a courier around to Whitcomb's estate across town, where no doubt the old aristocrat snoozed beside his wife of nearly forty years, to tell him his little lover was busy entertaining someone else tonight.

But of course Remont hadn't for fear something would happen to Demetri.

Wouldn't Whitcomb be shocked to know his much younger lover entertained a vampire in the expensive apartment he had purchased just a few months ago. Indeed, she had kicked and screamed like a child to get said apartment. Remont had read her thoughts enough to know she didn't wish to risk discovery by her lover, but she didn't want to let Demetri slide through her fingers either.

Remont had little doubt it had been Demetri himself to convince the little vixen that fucking anywhere but her apartment was a bad idea. Demetri thrived on danger.

Sadly, even now, as his lover had sex with another, Remont's blood still simmered in his veins remembering last night when they had made love so passionately. Remont had had more than his share of lovers in his time, and Demetri put them all to shame. The man had been born with an abundant skill for lovemaking.

But sadly, those skills did not cross over and translate into a highly emotional connection.

Out of nowhere a couple rounded the corner, surprising him. Remont had been too lost in thought, and now as they approached he removed the flask from his jacket, opened it, and took a long drink of brandy.

They were perhaps a decade older than himself. Both were dark-haired and moderately attractive, with pale skin and light eyes. The woman's laughter died as she spied Remont, and then she stared, not at all trying to hide it.

Remont noticed the second her gaze turned from fear to desire.

Her companion followed her gaze, his eyes narrowing as they came closer. No doubt they wondered why a man would be outside alone at this hour. Hell, it was sad, even to Remont.

It was not like him to behave so desperately, but perhaps he had just grown tired. Tired of being used. Tired of being the only one who cared about the relationship. Why did a couple live together and sleep in the same bed, if they did not share an exclusive sexual relationship?

The couple continued to stare, and Remont did not drop his gaze either, but merely smiled in return and read their thoughts.

The man's changed by the second, his gaze shifting slowly over Remont in a way that had excitement rushing along his spine.

Oh yes, they both wanted him, though their sexual fantasies differed a little. The woman saw both men in her fantasy, where the man wanted only Remont . . . while his companion watched. Funny how even the most masculine of men could harbor desires for another man, without their woman knowing it.

The man licked his lips, whispered in his companion's ear. If he could blush he would, especially since they thought Remont had been out on the corner deliberately trying to sell himself.

Remont smirked.

The closer they came, the slower they walked and the more they stared. Remont had never been vain, but he knew the power of his looks. King Leopold often said he was the prettiest man or woman in all the European courts.

"Good evening," the woman said, her French accent thick, her eyes sliding slowly over Remont. She grinned as her gaze stopped at the bulge in his pants.

"Good evening," Remont returned, his gaze skipping to the creamy slope of her ample breasts. The underside of a breast was the perfect place to bite a woman. Unseen by the victim, and it healed quickly. And her breasts were lovely, more than a handful each. It had been ages since he'd been with a female, and he felt his cock stir.

"Do you happen to have the time, monsieur?" the woman asked, stopping in front of Remont.

"Half past three, love," Remont replied, glancing at the apartment across the way. Just then the door opened and Demetri appeared, looking unkempt from his tousled, dark hair, down to the wrinkled, unbuttoned shirt that had been thrust haphazardly into his pants. His heart gave a hard jolt, and for a moment he almost jumped, not wanting to be caught spying.

"Would you like to join us for a drink?" the man asked.

Demetri's hand was on the door handle, and he had one foot out the door when Whitcomb's whore reached out from behind him, her long slender fingers brushing over the hard muscles of his abdomen.

Demetri's chuckle filled the night, and Remont thought he might be sick.

The woman cleared her throat. "Monsieur?"

Remont looked at the woman and then the man, both of whom watched him intently. "I have my own," he said, showing them the flask he never left home without. He took a drink from it before offering it to the woman.

She took the flask from his hand, and lifted it to her lips, watching him all the while, her thoughts turning more sexual by the second.

"Very nice," she replied, handing it to her friend, who took a long gulp.

So much for manners.

"Would you like to come to our hotel? It is just around the corner," the man asked, giving the flask back to Remont.

"It's late," Remont said, while chancing a glance at the apartment.

"Are you sure?" the man asked, his voice hinting at disappointment.

Demetri's deep groan resonated out into the night and the woman pulled him back into the apartment. Whitcomb's whore kissed Demetri passionately, her tongue nearly down his throat, her hand down his pants. A second later Demetri kicked the door shut with his foot.

"On second thought, perhaps I will," Remont said, biting the inside of his mouth, the blood easing the pain that sliced through him.

The woman grinned and winked at her companion, who also looked relieved and excited. "Wonderful! Do you live nearby, or are you also visiting?"

"I'm visiting too and staying with a friend. I do not think he would appreciate me bringing home a couple of friends."

"You are always welcome to spend the night with us," the man said, his gaze sliding past the band of Remont's pants.

Remont returned the predatory gaze. "Perhaps I shall. Either way, I look forward to getting to know you both."

They both wanted him desperately, and for the first time in many years, he was compelled to give them exactly what they yearned for. After all, why should he remain faithful when his lover fucked anyone he took a fancy to?

"Has anyone told you how very handsome you are?" the woman asked, wrapping a hand around Remont's elbow.

"Never," Remont lied, giving the apartment across the street one final, fleeting glance.

Remont left the hotel an hour before dawn broke over London. He heard the sound of someone knocking on glass and looked up to see the French woman waving from the third-story window.

He waved and looked away, disappointed in himself. Always he had refrained from participating in the very act that at one time had made him feel youthful and full of vigor. But he did not feel youthful or full of vigor. Rather he felt old, dreadful, and empty.

Why had he ventured back out tonight?

Or better yet, why had he made the mistake of falling in love with a man who would never love him in return? Torment is all he would ever know.

Fool.

Looking up at the graying sky he hurried his steps. The last thing he needed was to not make it home by sunrise. He might be one of the strongest of his kind, but he made it a point never to take chances, especially when it came to sunlight. He'd been burned a time or two, and healing always took a lot longer than expected.

Crossing the street, he rounded the corner and jumped to Darius's townhouse, and landed in the foyer.

The house was quiet, just as he expected. The only person usually up at this time would be Jacob, Darius's valet, who was one in a long line of servants who came from the same family who had always worked for Darius. They knew they served vampires and swore an oath of loyalty and silence. In return for said loyalty and silence they received an obscene wage, much like Remont and Demetri's servants.

As Remont walked up the staircase, he wondered if perhaps he shouldn't have stayed at the hotel tonight. Then at least he wouldn't have to face Demetri.

Or perhaps Demetri would be at the hotel—if he wasn't still with Whitcomb's whore.

He walked down the long hallway, turned the handle to his room, and walked in to find Demetri sitting on the edge of the bed, removing his stockings. *Shit!*

Demetri was naked to the waist, and Remont could see a series of nail marks on his lover's back. *The bitch.*

Demetri's dark brow lifted. "You are just now getting in?" he asked, clearly surprised, his gaze shifting over Remont in an assessing way. He hadn't bothered tucking his shirt back in his pants, nor buttoning his waistcoat for that matter. He looked a bloody fright, but for once he didn't care. In fact, he reveled in the jealousy he saw in his lover's blue eyes. For once the tables were turned.

"Yes, I am just now getting in," Remont said, dragging his gaze away from Demetri's powerful body. "Just in time, too. Daybreak is upon us." He pulled at his recently tied cravat. Jocelyn, or whatever the French woman's name was, had insisted on tying it for him. Remont had felt her lover watching him the entire time.

"Where were you?"

"I met a couple from France, and they invited me up to their room for a drink."

"A couple?"

Had he stammered? "Yes, a couple."

"It is unlike you to stay out so late," Demetri said, his tone cordial, but there was no denying the edge there. He stood, unbuttoned his pants, and slid them down his legs slowly.

Remont kept his gaze averted at all costs, and removed his jacket and waistcoat before bending to remove his boots.

"Are you coming to bed?"

Remont nodded, pulled his shirt up and over his head, tossed it aside. He didn't even bother removing his pants. He was too damn tired.

Lifting the covers, he slid beneath and closed his eyes, wanting nothing more than to forget the entire evening.

However, Whitcomb's whore's perfume still lingered on Demetri and was giving Remont a fierce headache. It was all he could do not to rip the pillow from the bed and go in search of a sofa to sleep on. But he would not be the one to act like a jealous lover.

"Are you feeling well?" Demetri asked, the bed dipping beneath his weight.

For God's sake.

"I am fine, Demetri," Remont replied, rolling onto his side, facing the wall. "I am extremely tired."

Demetri settled next to him, and then he moved closer. He sighed heavily, and then his hand came to rest on Remont's hip.

Remont's heart pounded in his ears.

Familiar, long fingers brushed up along his ribs, and back down again, over his hip.

To Remont's chagrin, his body stirred. He closed his eyes, hoping sleep would come soon.

Demetri moved closer, so close Remont could feel the heat of his breath on the back of his neck.

Remont dared not move. He tried to keep his breathing even, as though he'd fallen off to sleep already.

"What is wrong?" Demetri whispered, his breath stirring Remont's hair. Clearly he was not buying the sleeping act. "It isn't like you to be so quiet."

"You reek of her, Demetri. The smell makes my head ache." His voice held an edge that surprised even Remont.

Demetri's hand stilled immediately and fell away a second later. For once Remont was grateful for his lover's great pride that had now been sorely wounded.

Remont remembered Darius saying recently that he felt ancient. That he had lived a long life and felt no desire to live further. *Immortality is more unsettling to me than any of the dark gifts of our kind.* At the time Remont had thought those words incredibly sad, if not dramatic, but now he actually understood what Darius meant. *Certainly some think the ability to never die is a gift, but I do not feel that way. I never have.* Darius had said.

For the first time in nearly seven hundred and some odd years, Remont had to agree with his friend.

FIFTEEN

The house was strangely quiet.

Gabrielle sat up against the headboard, surprised to find herself alone in the big bed. She winced, her body aching, which reminded her of what had transpired in this bed in the past twenty-four hours.

It was hard to believe she'd given her virginity to a man she hardly knew. And a vampire at that.

Her stomach turned, knowing they had to speak of their differences one day. They could not avoid it, but now the very idea scared her.

She must not forget for a moment that she now lived in a different world. Living life as a creature of the night, save she was not a vampire.

But she had made love to one.

And it had been amazing. Indeed, she would never forget it for as long as she lived. Now she understood why the French called an orgasm "the little death." Indeed, she had "died" many, many times last night. *And I want to die again*, she thought to herself with a wicked smile.

Even the sheets felt strangely erotic against her naked body. Memories of the night before flooded her, of the pleasure she had experienced at the hands of Darius MacLeod. What a wonderful lover he was.

Excited to see him again, she pulled the bed curtain back and got out of bed. The room was dark, save for a candelabra that had been lit, the candles flickering by the slight draft the curtain had made. The shutters had been opened and the moonlight spilled in through the windows.

How strange it was to be waking just as others were getting ready for bed. She pulled the sheet from the bed and wrapped it around her.

Catching her reflection in the mirror, she gasped. Her cheeks were flushed and her hair was in serious need of a good brushing. Indeed, it would take a while to get the brush through the tangles. Perhaps she would need to take a long, leisurely soak in a tub.

She envisioned herself there, the warm water caressing her sore body, and perhaps Darius could join her—

She smiled inwardly. What a wicked woman she had become in such a short period of time.

Glancing over her shoulder at the closed door, she dropped the sheet and looked at her body. Last night Darius had stared at her and she had felt the blush race up her neck and face. Her body was far from perfect, but he made her feel comfortable.

And *his* body! Even now her blood stirred in her veins just thinking of his powerful body and large cock that had filled her to the womb.

The door shut abruptly, and she turned to find Darius standing there, holding a large box.

She gasped, and laid a hand against her pounding heart. "Darius! I didn't hear the door open."

He'd stopped short, his gaze sliding over her naked body. "I didn't mean to startle ye, lass."

Embarrassed to be staring at her naked body in the mirror, she covered herself with the sheet and went to him, going up on her toes to give him a kiss.

"I have a gift for ye," he said, tossing the box on a nearby settee. "But it can wait." He took off his gloves a finger at a time, all the while watching her, his gaze shifting over her in a way that made her insides burn.

Though she was covered by the sheet, she still felt naked. The room was cool and her body responded, her nipples tightening into firm buds. Excitement rippled along her spine, filling her with anticipation.

He tossed the glove aside and worked on the other.

"Perhaps I should take a bath," she suggested.

"Later," he said, throwing the glove aside. Shrugging out of his jacket, he then followed with his waistcoat.

As he undressed her heart rate accelerated and her palms began to sweat. Now this was a man who could make any woman weak at the knees. The kind of man who could make a woman crazy with jealousy.

The thought of him with another woman gave her a sinking feeling in the pit of her stomach. Why she should feel so strongly so soon after having met him made her question her sanity.

Oh, but we have not only just met. We've known each other before. We've loved before.

An image came at her abruptly. She stood at an altar in an old chapel with stained glass windows. She wore her hair long, much as she did now, falling in waves to her hips. The gown was light blue and fit tight at her shoulders and waist. A silver girdle rode low on her hips, and a crown of heather held the transparent veil in place.

Darius stood at her side wearing dark breeches and a dark tunic with a sash of his clan plaid. He looked at her with love and adoration.

Tears burned Gabrielle's eyes as they held hands and spoke their vows in front of a small crowd of friends and family members. She recognized Demetri, much as he was now, but dressed similar to Darius.

The memory faded as Darius's boots hit the floor, and Gabrielle's throat went dry.

He walked to her, reached out for her, his hands cupping her face. "I missed ye, lass."

"I missed you, too."

He grinned wolfishly, and bent his head to kiss her. He tasted so good and smelled even better, his scent consuming her, making her want to crawl right back into bed and stay there for days.

She placed her hands on his narrow hips, before cupping his high, firm buttocks.

He made a wonderful primal sound, low in his throat. A pleasing sound that made her smile.

Gaining confidence by the second, she quickly, and with amazing deftness for not having done so before, unbuttoned his pants and pushed them down over his hips to the floor, where she kicked them aside.

He grinned against her lips and picked her up in his arms, walking toward the bed they had spent so many hours in already.

She noticed the bloodstain on the sheets for the first time, and apparently so did he. He stiffened, looked at the blood and then at her. "Ye are mine, Gabrielle. Mine and only mine. I am your first and *only* lover. Understood?"

Loving the possessiveness in his voice, she nodded. "Yes, as long as you agree to the same. I will be your *only* lover, too."

His eyes had an intensity about them she had not before seen. This was the warrior from the past. A man used to fighting for what he believed in. A man who believed in loyalty and pledges. A man she had married in another life. "Aye, ye will be my *only* lover, Gabby."

Laying her down on the bed he immediately followed, his body flush against her.

She wrapped her arms around him, savoring the feel of his hard, muscular body. Her hands brushed up and down along his sides, and she smiled, feeling the goose bumps that followed. She grabbed his buttocks again and loved the way he tucked his hips, pressing his cock against her.

Pushing her legs open with his knees, he whispered against her lips, "Guide me home, Gabrielle."

With hand trembling, she wrapped her fingers around his thick cock and guided the engorged head into her moist heat. She winced, her tissues swollen and aching.

"You're still sore, lass. Will ye be all right, or should we wait for another time?"

She lifted her hips. "Do you want to wait?"

He actually trembled. "I do not want ye in pain."

"That is not the question I asked, Darius." She looked into his eyes, and he bit his bottom lip, obviously fighting an inner battle. The hard cock against her belly said he wanted her, and yet his eyes showed he didn't want to cause her pain.

She lifted her face, kissing him. Reaching between their bodies, he played with her tiny button.

Her body came to life under his touch, and already she reached for orgasm. Their tongues parried slowly, and he continued to play with her clit. Pulling his mouth from hers, he bent his head and took a nipple into his mouth.

His tongue brushed over the sensitive bud, flicking it over and over again. So many different sensations rocked her body, and she cried out with pleasure.

He kept it up for long, delicious minutes until she came with a satisfied moan. Though she'd climaxed, she still ached to have him fill her with his long, thick cock.

He kissed her throat, her neck, the pulse beating wildly there, and nipped at her ear.

Excitement rushed through her, heating her blood, making her crazy with need. She pulled his hair a little, bit his shoulder lightly.

His soft yet thoroughly masculine groan made her grow even bolder as she sucked on his earlobe, her tongue dipping inside.

Sliding into her gently, he let out a guttural groan that made her smile with joy. He looked at her then, his fierce eyes staring straight into hers. The smile slowly faded as he thrust again and again, his gaze unrelenting. Her blood burned with each thrust, and having him watch her so intently only added to her desire.

He bent his dark head, his silky hair falling over her breasts as he kissed her neck. A moment later she felt a sharp pain there, a piercing stab that disappeared as she climaxed. The release was so intense, lifting her up higher and higher. She felt as though her insides were exploding into a thousand tiny pieces.

Darius's satisfied moan let her know he'd reached orgasm as well, his hips pressed hard against her. So hard she felt herself drawing close to another climax. He ground his hips hard against her clit, and it was enough to have her crying out again, her inner walls pulling his cock further inside her body.

He collapsed on her, and she smiled to herself while her hands roamed the width of his broad shoulders and strong back. Her legs trembled with the force of that last climax.

She felt Darius's heartbeat, and for the first time it matched a rhythm similar to hers.

So many questions swirled in her mind, but she couldn't voice any of them. Not now. It was too soon, and she didn't want anything ruining what they'd experienced this past twenty-four hours.

Darius could hear Gabrielle's thoughts as clearly as his own. Had those questions been brought on by the fact he had bit her in a moment of passion, completely forgetting the pledge he'd made to himself when he first set eyes on her?

It had taken a second to realize his error, but by then it had been too late. One taste of her blood had sent him over the edge and the climax had been unlike anything he'd experienced before.

But he had let her down, and even more, he'd let himself down. He had made a promise he would protect her from everyone, and yet he had bit her without her consent. He could have made her into a vampire had he lost all control and drank her dry.

Isn't that what you want?

Ignoring the thought, he kissed her gently, savoring the moment of having her naked in his arms.

Her blood had tasted better than the finest champagne. An elixir, one he could not deny himself.

"Did I hurt you?" he asked, looking into her eyes.

Thankfully there was no accusation in those green depths. Nothing but immense, sexual satisfaction. A woman who by all accounts looked pleased with her lover. "No," she replied, lifting her head, kissing him softly.

All the fear he'd been feeling melted away under that kiss. He would never tire of this. Never tire of the moments he'd been denied with Rose. Back in those times, he and his wife had only shared a handful of stolen moments together. War with England and other clans had kept him away from home much of the time. When he had come home that last time, she had become more of a stranger than wife, and he could blame only himself.

"I would love to take a bath," she said, going up on an elbow. How he loved just staring at her. So beautiful and fragile. When he had seen the blood on the sheets, his heart had leapt with not just joy, but possession. Like with Rose, he had been the first man to touch her, and he would show Gabrielle all the ways to love.

"Did you not hear me?" she asked, her brow furrowing. Even when she frowned she was gorgeous. "You looked a million miles away."

He reached out, cupped her face. "Ye do not wish to stay in bed with me all day and night? I'm hurt, lass."

Her full lips curved into a sexy smile. "I would love to stay in bed all hours of the day—but only after I take a long, hot bath. If only to soothe my poor, sore body."

Indeed, she would be sore.

He rolled off her, bringing her with him, until she lay on top of him.

"I think I can accommodate ye, lass."

"Could ye now?" she said, doing her best to imitate his accent—but failing miserably. "Ye could use a bath yerself, lad."

He couldn't help but laugh at her horrible accent. But his laughter was interrupted by a knock at the door. "Darius, I must speak with you."

It was Demetri, and by the tone of his voice it must be urgent.

"I shall see to that bath, love." He kissed her nose, eased her off of him, and left the bed.

Gabrielle stared at the strong, broad shoulders, narrow waist, and high, tight ass and sighed.

He glanced back at her, saw where she was looking, and tried to frown but failed. Instead, he gave a cocky smile that made her laugh.

"Just relax, lass. I'll see what my brother needs—and then I'll spend all night fulfilling your needs."

SIXTEEN

Gabrielle watched as Darius pulled on his pants and shirt. Good Lord, she couldn't get enough of the man.

"See ye shortly," he said with a devilish smile, and a second later the door opened and closed. She heard Darius and Demetri speaking in hushed tones, and a moment later they walked away, further down the hallway.

Her stomach twisted. Did they not want her to hear what they spoke about? Did Demetri have information about her uncle or Sutherland?

She tried not to worry about what might be wrong, or that perhaps she had truly endangered Darius, his brother, and Remont. She had spent too many days being miserable while living in her uncle's home, awaiting her wedding to Sutherland. Now she wanted only to experience love.

Love?

Was she already in love with Darius MacLeod?

Or was she mistaking lust for love?

After seeing all the images of them together in a previous life, she felt safe to say she did love him, or she would come to love him just as she had loved him before.

But aside from the fact that Darius had loved his wife, what had transpired between them? How had he gone on to become a vampire—and how had his wife died?

She had so many questions to ask him.

Be careful, daughter. You might not want to hear the answers you seek.

The room turned cold, and she pulled the blanket tighter about her.

I am happy, Mother. For the first time in a long while I am doing what I desire.

There is nothing wrong with that, child. But at what cost will you love him? He is not human. He will never be human . . .

Darius is good to me and I care for him deeply, Mother. He has protected me, where your own brother handed me over to the horrible Lord Sutherland. Would you prefer I marry a man who has killed his previous wives and would no doubt kill me in time?

I visit your uncle in his dreams and shall continue to haunt him for what he has done to you. Be careful, Gabrielle. If MacLeod is to bite you, he will make you into what he is. Do you want to live as such a creature for the rest of your life? You were given the gift of healing, and how can you continue to heal if you are made into a monster?

He is not a monster, Mother. He isn't, nor is his brother or Remont. I love him, Mother. I loved him in another life, and we are getting a second chance.

Ask him how his wife died, Gabrielle. Or since you were that wife, do you remember?

A fierce breeze rushed through the room, blowing out the candles, leaving Gabrielle in darkness. She didn't bother to light them again, but instead looked toward the fireplace where the embers burned.

Tears stung her eyes. For so many years it had been just she and her mother, who she trusted with all her heart. And all she'd ever wanted was her support. In this situation though, her mother would never give her peace, not for as long as she stayed with Darius. Why could she not just be happy for Gabrielle?

Remembering her mother's comment about Darius biting her and making her a vampire, Gabrielle nodded, and lit a candle, a trick she hadn't shown Darius yet, but would one day.

Taking the candle from the holder, she walked to the mirror, lifted her chin, and looked at her neck, but could not see any marks in the waning light. Leaning closer, she bumped her head on the mirror and nearly set her hair on fire with the flame from the candle.

Darius appeared in the mirror from behind her, and she screamed. She had not heard him come in, and his finding her in front of the mirror yet again was downright humiliating. She noticed though that in the reflection there was no mark over her heart—like there was over his.

He extinguished the candle and set it on a nearby table. "Careful lass, ye do not wish to burn that beautiful hair of yours."

"I didn't mean to."

To his credit, he tried not to smile but failed miserably. "I did not mean to startle ye. I said your name, but ye didn't hear."

She went into his arms, pressing her cheek against his chest. She closed her eyes, taking comfort in the slow, steady beat of his heart.

"Are ye trying to seduce me back to bed, lass?"

She looked up at him. "What do you mean?"

He nodded toward the mirror and she glanced over her shoulder, seeing her bare bottom reflected.

"I should put on the pants," she said, not budging.

"No more breeches for ye, love." He took her by the hand, toward the settee and the box he'd arrived with earlier. "Before I become distracted yet again, this is for you," he said with a wolfish smile.

Gabrielle's heart did a little flip inside her chest. She had never received a lot of presents and the gifts Sutherland or her uncle had bought her had not been given out of affection. "You didn't have to buy me anything."

"I wanted to. I just hope ye like it."

"I know I will." Gabrielle opened the box to find a gorgeous gown of light yellow muslin with a pink silk underskirt. The detailing was exquisite, with tiny flowers embroidered throughout. Beneath the gown was a new chemise, petticoats, silk drawers, and stockings. "Darius, they are beautiful. Thank you!" She held the gown up to her body and looked at her reflection. "It's absolutely perfect." Her throat tightened and she blinked back tears.

"There are slippers as well," he said, pulling the cream silk shoes from beneath the undergarments.

"Do ye wish to try it on?"

"Yes, but only after I bathe." She went up on her toes, kissed his cheek. "Thank you so much, Darius. They are all so lovely."

"Ye are most welcome, Gabby. I took the liberty of buying a few more gowns that need small alterations. They will be arriving by tomorrow evening." He smiled, but she sensed he had something else to tell her.

"What did Demetri want?"

"Ye are intuitive, aren't ye?" he said with a warm smile.

She blushed. "I have been known to be."

"I fear we must leave London, posthaste."

Her stomach coiled. She *had* put them all in danger.

"Remont and Demetri attended a party last evening. They learned that your uncle is aware ye are here."

Her heart skipped a beat. "How?"

"Spies are watching the townhouse."

She remembered looking out the window and seeing the young man staring up at her. That stupid mistake had put them all in danger. "I am so sorry, Darius. I wish I wouldn't have brought this on you. Yesterday I looked out the window, and I saw a boy watching me. For an instant I wondered if he could be spying, but dismissed it. Forgive me for not telling you."

He lifted her chin with gentle fingers. "Do not worry. You are well worth any risk, Gabby." He kissed her forehead.

"I wonder if you were followed to the dressmaker's."

He shrugged. "I'll say the dress is for my mistress."

She frowned. "Mistress?"

"Yes, every man in London has one."

She was shocked at the murderous thoughts racing through her mind at the thought of Darius having a mistress.

The corners of his mouth lifted, and it was obvious by the boyish smile on his face he was pleased by her jealousy. He cleared his throat. "Let me rephrase that. Every *unhappily* married man has a mistress, Gabrielle. I do not fit that category."

"Because you are not married?"

He cupped her face with his hands, kissed her gently. "Because I am extremely happy with my lover."

She grinned like a child in a candy store.

His thumbs brushed along her cheeks. "I have never been happier than I am at this moment, Gabrielle. I have felt dead for centuries, living life day after endless day. When I saw ye at the Vanderlines' ball I knew I must have ye. Ye were taken from me once. I will not lose ye again. Not to anyone. I am not afraid of Sutherland or your uncle. We shall leave at sundown tomorrow evening."

"What if they follow us?"

A murderous gleam shone in his eyes. "I hope they do. I shall give them a fright they will never forget."

"Sutherland still scares me. He is unpredictable."

"Sutherland will not harm ye. I will not allow it. Demetri will not allow it and Remont will not allow it. Trust me, Gabrielle. Trust *us*. Ye are safe. Ye will have all three of us, and we are a force to be reckoned with."

She did not doubt it, especially after what she had seen the night of the robberies. "Perhaps we should leave tonight?"

"It is too late already. Plus, your uncle and Sutherland's men are watching us intently. That is precisely why Demetri and I are going out this evening in order to be seen."

"What of Remont?"

"He will stay with ye this evening. I cannot leave ye alone without any protection, and if I stayed, then Sutherland would surely know ye were here. I know Remont looks like he could cause little harm, but he is the oldest, and thereby the strongest among us."

She nodded, relieved to know she would not be alone tonight. "When will you return?"

"As soon as possible. I'll make sure I am seen at a few different parties this evening."

"Be seen with other women?" Her voice broke. She hated that he would be flirting and charming other ladies.

His thumb brushed along her jaw, over her bottom lip. "Aye, it will help the guise if I am in the company of other women, but know this, Gabrielle. I want only ye—and no one else, lass."

She held his gaze and knew he spoke the truth. He didn't want to leave her. In fact, he yearned to return to the bed just as she did.

He took her by the hand. "Come, your bath should be just about ready."

"Already?"

"Aye." He led her into a smaller sitting room, where steam rose from the surface of a bathtub. He had even set several fluffy drying cloths nearby.

"Very impressive," Gabrielle said, itching to sink into the bath. "It smells delightful."

"That is the oils ye smell. Jacob, my valet, always adds them."

"I shall thank Jacob next time I see him."

"I'm sure he would appreciate that. And now it is time for ye to take your bath." He took the gown from her and helped her into the tub. She eased down into the warm water with a contented sigh.

Darius laughed as he sat down in a nearby chair to watch.

How easy it would be to get used to this. To being treated like a princess. She lay back against the tub's edge, closing her eyes, savoring the feel of the water against her sore extremities.

"Tell me about Scotland," she said, opening her eyes to find him watching her intently, one elbow propped up on the chair's arm, chin in hand. His gaze slid down her body. The lack of bubbles meant he could see everything. "What do ye want to know?" he asked, his gaze returning to her face.

The heat in those blue eyes sent her pulse racing. "About your home. Where you were born and where you grew up. Everything."

He ran a hand through his long hair, something he'd done before when she asked him a personal question.

"My father was a clan laird, and my mother was a daughter of a rival clan. Their marriage was meant to achieve peace, but it was a long time coming."

"But did it?"

"Aye, it did. As ye can guess, I had a somewhat privileged upbringing. As I said before, I was raised in the highlands of Scotland."

"Where you live now?"

"No, but just a day's ride from there. I built a lovely manor house between two large hills."

The place she saw in her dreams.

"Were you always at war?"

"Aye, for as long as I can remember. It was a way of life. Our father trained my brother and me, along with other children of the clan. I think that is why so many feared us, because fighting was ingrained in us at such an early age."

She smiled, imagining Darius as a child. She wondered if ever they had a child, if it would look like Darius and have dark hair and ice blue eyes, or have her fair coloring.

Could he even have children?

The smile slowly faded, and she looked away, toward the fire before he could sense something was wrong. "Did Demetri have a wife?"

"No, but the ladies loved him, and he broke many hearts. I remember one occasion when he actually juggled three mistresses."

"How scandalous."

"Aye, it was scandalous."

"And now?"

Darius shrugged. “He loves Remont.”

“Has he always loved Remont?”

“One always loves their maker.” He pursed his lips, as though deep in thought. “The bond is incredibly strong. I love Remont, but not in the same way my brother does.” He sat forward in the chair. “Obviously.”

Gabrielle nodded, and taking the sponge, began to scrub at her skin. She could feel Darius’s eyes follow her movements.

“Rose fell in love with Demetri before she fell in love with me.”

Now that surprised her. “Why do you say that?”

“A man knows when a woman desires someone else.”

“But you are twins.”

“Aye, we are, but that does not mean our personalities are alike.”

“What did you do when you realized Rose liked Demetri?”

“What can a man do, but buy pretty trinkets and gowns to win a woman’s affection,” he said with a wink.

“I’m sure she was pleased to have married you in the end.”

“Aye, she told me as much. We came to love each other very much.”

He stood, came over to the bath. “Let me wash your hair.”

“Are you sure? It will not be easy with all the rats and snarls.”

“Which I helped create,” he said with a wicked smile.

He went down on his haunches, and she relaxed while he soaped her hair, taking his time, working it into the long strands and rubbing her scalp.

Closing her eyes, she moaned. “That feels positively heavenly.”

“I am happy to oblige.”

His hands fell away, and she opened her eyes to find Darius grabbing a pitcher. “Let me rinse it for ye.”

When he was finished, he set the pitcher aside and proceeded to remove his shirt and pants.

"You're going to join me?" she asked, excitement rushing through her.

"Since I am already wet," he said, motioning to the water spots on both articles of clothing, "I thought it might be wise to do so, and I would be a fool not to with such a lovely lass tempting me."

Soon he had settled in behind her, and she lay back against his powerful chest and stomach.

He soaped his hands, and brought them up her arms, over her chest and her breasts.

She hid a smile and closed her eyes as his fingers rolled over her nipples, drawing them into tight little buds. Her body came to life under his wonderfully talented fingers. One hand slid down her belly, over her mons, where he touched her sensitive button, drawing circles around it, flicking it. The oils only added to the sensuality of the moment, and as he slid a finger into her, she arched against him.

As usual, he seemed to know just what she needed and when she needed it, and soon she needed more than just the pleasure of his hand.

She felt his cock, long and hard against her lower back and buttocks. Turning slightly, she kissed him. His hands moved beneath her arms and he lifted her so that she faced him.

His cock rose between them, long and thick. "Ride me, Gabby." His eyes darkened as he lifted her slowly onto his rod. When she looked into his eyes again, she could not believe the heat there. She moved her hips a little and soon found that holding onto the tub's edge gave her leverage.

Bending his head, he kissed one breast and then the other. Taking a nipple into his mouth, he flicked his tongue over the sensitive bud, suckling her while pinching and pulling the other with gentle fingers.

Her head fell back and she moaned as he sucked harder, tending to one breast and then the other.

It didn't take her long at all to reach climax, and she cried out his name as her sheath tightened around him.

His mouth left her breast, and kissed a path up to her neck. He placed a kiss there, above the erratic pulse, his breath hot against her throat. For a moment she paused, half expecting the prick of his teeth against her skin.

Then he lifted his hips against her, and she rotated hers. He came with a low, guttural moan that told her she had done well and ridden him to completion. To her surprise she came again, her arms wrapping around his broad shoulders as she rode out the final tremors.

A sharp pinch at her neck made her wince. She could feel him suck, and could not believe the sensations that wracked her body as she cried out his name on a sigh.

SEVENTEEN

Gabrielle, having finally dried her hair and dressed, found her way down to the library. She had not yet seen Remont and looked forward to speaking with him. But first she wanted to find a good book or two to read, especially for the journey to Scotland.

She loved libraries and the smell of old tomes in leather-bound covers of various colors. For whatever reason, she felt a strange comfort when surrounded by books, and Darius's library did not disappoint. Mahogany bookcases took up two entire walls, and they were stuffed. Indeed, there had to be hundreds of books, all begging to be read.

Gabrielle's mother had urged her to read from a young age. She herself had little talent with pen and paper, but she appreciated all types of works, from poetry to fiction, and even diaries.

She often thought her mother's life would make an interesting tale, but now that she had met Darius, she wondered how many volumes it would take to tell his life story. After all, five centuries was a lot to fit into a few hundred pages.

"If you think five centuries would be difficult, then can you imagine how many volumes seven centuries would take?"

Gabrielle gasped and turned to find Remont standing nearby, dressed casually in breeches, Hessian boots, and a surprisingly simple linen shirt. He had not even bothered with a cravat, and his hair looked a bit mussed up, as though he'd been running his fingers through it, or perhaps been out riding. Whatever the case, she thought him exceedingly handsome.

"Seven centuries. Indeed, that would be an amazing tale."

He walked toward her, his long, elegant fingers brushing along the back of a chair. "I suppose it would be entertaining, but I prefer to keep my life private. Let people wonder and think what they wish."

She smiled, already enjoying his company.

"I have many tales to tell," he said, taking a seat in a high-backed chair, motioning for her to join him. She did, settling onto the settee near the fire. How handsome he was. Not a single line on his face, or a blemish. And such high cheekbones. "But I would hate to bore you."

"You will not get off so easily, Remont. Tell me everything. I want to know all about you, and we have all night to talk."

He smiled, and looked into the fire. "I suppose it would make more sense to tell you how I met Darius and Demetri. Actually, I shall have to start with Demetri since it is he I met first."

Gabrielle tucked her feet beneath her.

"I had journeyed to Scotland after a friend and I parted ways in London. Back then I enjoyed painting, and I had been staying at an inn that sat near a beautiful loch where I walked each night. One evening, the moon was shining down on the still waters, and I rushed back to the inn and grabbed my paints and returned."

As she stared at him, she caught a glimpse of his emotion—of his intense sadness, but could not tell if it came from the memory of the past or if it was from the present.

"I was setting up my things when out of nowhere walks this man, and of all things he's wearing this skirt, or a kilt as they are called. Mind you, I had not been in Scotland long, and I had only seen a few men wearing them."

"I imagine Demetri put them all to shame?"

Remont's brows lifted. "Indeed, he did. I sat near a copse of trees, so he didn't know I was there. And I confess that I did not alert him to my presence. I should have, especially when he started undressing, but I probably couldn't remember my own name at the time."

Gabrielle grinned.

"I think he must have been so tired, dirty, and dusty from the fighting, that he wouldn't have cared had he known I was there, watching him. You must remember that during that time Scotland was fighting for her independence, and he and his brother had spent their lives at war. It's all they knew, so when I saw him I was struck by the power he exuded. So strong, the muscles flexed beneath his skin as he moved. I was completely entranced."

"How long did it take for him to realize you were there?"

"I honestly couldn't tell you how long he was in the water. I don't think I even drew breath until he stepped from the loch. The image of the water sluicing down that powerful body is something I shall never forget. I had never wanted anything as badly as I wanted him at that moment."

Gabrielle's heart clenched. "You love him?"

He looked at her, smiled softly. "I do. I always have."

She had never thought about two people of the same sex being attracted to each other, desiring each other just as she desired Darius. She had known they existed, but she never thought she would have the opportunity to sit and talk with someone who would be so forthcoming about it. "Did you turn him into a vampire then and there?"

"No, several days went by. One night when we were making love, I bit him in the heat of the moment, as they say. I hadn't planned on it, and I was shocked when he told me he wanted to be what I was. He had apparently known what I was, even after I had taken such pains to hide it from him. Little did I know he had followed me the night before and had seen me feed. He asked me millions of questions, and I could tell he was intrigued, especially when he learned that vampires lived forever and never aged." He laughed. "That is quite appealing to someone as handsome as he, and he asked me to make him what I was."

"That could not have been an easy decision."

"It wasn't. I felt extremely guilty afterward, but the thing of it was, Demetri has always loved the dark gift and all it entails."

"The thought of never growing old *is* intriguing."

Remont shifted in his chair. "Yes, becoming immortal and never aging is tempting, but it is not for everyone."

"Are most vampires young?"

"Not necessarily. Making a child into a vampire is positively forbidden. It has been done, but those who made them were condemned and killed. There are many vampires of my age, and older."

"How old were you?"

"Just shy of my twentieth year."

Not much older than herself. "How do you make someone into a vampire?"

"I bite them in the neck."

Gabrielle's heart pounded in triple time. "Does that person always know when they've been bitten?"

Not always. "Oftentimes we seal the wound. Sometimes we do not."

She touched her throat. "How does a person know?"

His lips quirked. "You are not a vampire, Gabrielle, if that is what you are asking."

Her cheeks burned under his intense gaze. "What of those men in the woods? Darius bit them and drank their blood."

"Sometimes feeding will kill a person. It takes great discipline and care. Far more discipline than you could possibly know. Darius has been a vampire long enough to know how to kill, when to kill, and especially when not to kill." He brushed a long-fingered hand through his pale hair. "Oftentimes the person will not even know what has occurred. They might feel weak afterward, and perhaps a little sick, but they recuperate quickly."

"Have you turned many?"

"Turning is a delicate exercise, and one must always be careful to drain the person to the point of death. At that moment, when their heart nearly stops, you draw a final time. That person will die to their human life and awaken a vampire. The initiation does not end there. The new vampire must feed from its master, and only its master. If it does not, then it will die. So to answer your question, I have not turned many vampires."

"Who was your maker?"

He swallowed hard, looked at the fire again. "His name was Geoff, and he had been born several centuries before me. He wanted a companion of the age, he'd said, and once I came to accept my new life, I grew to love him."

"Did you not harbor resentment toward him for taking you from a good life?"

"I did, but I soon learned to accept my gifts. You would be amazed at how many of us there are in the world, and as in any society, one must adapt."

"But you enjoyed it more after making Demetri?"

"Very much so," he said with a boyish grin. "I enjoyed Darius's company as well."

"You didn't tell me how you made Darius."

"Both Darius and Demetri had been fighting in a battle near Stirling when Darius was struck down. He suffered a horrible wound to the belly. A mortal wound to be sure. I found him before Demetri did. Indeed, at first I thought he was Demetri, but I realized my mistake almost immediately. The two are not at all the same in heart. As he lay there dying I kept asking Darius over and over again if he wanted the dark gift. He did not seem to understand, and he was moments from death when Demetri appeared. Demetri told me to turn Darius, as he could not change him himself since his powers were too new. Because I adored Demetri, I changed Darius."

"Without his consent?"

"Without his consent." He glanced at her. "I always regret having done so, especially after what happened to Rose."

"I'm sure he understood. He would have died had it not been for you."

"Perhaps he would have preferred death over losing his wife."

She sat forward. "How did he lose her?"

Remont reached into his pocket and drew out a flask. He took a drink. "I would offer you a drink, but I have a feeling you would not care for it."

She wondered if it was blood.

"You are ignoring the question."

Remont nodded. "Yes, I am. It is a question I cannot and will not answer. It is Darius's place to tell you when the time is right. For now just know he is a good man, and he would do nothing to harm you."

She smiled, unable to hide the intense happiness she felt.

"I have heard you have some secrets of your own, Gabrielle."

Feeling her cheeks grow hotter, she shifted. "What do you mean?"

"I understand you are a witch who brought a young boy back to life. A boy who had been struck by a carriage. To bring someone back from the brink of death is quite an undertaking."

"I could not help it. I felt responsible."

"Responsible because Sutherland was groping at you?"

"You're reading my mind again."

He laughed. "I can't seem to help myself. A habit, I suppose. Aside from this gift to heal, what other powers do you possess?"

"Well, I can cast spells, and like you, I can read minds."

"Indeed . . . prove it."

She watched him intently, probing his mind. It was not easy. In fact, his power shocked her. Finally, she sensed his pain, an overwhelming sadness he did not show on the outside, but one that nearly consumed him emotionally.

The valet knocked at the door and entered a second later, carrying a tray with a pot of tea and two cups and saucers. Gabrielle continued to concentrate on Remont's thoughts while the valet poured their tea. Suddenly, she saw Demetri standing in a doorway, a woman kissing him. It was obvious by the state of their clothing that the two had been intimate.

Had Remont watched Demetri with this woman, or had he read Demetri's thoughts? Whatever the case, she ached for her new friend. The valet left and closed the door behind him. "Why don't you leave him?"

Remont's eyes narrowed. "Leave him?"

Gabrielle oftentimes said exactly what was on her mind, without thinking about the consequences beforehand. She could tell by Remont's expression that this was one of those times. "Forgive me. It is none of my business. I saw an image of Demetri with a woman."

"You actually read my mind?" he said, disbelief in his tone.

She winced. "You asked me to prove that I could."

"Indeed I did." He looked away. "Do you think me weak for staying with him all these years?"

"Not at all."

He didn't look like he believed her. "Honestly, I do not know why I put up with it."

"Perhaps because you love him."

He sighed heavily. "Yes, I do. Too much, I think."

"He loves you, too."

He laughed, but it didn't reach his eyes. "Demetri does not know what true love means."

"I can tell he loves you."

"Love and desire are two different things, Gabrielle. You yourself know that, even at your age. You asked yourself that very question earlier tonight, did you not?"

And now it was her turn to be surprised. She nodded. "Yes."

"Touché" he said, taking a sip of tea. "I think perhaps we have been together for too long. Perhaps we became too comfortable."

"But you love him?"

"Yes, but that is not enough. I grow tired of wondering who he is with and when he will finally come home. Perhaps one day he won't come home at all."

"Have you ever stayed away for a night?"

"No, because I never wanted to stay away. I never wanted to be away from Demetri."

"So does Demetri mind if you share another person's bed?"

"I think it would bother him."

"Does he not know?"

"I have never been unfaithful." He sighed. "Well, I hadn't been unfaithful until quite recently."

"And you feel guilty?"

He nodded. "I'm disappointed more than anything and furious with Demetri, because I did it out of spite."

"Maybe it would do Demetri some good to know that he is not the only one in your life."

Gabrielle sensed his fear. Remont had been in love with Demetri for over five hundred years, and those feelings did not go away overnight. "He would probably leave."

"And would that be so horrible? Would you like to be with someone who is not faithful, or be with someone who wants to be with you and only you?"

"It's difficult with our kind, Gabrielle. We feed, and the act itself is erotic. So erotic that oftentimes it leads to . . . other things."

Which made her wonder about her future with Darius. Though he told her he would be her only lover, what would happen if a woman came along that made him feel differently? Perhaps another vampire. She could see no resolution, save becoming a vampire herself . . . which terrified her.

"I would think long and hard about that first, Gabrielle. You must be sure you want this life, because if you do become a vampire, you *will* live forever."

EIGHTEEN

Darius walked in the bedchamber just as Gabrielle finished brushing out her hair. All night he'd thought of her, wondering what she was up to, yearning for the moment he would return, and take her to bed.

He closed the door behind him, and she set the brush down and stood. "You're finally home."

Home. Just hearing the words from her lips made him smile.

His gaze shifted down her body. She wore one of his shirts, which hung to the middle of her thighs. "I have a greater appreciation for that shirt now." He turned the lock.

She grinned and twirled around, the shirt flying up, showing her lovely bottom. "I'm glad you like it. It's quite comfortable."

Blood heated his groin, his cock aching. "If this is what will greet me upon every return, then perhaps I shall refrain from purchasing ye more dresses."

She took the few steps that separated them. "Did you have a nice evening?"

"Yes, and did you have a nice time with Remont?"

"A very nice time," she said with a wide grin. "He is a wonderful companion and has so many stories to tell. In fact, he told me a few about you."

He untied his cravat. "None too telling, I hope."

She laughed. "No."

"I hope I did not do myself a disservice by leaving ye here alone with Remont. I forgot how charming and engaging he can be."

"Yes, he is. Speaking of charming, did you *charm* any ladies this evening?" She lifted a brow as she awaited his response. Despite her effort to block him, he could read her mind, knew she worried that he might find another lover.

"I did try to charm a few women, but only because I had to prove I didn't have a beautiful young woman waiting for me at home."

"Flatterer."

He pulled her into his arms. "I missed ye."

"I missed you, too."

Her words pleased him immensely. She trusted him. He felt it, but he also felt her insecurity about their future. How would they ever be able to get over such a hurdle?

"No one can compare to ye, lass."

He saw the vulnerability in her eyes slowly slip away.

His hands moved to her shoulders and he bent down, kissed the side of her neck. Her heart was beating so fast, he wondered if it was from desire or fear.

Her arms encircled his waist. Pressing her cheek to his chest, he knew she heard his slower heartbeat. He held her tightly to him, one arm about her waist, the other at the back of her neck. "Look at me, Gabrielle."

She did, and what he saw in her eyes took his breath away. She desired him. "I have waited too long for ye to return to me and I would never ruin that. I went tonight because I had to. This is where I want to be, here with ye. I can hardly wait to leave the city tomorrow evening and return home."

She leaned into him, and he knew she must feel the hard length of his cock. Her eyes widened. "You *did* miss me."

He laughed before he kissed her. "See what ye do to me?"

"I am glad."

He lifted her in his arms, and she wrapped her legs around his lean waist, locking her ankles at his back.

His hands cupped her naked buttocks, squeezing the high, firm mounds.

Soft lips left Gabrielle's to journey over her jaw, over her throat, and then up the other side.

Her channel grew wet, the flesh between her thighs tingling with anticipation as the hard ridge of his sex rubbed against her sensitive bud.

He took a few steps toward a large side table. Resting her bottom on the edge, he went slowly to his knees, bringing her legs over his shoulders.

She gripped the sides of the table as he licked her slit, his tongue lifting her delicate nub, over and over again.

Her stomach coiled in a tight knot as she climbed toward orgasm. How exquisite his tongue felt laving her sensitive folds, dipping inside her hot, dripping channel.

Her climax came, and she shifted, nearly toppling the table, but Darius braced it with a foot. She looked down at him as he continued to pleasure her, and was stunned by how excited she became just watching him.

Even after the orgasm he continued to stroke her, his long tongue slipping into her heat before circling her tiny button, over and over again. He slipped a finger into her, and she arched her hips, moaning when he slid another finger in.

With his other hand he reached up, palmed a breast, weighing it with his hand before playing with the nipple. He rolled the taut bud between thumb and forefinger, pulling it, pinching it lightly.

His fingers began pumping in and out of her slowly while he continued to taste her, his tongue bringing her to orgasm again and again.

The multiple sensations were almost too much for her. She came again, her insides pulsing around his long fingers, coating them with her dew. "Darius," she said, her inner muscles still throbbing, her legs shaking from the intensity of her climax.

"Yes, love."

"I need you."

He didn't ask her to elaborate, but stood, his cock rising above the band of his pants. She stared at his large, thick length while he unbuttoned his pants, took his cock in hand, and guided it toward her dripping entrance.

She opened her legs wider as he inched inside her.

He pulled the tip of his manhood out, and she looked down to see it glistening with her essence.

Her intense need must have shown on her face, but she didn't care. She wanted him to know how desperately she needed him. "Darius, please."

He thrust into her, and they moaned in unison. His strokes were slow and fluid, the table shifting with each thrust.

The now familiar stirring grew more intense as she pushed toward orgasm. For once she did not guard her thoughts or her emotions from him. Instead, she wanted him to feel what she felt.

As the first flutters of her climax hit her, she moaned, reveling in the feel of her lover filling her completely.

Darius would never forget Gabrielle as she was at this moment. Those haunting green eyes staring at him with such desire.

He could hardly believe that just days before she had been a virgin. How comfortable she had become with sex in such a short time.

To his shock she pushed her thoughts at him, her joy and exultation, and as he came, he reveled in the knowledge that she truly and deeply cared for him.

Across the street from Darius MacLeod's townhouse a man rested against a tree, inhaled deeply of his cigar, taking the smoke into his lungs. Smoking always calmed him, and as he blew out a trail of cigar smoke, he cursed Gabrielle Fairmont and her lover. He had been made a fool of one too many times in these past weeks since she'd disappeared at the Vanderline ball.

Fool or no, he wanted Gabrielle Fairmont in his bed, if only to fuck her once before he squeezed the life out of her.

And that day was coming very soon.

His sister had asked him just last evening why he did not pursue another woman. After all, he could have any number of women. His wealth made that possible, even at his age, but he yearned for only one. And that woman was the beautiful blonde with haunting green eyes who had all of London talking about her beauty and her ability to heal.

Ironically the whispers of her being a witch had soon died down, and now the rumor went that Gabrielle was descended from angels, put on earth to save the helpless.

It had been angels who whisked her away that night at the Vanderline mansion, many said. He knew the truth. She'd escaped him, and had no doubt planned it all along.

Sutherland shook his head and took a long drink from a near-empty brandy bottle.

She might have fooled everyone else, but he knew her secrets. Had watched her witchcraft with his own eyes.

As though his thoughts conjured her up, Gabrielle stepped near one of the windows. Her hair fell around her like a veil, and while the window was not low enough that he could make out what she was wearing, it looked very much like a man's shirt.

His blood ran cold.

Damn Darius MacLeod.

A second later the Scot appeared, pulled her into his arms, and kissed her passionately.

Sutherland trembled with anger.

"I shall have the last laugh," he said, dropping the cigar, crushing it beneath his heel, before draining the contents of the bottle. He walked around the corner to where his carriage awaited. Opening the door, the beautiful redhead smiled. "Are you ready for me?"

"Yes, it is time to make your grand entrance, my dear."

"And what of the money?"

Greedy bitch.

He patted his waistcoat pocket. "Here, when you have done your job."

With a nod, she stepped out of the carriage and walked toward Darius MacLeod's townhouse.

NINETEEN

Gabrielle had just dozed off when she woke to the sound of voices, which seemed to come from just outside the bedchamber.

The bed curtain was opened just enough to see some of the room. Fortunately, she was able to see Darius. He stood at the chamber doorway, wearing only his pants.

"But I want to come into your chamber, Darius," came a soft, feminine voice. "I want you desperately."

Gabrielle's stomach tightened. Could it be an old mistress? She listened intently, willing her heart to stop pounding so hard.

"Bernadette, I am too tired this evening."

"But I have come all this way, my love. You promised me the night of the Vanderline ball that you would come to see me again, and yet I have not heard from you since."

"Ye really must leave."

Bernadette leaned into him. "Darling, do not send me away. My driver will not be back for at least an hour."

"Ye should have sent word beforehand, Bernadette," Darius said, lowering his voice. "I could have saved ye the trip."

"I have dreamt of your cock for weeks." Bernadette rubbed against him. "In fact, I can hardly wait to feel you inside me again. No one can fuck me like you do."

Again? Jealousy rushed through Gabrielle. When exactly had they made love? Hadn't he been in London for just a few weeks?

"I'm so hot for you, Dari."

Gabrielle felt nauseous. Though she told herself she shouldn't listen, she couldn't bring herself to cover her ears. Instead, she bit into her bottom lip to keep from saying anything that would only make the situation worse.

"Bernadette, ye have to go."

"But I don't expect Harold home for hours."

"Bernadette, please." His frustration was evident in his tone and body language.

The woman must have been drinking this evening, or she would have recognized he didn't want her.

"Come, let's go to bed, Dari. We can be quick about it, and then you can get the sleep you want so badly."

"Bernadette, please."

"I will even let you bite me again."

Gabrielle's breath lodged in her throat. Darius had bitten the woman? She remembered what Remont had said about biting during sex.

Absently, Gabrielle rubbed the side of her neck. It was still sore, but she felt no puncture wound.

"Bernadette, I am flattered that ye came all this way to be with me, but I am with another."

"Another?" she said, her voice deadly calm.

The woman rushed across the room, and Gabrielle pulled the covers over her head.

"Bernadette!" Darius yelled, just as the curtain was ripped open.

Bernadette pulled on the blanket, but Darius was faster, saving Gabrielle from further embarrassment. "Who is it? I must know."

"It is time for ye to leave, Bernadette," Darius said in a firm tone.

"Darius, is everything alright?"

Gabrielle recognized Demetri's voice.

"All is well," Darius replied, sounding frustrated. "Bernadette was just leaving."

"Who is the whore in your bed?" Bernadette asked.

"I am no whore," Gabrielle said, unable to take another second of the woman's abuse. She was tired of people assuming so much about her.

"Yet you cower in *my* lover's bed, hiding your face for fear I will see you."

Gabrielle sat up, uncaring if the woman saw her or not. "He is my lover, not yours."

Bernadette's eyes narrowed. "Well if it isn't Sutherland's missing fiancée. You are engaged to another, and you say you are no whore?"

"I will not marry Sutherland, and who are you to speak of whores? Are you not married?"

"Bitch," Bernadette spat, swinging at Gabrielle, but Darius was quicker, grabbing her by the wrist.

"For God's sake," Demetri said, rolling his eyes. "My brother has another woman in his bed. A woman he cares for, and therefore, I suggest you leave, madam—before someone throws you out."

"Come, let me call the driver for ye," Darius said, but Bernadette ripped her hand away.

"I hope you are hanged for witchcraft, you little bitch."

"Enough!" Darius said, pulling her toward the door.

"Here, let me escort her home," Demetri said, the side of his mouth lifting in a devious grin.

"How pleased you must be to have bested the powerful Sutherland, Darius. He will be shocked to learn you have been with his little virgin—or not so virginal—bride."

"Gabrielle is *not* marrying Sutherland," Darius said, his voice edged with steel.

The fake smile slid from Bernadette's face. "How protective you are of your little lover."

"I am not afraid of Lord Sutherland," Darius said, his jaw clenching.

Bernadette smiled, but it didn't reach her eyes. "Perhaps you should be."

"Sutherland does not scare me, Bernadette."

"Nor me," Demetri replied.

Bernadette's gaze shifted over Demetri. "Why don't you worry about your own lover? I met a young couple earlier this evening who told me Remont *entertained* them the other night. Indeed, that is the only reason they attended the soiree. They had hoped for a second act." Her eyes widened. "And there he is. Were your ears burning, Remont?"

Remont lifted a brow, but said nothing.

Demetri's eyes narrowed as he stared at Remont, but to his credit he said nothing.

"Bernadette, it is time for ye to go," Darius said, clearly at the end of his rope. "I shall see you out."

"I am sure we will meet again," Bernadette said to Gabrielle in a mocking tone as she tried to pull away from Darius's grip, without success.

Darius glanced at Gabrielle. *Do not fear, lass. I shall return.*

She nodded as he walked Bernadette out of the room.

Gabrielle closed her eyes and focused on Bernadette's thoughts. Tonight's visit had not happened by chance. Sutherland had orchestrated it.

Knowing Sutherland was nearby made the hair on her arms stand on end.

If only they could leave right now. Or, even better, if they could jump from London to Scotland, but she knew that was impossible. No, they would travel by carriage at night, and hope Sutherland or her uncle did not follow.

A knock sounded on the door, bringing her from her thoughts. "Gabrielle," Remont said, approaching the bed, "are you all right?"

Her throat tightened. So many emotions rushed through her, most of all fear. And not fear for herself, but for the three men whose uncomplicated lives had suddenly turned complicated, and all because of her. "Yes, thank you for asking."

"Do not worry about Bernadette. She would have a lot to explain if she started telling people what she saw in another man's bedchamber."

"Sutherland sent her."

He nodded. "Yes, I know."

"He will follow us to Scotland."

"Perhaps, but he will never get his hands on you. We do not fear him, and if he is foolish enough to follow us to Scotland, then he deserves what is coming."

She didn't need to ask what that might be, but instead nodded.

He winked. "You'll be fine, my dear. We will not let anyone hurt you."

"Thank you," she said, squeezing his hand. "I'm glad we are leaving London."

"After a few weeks in the highlands, you might feel differently."

"As long as Darius, Demetri, and you are with me, I won't have time to be bored."

"I'm not so sure about that."

"I'm sorry Bernadette told Demetri about the young couple you were with."

He shrugged. "I think it's rather ironic that the first time I'm unfaithful in centuries, I'm caught red-handed, while Demetri can have a different lover every night and no one is the wiser."

"You must have made quite an impression if the couple was out looking for you."

He smiled softly. "I have been alive for many years," he said with a wink. "Even so, I didn't want Demetri finding out like this."

Gabrielle hugged him. What a kind and gentle man Remont was. Not at all what she expected a vampire to be, especially one as old and powerful as he apparently was. How alike they were in their loyalty.

Darius walked in and Remont stood. "I hope that is the end of the excitement for one night."

Darius sighed heavily.

Remont stood and clapped Darius on the back. "Do not fret, my friend. Now get a good night's sleep, you two. Tomorrow is a new day, or should I say night."

Darius shut the door behind him. "I am sorry ye had to endure that, Gabrielle."

"How did she get into the house?"

"An open window in the parlor. I've asked the servants to double check all the windows and doors to make sure they are locked."

"Was she your mistress?"

"I met her the night before I met you in London, and yes, we did have sex, but it was nothing more than that." He unbuttoned his pants, slid them past his narrow hips and perfect buttocks. Turning, she could see his cock, large and thick, even when he wasn't aroused.

Her nipples hardened.

Slipping under the covers, he pulled her into his arms. "I swear to you that I have not slept with another woman since meeting ye, Gabrielle."

She instantly relaxed as he kissed her once, twice. Small, gentle kisses. Already she could feel his cock swell and harden.

Goose bumps rose all over her body, and not from the cold, but his touch.

Her hand rested on his stomach, over the thick muscles there, and trailed lower still to his cock.

"Go up on your knees," he whispered.

She frowned, but did as he asked.

Her heart accelerated as he moved behind her. He touched her slit, circled her tiny pearl.

Arching her back, she released a moan. He slipped a finger into her heated core, then another. He bent over and kissed her spine, inch by inch. All the while his fingers worked their magic. He cupped one breast, toyed with the nipple.

She came with a low-throated moan, her sheath contracting around his fingers.

When the climax subsided, he slid into her slowly, adding only an inch at a time until he filled her completely.

"That feels so good," she said, looking over her shoulder at him.

His eyes were half-mast, full of desire. She licked her lips, looking at his wide chest, hard stomach, and that part of him that was slick from her honey.

His strokes increased, and she grabbed for the headboard, her fingers curling around the rail. She felt herself building toward climax again, and arched her back, her buttocks high in the air.

"Come with me, Gabrielle," Darius said, his strokes increasing, faster and faster. The headboard hit the wall over and over again. Her cheeks burned, knowing others would hear it, but she didn't care.

He kissed the back of her neck as he ground into her.

And as though on command, she came at the same time he did.

Remont hesitated outside the bedchamber he shared with Demetri. Thanks to Bernadette, he now had some explaining of his own to do.

Why the bloody hell was he so nervous? After all, Demetri slept with different people all the time and never had to sit down and explain himself.

Taking a deep breath, he pushed the door open.

Demetri lay in the middle of the bed, his back to him. Perhaps he had fallen asleep already?

Or perhaps he would turn a blind eye to Remont's wandering ways—just as Remont had ignored all his legions of liaisons these past five centuries.

"Was Bernadette telling the truth?" Demetri asked, his voice surprisingly calm.

Damn. Remont closed his eyes and counted to ten.

"It isn't important, Demetri."

"Is it not?" he asked, the rage returning to his voice yet again. Demetri went up on his elbows, and the blanket fell down to his muscular stomach, exposing the hard planes there.

Remont's mouth went dry and he forced himself to maintain eye contact.

"I do not even recall their names."

"Their?" Demetri shot off the bed like it had caught fire. Remont lifted a brow, but refused to drop his gaze past his lover's lovely, wide chest.

Demetri, only just now realizing his naked state, ripped the blanket off the bed, wrapping it around his waist. "So she was not lying. There were two—at the same time?"

Remont swallowed past the lump in his throat. Dear God, he hadn't been this nervous for ages. "Yes, there were two at the same time."

Demetri closed his eyes, ran a hand down his face.

As strange as it was, and as painful as it was, Remont felt like a large weight had been lifted from his shoulders.

Demetri planted his hands on his narrow hips. "Where was I when you were experiencing this ménage à trois?"

"Fucking Lord Whitcomb's mistress, I believe."

The nerve in Demetri's jaw twitched. "Where did you meet them?"

He wasn't about to tell him he'd met the couple outside Whitcomb's whore's townhouse. That would be too humiliating. Plus, it would no doubt stroke Demetri's ego knowing Remont had been so desperate. "I think it was at the Vanderlines' ball."

Remont could see the wheels turning in his lover's head. "What did they look like?"

For the love of God. "It doesn't matter, Demetri. It happened, it's over, and that is all there is to it."

"It matters to me."

"Why?"

Demetri walked toward him, and Remont nearly took a step back, but forced himself to not move a muscle. His lover had never bullied him, and he sure as hell wouldn't start now.

Stopping just inches away, Demetri's blue eyes narrowed. "I didn't know you were so unhappy."

"I never said I was."

"But you are taking other lovers."

"I did not think you would mind, especially given you have other lovers as well."

"That is different, Remont."

"In what way is it different? Fucking is fucking, Demetri."

Demetri flinched as though he'd been slapped. "We have always had an understanding."

"I don't recall ever having such a discussion," Remont murmured, moving away from him, untying his robe. "I'm tired. Perhaps we can speak about this another time."

"Why are you so tired? Did your lovers take all your energy?"

"I am mystified by your reaction, Demetri. Why is it that you can fuck whoever you want and it makes no difference, yet when I do the same, I am chastised? Look at you. You're furious, and you have no right to be."

Demetri's brows furrowed. Ironically he probably never had thought anything was wrong with his own behavior . . . until now.

"I am tired," Remont said again, sidestepping Demetri and removing his robe, tossing it over a chair.

Lying down, he pulled the sheet up. It was hardly enough to keep him warm, but he would not ask Demetri for the blanket that was still firmly wrapped around his hips.

Apparently he would not have the chance, as Demetri headed for the door.

"Where are you going?" Remont asked.

Demetri looked at him, his blue eyes full of hurt. "It doesn't matter."

He nearly asked for the blanket but refrained, knowing Demetri would walk naked through the townhouse and that would not do.

Demetri looked at Remont for what seemed like minutes, but was actually seconds. He shook his head, walked out the door, and slammed it behind him.

TWENTY

Scottish Highlands
One week later

Darius's manor house was exactly how Gabrielle had seen it in her dreams. Up close it was absolutely breathtaking. Four stories high, and made in an L-brick design, the glorified hunting lodge, as Darius had called it, was impressive.

Ivy clung to the dark gray stone, and candles lit up each room, it seemed. No doubt in preparation for the master's return.

Remont, Darius, and three carriages full of servants and other items had followed directly behind the carriage she and Darius traveled in. It had taken them less than a week to make the journey, stopping at pleasant inns along the way. Strangely, she had already started to become accustomed to sleeping all day, and only going out at night.

It was a good thing they left London. There she had been trapped, and even though Darius's townhouse was beautiful, she did not like the idea of being caged.

How tempted she had been to go out on her own, to just walk out on the porch, lift her face to the sky, and feel the sun beaming down on her.

But Darius had not allowed it, saying he feared Sutherland and his spies were watching. So Gabrielle had stayed in, away from the windows, scared that somehow her ex-fiancé would ruin the happiness she had so recently found.

And she was happy.

Intensely so, and she did not care that her mother, or anyone else, would not approve.

Each night Gabrielle's mother visited her in her dreams, and at first those dreams were always filled with warnings about Darius. But apparently even her mother was giving in, and instead her warnings were more about Sutherland and her uncle.

"It hasn't changed at all," Demetri said, his voice wistful, as though he remembered another place and time.

"It's lovely." Gabrielle looked at Darius, who stepped out of the carriage and grinned. It was evident he was thrilled to be home, and to have them all with him. He could not stop talking about it the entire way.

"For the love of God—is it raining now?" Demetri asked in disbelief, wiping a rain splatter from his brow. "Bloody hell!"

Remont laughed, but sobered instantly when Demetri shot him a nasty look.

"Ye sound as though ye have never been to the highlands, brother," Darius said, taking Gabrielle by the hand. "Did ye forget how cool and windy it gets?"

"No, I did not forget. I remember, and that is precisely why I live in Venice."

They started for the manor, and Gabrielle thought back on the book she'd found in Darius's library about Scotland's fight for independence. She had scoured the names on the pages and had been shocked to find the MacLeod family name throughout, and even once there was mention of twin brothers who fought so valiantly for Robert the Bruce.

Looking at the brothers now, dressed in the clothing of wealthy nineteenth-century aristocrats, one would never know they were once warriors who fought hand-to-hand combat with the English.

And Darius had died on the battlefield. Had Remont not come along when he had, the man she was falling in love with would not be here today.

Remont glanced at her, and smiled.

Why did she always forget to watch her thoughts when around these men?

Darius lifted the doorknocker, but never had a chance to use it, as the door opened.

A small, matronly woman with gray hair smiled up at them. "Welcome home, sir. Oh, and the rest of ye as well."

"Thank ye, Eleanor. It is nice to be home."

"We will take good care of all of ye. Fine care, indeed." Her gaze shifted to Demetri, and her eyes widened. "Well as I live and breathe. I never thought to see your handsome face again, my boy. It's about time ye came home!"

Demetri smiled for the first time all week. "It was my brother's idea."

"And a good idea it was. Good for ye. Now come, let me get you out of those wet clothes."

"Well, Eleanor, I didn't know you felt that way about me," Demetri replied, his voice low and seductive.

The old woman's brows furrowed into a frown. "Ye are not so old that I can't bend ye over my knee and paddle your bottom, Demetri."

"Jacob and the others will be bringing our bags in," Darius said, cutting off his brother's reply. "Eleanor, will ye be sure and see everything is put where it belongs?" Darius kissed her cheek. "Oh, and please forgive my bad manners. This is Gabrielle, who will also be staying with us. And of course ye remember Remont."

"How could I forget that handsome face," Eleanor said, embracing Remont before turning to Gabrielle. "It's nice to meet ye, lass."

"Thank you."

Gabrielle took in her surroundings as they walked into the landing. Everything was so elegant and yet masculine. Rich wood tones and plush rugs. Artwork that must have cost a fortune. "What lovely paintings."

Darius smiled. "Thank ye. I painted those many years ago."

"You are the artist?"

He nodded. "I was not lying when I told ye that I painted."

"Indeed," she said, reminded yet again of how very little she knew about him. Perhaps this visit would fix all of that.

Demetri was already up the stairs when Gabrielle, Darius, and Remont ascended. "He does not seem himself of late. Have ye noticed that?" Darius asked, looking at Remont.

Remont shook his head. "Perhaps he was not quite ready to leave London yet. You know how he loves the city."

At the top of the stairs they turned right. Darius stopped and opened the fourth door they came to. "Remont, here is your room. I hope it is satisfactory."

Gabrielle peeked in. It was beautiful, the walls painted a dark hue that offset the white marble fireplace. A huge four-poster bed looked almost small in the large room. "Thank you, Darius. It shall be perfect."

A door shut loudly, seemingly from the very next room. No doubt Demetri's chamber.

"We shall see ye shortly," Darius said, taking Gabrielle's hand within his own. He was so happy to be home. She could see it in his eyes, and in his demeanor. He felt safe here, as did she.

Darius's room was at the end of the hallway, and was massive. Everything had been well thought out, from the furniture, to the drapes, to the carpet beneath her feet. "It's beautiful, as is the rest of the manor. You must be successful to have such lovely things."

He shrugged. "When ye live long enough, ye begin to realize what you're good at."

"And what would that be?"

"I own many businesses throughout Scotland, England, and Wales, and even in America."

Her heart leapt. "Have you ever been to America?"

He nodded. "Many times."

"I should like to go one day."

"Then I shall take ye."

He opened his arms and she went into them, resting her head against his chest. "Your heart pumps so slowly—except on certain occasions."

"And what occasions would that be?"

She grinned. "When we make love."

Smiling, he bent his head and kissed her. "I want nothing more than to make love to ye, but I shall have to refrain until later. I must tend to some matters first.

"And after you attend to business."

"Then I shall attend to you."

Remont sat on the edge of the bed, watching Demetri pace the carpet. He hadn't been settled in his room for five minutes when his lover came bursting through the door.

"What is happening to you?" he asked, coming to a halt before Remont. "You have been acting strangely for a week now. Hell, the carriage ride here was excruciating."

Remont ran a hand through his hair. "Isn't that why you spent so much time riding your horse *beside* the carriage, so you wouldn't have to suffer my company?"

Demetri closed his eyes, sighed heavily. "That is not at all what I meant. You test my patience, Remont."

Remont could tell that Demetri tried to probe his mind, something he had not attempted for years. Perhaps they had grown too comfortable and that is why they now felt like strangers, with nothing to say except for the obvious, pointless questions.

And for the sake of his sanity, Remont knew he had to let his lover go. "You are right in some ways, Demetri. I've been giving our relationship a lot of thought, actually, and I think we might both benefit from spending time apart."

Demetri's ice blue eyes narrowed. "You waited until we came all this way to tell me this?"

"It's a decision I made during our trip."

Demetri shook his head in disbelief. "Perhaps I should leave."

"Do what you must," Remont replied, feeling quite sick.

"You do not care either way?"

"I will be content with whatever you decide, Demetri. I shall stay on for a while longer . . . at least until I know Sutherland and Gabrielle's uncle are no longer a threat."

"Perhaps if I leave you will be happier. And you could always invite your French couple to visit you."

"I do not want them to visit."

"You're lying."

"I am not lying, Demetri. I do not want them to visit me here. I don't want them, period. Once was enough."

"You think of them. I see it in your thoughts. I know what happened."

Remont stood, exasperated that things had finally come to this. "Do you?"

"Yes."

"How is it you knew I was having sex while you were busy fucking Lord Whitcomb's whore at the same time?"

Demetri blanched. "Is that why you were with them?"

"No," he said too quickly.

"Were you with them just the one time?"

"Were you with Whitcomb's whore just once?"

"Yes."

Liar. Remont bit his bottom lip. How many other things had he lied about?

"I am not lying to you," Demetri said, "I was only with her that night."

"So now you read my thoughts?"

"I cannot very well help it now, can I? You are not the same." He ran a trembling hand through his thick, dark hair. "You don't want me touching you, and you can barely tolerate sitting next to me."

Demetri crossed the room, stopping just inches from Remont. "Do you care for me?"

Remont's insides twisted. "Of course I do."

"Do you want me?"

"I don't know."

Demetri's eyes widened in disbelief. His gaze searched Remont's face, and it was all Remont could do not to take the words back and tell him that he did want him. That he would always want him, and that no one could ever take his place. But he had come too far and suffered in silence for far too long to go back to the way things were.

Stay strong, Gabrielle had told him. And that is exactly what he planned to do.

"So that is the way of it," Demetri said, his voice deadly calm. "I shall make this easy for you then."

He headed for the door. "I will leave. Good-bye, Remont."

Remont didn't say a word, but his throat felt so tight he couldn't swallow.

With a final glance, Demetri walked out the door, slamming it behind him.

TWENTY-ONE

"Get away from me, ye beast!"

Gabrielle's heart slammed against her ribs as she rushed from the dining room.

Darius called out to her. "I will not hurt ye, lass. Trust me. I love ye Rose."

Rose? Why was Darius calling her Rose?

She looked behind her. He was running toward her, and by the time she turned around, he stood in front of her, stopping her progress.

How in God's name had he gone from being behind her, to being in front of her?

It was physically impossible—unless he really was a vampire. Fear rippled through her as she looked into his ice blue eyes.

Clan members had been talking about his death on the battlefield at Bannockburn. How then could he arrive home two days later, without a wound or scar?

It did not end there. He slept throughout the day, and stayed up all hours of the night. Friends dropped by less often, too afraid of what he had become.

Tonight at dinner she had seen his fangs, which explained why her neck hurt for hours after they'd made love last night. He had kissed her there, and she had felt a sharp prick on the tender skin of her throat. She touched that place now, her heart trip-hammering. Dear God, was it too late? Would she become a creature as well? She laid her hand on her round stomach. And what of the child that rested in her womb? What would happen to the babe?

"Stay away from me, Darius!" She raced from the room, certain she heard his steps behind her, yet when she looked back he wasn't there. She raced for the steps, looked back once more, and lost her footing.

She grabbed for the balustrade, but missed it.

It happened so quickly. One moment she teetered on the edge, the next she was falling fast. She could hear her bones breaking as she tumbled—and then, she hit her head hard and black rose up to greet her.

Darius screamed her name over and over again, his voice full of pain and fear.

Gabrielle awoke with a start, her heart still pounding like she'd run a great distance. She blinked a few times, looking about the room, and recognized the library in Darius's home in the Scottish highlands.

From the moment she'd walked into the house, she had been inundated with thoughts of Rose. It seemed as though the woman wanted to torment her.

Was Gabrielle really this woman in a past life, or did they simply just look alike?

Whatever the case, she needed peace. She could not afford many more sleepless nights. Even last night she'd awoken from another dream, much like the one she'd just experienced. Not wanting to bother Darius, she'd slipped on her chemise and robe, and gone in search of a good book, hoping it would take all the strange emotions away.

But reading could not rid her of Rose, and her tragic end. However, she now understood Darius's sadness, the strange look in his eyes whenever Gabrielle brought up his dead wife.

Chilled, Gabrielle pulled the blanket tight around her shoulders and stared into the blazing fire. Candles that had been lit earlier had now burned down, casting the room in eerie shadows.

How did Darius, his brother, and Remont find the blood they needed to satisfy their thirst? Did they slip out in the middle of the night, finding a victim? Darius had told her he did not kill many, only those who deserved it. But what of Demetri and Remont? Did they kill each night, or just feed from some unsuspecting person who would not remember what happened? What if they could not find victims? Would they start feeding from animals?

"Gabrielle?"

Gabrielle's heart jumped to her throat. She'd been so lost in thought she hadn't heard the door open.

Darius walked toward her and pulled her into his arms. He loved being home, and seemed so relaxed. "Ye weren't in bed. Could ye not sleep?"

"No."

"Nightmares again?"

She nodded. "Yes, it seems I cannot escape them."

Darius's fingers curled around Gabrielle's.

Though he rarely made a habit of reading her thoughts, he did so now, wanting to know exactly what tormented her, so perhaps he could help her.

He concentrated and was shocked to see Rose's final minutes, where she had raced from the dining room, to get away from him.

He could feel her inner torment, the concern of being with him, and what that would entail. Could she live with a man who was immortal? What if they wanted more children? Could she become pregnant with a man who was by all accounts dead?

Little did she know he too had agonized over those very concerns since the moment he took Gabrielle to bed. It all came down to one thing—what would happen if he did make her into a vampire? Would the powers she already had intensify, or would it harm her or even kill her? And perhaps she did not want to become a vampire at all.

The vision ended with Rose falling down the stairs.

Shaking away the horrible image, Darius took her by the hand. "Come, there is something I wish to show you."

Her brows furrowed. "What is it?"

"Ye shall see soon enough. First ye will need to dress warmly."

"We are going outside?" She looked toward the window. "Isn't it too cold to go for a walk?"

"I shall keep ye warm, lass."

"Promise?" she asked, her soft, full lips curving in a sensual smile that made his blood warm and put his fears at ease.

"Aye, I promise."

They walked for what seemed like forever. Surprisingly, it wasn't as cold as Gabrielle had thought, and Darius had kept true to his promise and kept her warm.

Finally, when they reached the top of the hill, Darius turned around and told her to do the same.

The manor house, slightly hidden by the trees, stood out like a beacon, every room lit up. The top floor had several stained glass windows, which only helped add to the manor's ambiance.

"It's positively beautiful."

He grinned, obviously pleased. "I used to come up here on occasion and watch the sun rise. I know it sounds silly, but that is the worst part of being a vampire. Not being able to see the world in color. Not feeling the sun upon my skin. Just small things that ye take for granted. Ye have no idea what I would give to have just one more chance to see the sunrise."

He turned to Gabrielle, took her hands in his, and kissed them softly. "One day, when it is safe to do so, I want ye to come up here, to this very spot, and watch the sunrise for both of us. It will take your breath away," Gabby.

Gabrielle's throat tightened with unshed tears as she looked into his handsome face. "I will. I promise." Resting her head against his shoulder, she felt some of the fear and anxiety she'd been feeling since waking from her dream dissipate. "I'm afraid, Darius."

He put her at arm's length. "Afraid of what?"

"Everything. I'm afraid of how I feel when I'm with you, and how I feel knowing that my past could catch up with me at anytime. That Sutherland and my uncle will never stop searching for me. I'm afraid that we're so different we won't be able to stay together."

"I will never let Sutherland get ye, and ye know that. When it comes to our differences, ye have to believe that everything will work out."

"I just feel that something very bad is going to happen. I sense it. I know it. I've always been able to see things, sometimes before they happen. When I lived in the convent I could not use my powers, and they became weak. But now that the door's been opened, I cannot close it. Just yesterday I had a strange vision of my uncle. He lay dead in a ditch, murdered, and then I saw Sutherland. I honestly feel that my uncle is dead, Darius."

Darius lifted her chin with his fingers, and stared into her eyes that were filled with tears. "Ye have no control over what happens to your uncle, Gabrielle. If the image ye saw ends up being fact, then ye must remember that he sold ye to Sutherland in order to pay off his debts. Your uncle did not care about your welfare. He only wanted ye for what ye could give him, love."

"I know you're right. I just wish I could get all the thoughts out of my head. I will not have peace until I do."

"Ye are safe from both of them, Gabrielle. Ye will never be forced to marry Sutherland, and face a fate like his other wives. Ye are strong, lass."

She knew what he said was true, but she could not shake the feeling that had plagued her since waking. Hopefully Sutherland would stay away and leave them all alone. If anything happened to Darius, Remont, or Demetri, she would never be able to forgive herself.

Gabrielle closed her eyes, content to hear the slow rhythm of his heart. His large hand moved up and down her back. "I'll never let him hurt ye, Gabrielle. Ye shall be safe. I promise ye."

TWENTY-TWO

On his way to have a drink at the only pub in town, Demetri walked past an old graveyard, all the while wondering why his brother loved the area so much. There was just so little to do.

He enjoyed living in big cities where there was always somewhere to go, someone to see . . . and someone to feed from.

But now he was in the highlands, too close to where he had been born and raised, and it all felt too familiar. Too many memories from a time he would just as soon forget. That world was long gone, and he had no idea, aside from missing Rose, why his brother clung to it. Perhaps now that he had Gabrielle he could let it go. Maybe he would even come to Venice.

As it was, Demetri didn't know if he would have a home in Venice any longer. Remont had been acting so strangely of late, and Demetri had been shocked to learn of his liaison. How did he know that had not been one of many?

Shaking away the images of Remont and his two lovers, Demetri crossed the heavily rutted road and opened the door to the warm and inviting pub with its dark-paneled walls and gaudy chandeliers. He lifted a brow. Interesting choice for a pub in the middle of nowhere.

The few patrons stopped what they were doing, looked him over, and then went back to conversing. All but one, a young man with green eyes and blond hair who worked in the pub cleaning tables and such.

Demetri removed his jacket, set it on the back of the chair, and sat. The boy scarcely blinked.

"What can I get ye?" the old man behind the bar asked.

"Madeira please."

"Don't have any, but I got a bottle of red wine, or perhaps a nice, dark ale?"

Demetri winced. "Wine would be fine, thank you."

Laughter sounded from upstairs. Demetri looked up to find a young woman and her companion descending the stairs. The lady couldn't be a day over twenty, very close to Gabrielle's age. Her companion, a much older man, leaned in, whispered in her ear.

She laughed aloud as he pressed a coin or two into her hand. Demetri read her thoughts instantly. The two had met here for a liaison. Her companion was a married man with a devoted wife at home and four children, all under the age of eight. And now the man must return to his wife and brood.

The woman leaned in, bit the lobe of his ear before whispering what she would do to him on his next visit. The man left after pinching the woman's behind, and the pub's door closed behind him.

The whore must have sensed his perusal, for she turned, catching Demetri's gaze. Her lips curved and she sauntered toward him.

He could smell her sex from here. The scent pungent since she'd just been fucked.

She nodded at the other men who watched her walk toward Demetri. She knew they all wanted her, and she reveled in it. At the age of fourteen, she had started whoring to make ends meet, as she was tired of working as a nurse for the privileged. One of those homes happened to be her fat lover's, and she'd cared for his four children—until his wife caught on. They had moved to the country and the whore had followed behind.

Each night it was the same routine. He would be her first client. He didn't mind that she fucked other men, just as long as he was first each evening.

Demetri could hardly wait to bite her. No, he would not drain her, not by half. Nor would he make her a vampire. But he would use her. Perhaps even fuck her . . . after she washed. Lord knows Remont had not been in the mood of late, and his balls were full and heavy.

"How ye doin' tonight, love?"

Her teeth were disappointing, with a large gap between the two bottom ones. Aside from that, she had the face of an angel.

"Very well, thank you," Demetri replied, taking the glass from the young boy, who looked irritated by the whore's attention.

"Buy me a drink?"

He nodded for the barkeeper to oblige.

"Have a seat?" he asked, and she plopped down beside him.

Her strong perfume nearly gagged him, but she also amused him, and he could certainly use some form of entertainment.

"Ye new in town?"

"You could say that."

"Will ye stay long?"

"No."

He could tell the news disappointed her. "You do not like the country?"

"I prefer the city."

"Do you?" She pouted. "I prefer the country myself."

Demetri stared at her until she was shifting on her seat, extremely nervous. "He will never leave his wife, you know."

The smile slipped from her lips. "Wot?"

"Your lover who just left. He will never leave his wife. He tells you he will, but he won't."

She lifted her chin, licked her lips. "I don't know what you're talking about."

Demetri watched her closely. "Oh, but I think you do. Your rich lover promises you everything, and yet, all these years later you are exactly where you started."

"He will marry me one day."

Forcing himself not to laugh or crack a smile, he shrugged. "He tells you that to keep you from leaving. He could not bear it, for you are the only thing that he cares about."

She smiled. "How do ye know?"

"I can read people's minds."

She laughed, hitting him playfully, her hand lingering on his arm.

"You've learned what he likes in and out of the bedchamber. You treat him like a king, knowing his wife will never do the things you do."

She swallowed hard and glanced over her shoulder, but he knew no one paid them any attention, save for the boy.

"You are young and beautiful now, but soon your looks will fade and you will still be here, in this old run-down inn, waiting for your married lover to come visit for his few minutes every day. Yes, he'll bring you trinkets, flowers, anything to keep you here. You are like chattel, bought and paid for."

"Why are you saying this?" she said, her voice cracking, her eyes narrowing. "I don't even know ye." She dabbed at her eyes with the sleeve of her dress.

Perhaps she should have taken up acting instead of whoring.

"No, you don't know me, but I know you and your kind. You are in every pub, in every city, and in every country inn like this one." He drained the glass of mediocre wine, leaned toward her. "Set yourself free from this life while you can. He is nothing to you, and soon he will not even bother coming by. He has never belonged to you and he never will."

A tear ran down her face and she brushed it away. "It is so hard to leave."

"This is all you have known, but trust me when I say that there is so much more opportunity out there. Do not waste the rest of your life here."

She nodded, even though he knew she would never leave her fat lover.

She licked her lips. "Do you want to come upstairs?"

"Certainly," he said, already standing, surprised she'd want to fuck him after his tirade.

They climbed the stairs to her room, and the patrons let out whistles and crude remarks. Demetri ignored them as she opened the door to her room.

"Just give me a moment," she said, taking the soiled sheets from the bed and rolling them into a ball while she straightened her coverlet. "Shut the door, love."

Doing as she asked, Demetri shut the door behind him.

A washbasin of rose water and soft towels sat nearby, assuring him that she at least washed between partners. Or he at least hoped that was the case.

She began undressing, exposing her slender, well-toned body. He could tell she enjoyed doing this by the way she watched his face intently. Expecting his reaction, perhaps even his gratitude.

She stepped behind a screen and washed herself before walking toward him, her curvaceous hips swaying. Straddling him in the chair, she pressed her bare mons against his still soft cock.

Despite the fact she had cleaned herself, he could still smell her musky scent mixed with the fat man's semen.

"What do you want?"

She pressed her full breasts against his chest, rolled her hips, and arched her back. "I'll do anything you desire."

"Truly?"

"Of course," she said, placing a hand on his cock, molding the material of his pants around its length. "Nothing is forbidden." She bit into her bottom lip. "Mmm, and ye are a big one to be sure."

He brushed her hair aside, kissed her neck.

"Mmm, that feels positively delightful."

"Does it," he whispered, noting the hair on her neck stood on end.

He held her in place, bracing one hand on her hip. Then he bit down hard.

She cried out in pain, but only for a moment. To his surprise she moaned, rocking her hips against him, rubbing her sex against his cock over and over again.

He pinched a nipple and she gasped, her sex throbbing against him as she climaxed hard. He drank from her more than he should have, but he had been deprived for too long.

"I want you inside me," she said, her eyes dark, her hips arching against his cock.

How tempted he was to fuck her, but for some reason he could not get Remont out of his mind.

He drank a little more, until her eyes rolled back in her head. A second later she sagged against him. Lifting her, he laid her down on the bed and covered her with a blanket.

He left a fistful of coins on the table. She would sleep for an entire day and forget everything that happened after her fat lover had left.

Demetri left the inn by way of a window. Wiping the blood from his mouth with his sleeve, he looked up the road to the castle, and then glanced in the opposite direction, which lead back to London. Perhaps he should return to Venice. Back to life as he'd known it. But a life without Remont . . .

Damn it!

With stubborn determination he jumped to the manor, hoping to find Remont.

The sound of a piano filled the manor, and Demetri followed. Remont had always been a skilled musician, and he played now for Darius and Gabrielle, who sat hand in hand listening, the very picture of marital bliss.

Darius motioned for Demetri to join them, but instead he stood at the doorway, watching.

The music ended and both Darius and Gabrielle clapped loudly. Demetri clapped as well, and Remont turned, obviously surprised to find him standing there.

"That was wonderful," Gabrielle said with a wide smile.

"Indeed," Darius agreed. "I look forward to hearing more, but first I must tend to business matters."

His brother never could lie well.

"Gabrielle, you are welcome to stay," Remont said, his voice almost pleading.

"Actually, I am going to rest before dinner."

Without another word, the two left the room, leaving just Demetri and Remont.

"We must talk, Remont."

Remont lifted a tawny brow. "I thought we already had. In fact, weren't you leaving the manor?"

"I did, but I chose to return."

Remont rounded the piano and sat down in the nearest chair, his long legs sprawled out in front of him, in a very uncharacteristic way.

Demetri took the chair nearest him. "Tell me what you are thinking."

"I am tired."

"Of me?"

"Yes."

He hadn't even blinked. For God's sake, he could have at least lied. "What have I done to change your heart?"

"You have always held my heart, Demetri, and well you know it."

"So what has changed?"

"Nothing." Remont stood as though the chair had caught fire. "Everything."

"That makes no sense."

"I know it doesn't. I only know I cannot live this way another day. My stomach is constantly in knots, and my heart aches. I just want it to end, Demetri, and the only way I know to make it end is to leave you."

Demetri felt like he'd received a blow to the gut. "You wish to leave me?"

He nodded, and looked into the fire. "It's the only way either one of us will ever have peace."

"Why do you suddenly feel this way? What has changed your heart?"

"It started in London. The night when Darius asked us to attend the soiree to find information about Sutherland and Gabrielle's uncle."

"And we did find that information."

"Yes, but instead of going straight to your brother with the news that he was in grave danger, you instead chose to meet up with a woman, knowing full well I would run back and tell your brother the news."

"You yourself had a liaison that night, too."

"Only because you were with another. Yes, I went to Darius's right after the soiree but he was behind closed doors with Gabrielle, so I did not disturb them. I was not tired so I went for a walk, and that is when I saw the French couple. I knew you were with Whitcomb's mistress, and something within me yearned for revenge. That is why I did it, and for no other reason. Just to hurt you."

The news shocked him to the core. Remont hadn't slept with the two out of desire, but rather because he wanted revenge. "I forgive you."

"*You* forgive me?" Remont's false laughter filled the room. "I am unfaithful one time in countless years and you forgive me." He shook his head. "I cannot bear to be with you any longer, Demetri. We must end this, and it must end now."

Demetri's stomach churned, and he stood. "You cannot mean it."

"But I do, Demetri. We need to spend time apart."

"For how long?"

He shook his head. "I don't know. A week. Maybe two. A month. Perhaps forever."

Demetri ran a hand through his hair, fighting the urge to cry. "What will time apart do for us?"

"I don't know."

Demetri walked toward Remont, whose eyes narrowed at his approach. He grabbed him by the back of the neck, his fingers weaving into the soft, blond locks, their lips inches from each other. "I want you. I've always wanted you."

Remont swallowed hard. "But it is not enough."

Demetri's eyes searched his. He loved him so much his heart ached. Everything about him, from his incredible eyes, the fine bone structure, to the soft, full lips. They had spent every day together for five centuries. Life without him was unthinkable.

Unable to help himself, Demetri kissed Remont.

Though he was unresponsive, Demetri kept at it, kissing him softly, his tongue running along the seam of his lips. He captured his face between his hands, and kissed him harder, demanding a response.

Remont opened just a little, whether to say something or to accept the kiss, Demetri would never know because he wouldn't give him a chance. His tongue slipped in, tracing the recesses of Remont's.

Remont tried to push against Demetri's chest, but he stood firm.

"I want you," Demetri said against his lips. "I've always wanted you. From the moment I knew you were watching me in the loch."

Remont pulled away enough to look at him. "What?"

"Yes, I knew you were there. Had seen you from a distance, painting. I could not believe your beauty. How graceful you were. Like the most beautiful of statues come to life. Everything about you intrigued me." His gaze shifted lower. "Most of all your gorgeous mouth."

Remont's brows furrowed, his look of surprise telling Demetri he heard every word. "Oh yes, you were so unlike anyone I had met, dressed in those fine silk clothes." His gaze swept over Remont's face. "You are as beautiful now as you were then."

"I didn't know you saw me first."

"I never had the courage to tell you before."

"Why?"

"Because, I have never been close to losing you. I don't want to lose you, Remont. I can't imagine not having you beside me." He kissed him then, and this time his lover responded. His mouth opened completely, his tongue brushing against Demetri's.

Relief such as Demetri had never before known washed over him. "I love you."

Remont straightened.

"I have always loved you, Remont. From the first time you kissed me. From the first moment I tasted your lips. It's always been you and only you."

"No it hasn't been, Demetri. Perhaps you do love me in your own way, but if you truly loved me, you would not have to venture out each night to have sex with someone else."

"But it is only sex."

"To you it might only be sex, and just another night, but it isn't that way for me. I had sex with another and I still cannot forgive myself for it. I feel guilty, and I keep asking myself what for, especially since you fuck whoever you choose and it doesn't bother you in the least. In fact, you can come home and give me each and every detail. If I were to do the same you would come out of your skin."

Demetri opened his mouth to deny it, but then realized he couldn't. It was true. His recent behavior proved as much.

Remont ran a trembling hand down his face. "We've been living a lie for far too many years, Demetri. I want you. I've always wanted you. No one makes my blood burn the way you do, but no one hurts me the way you hurt me, and I am getting too old."

Demetri's blood stirred in his veins as Remont's gaze slipped from his, over his chest and down his belly to his cock. His gaze shot back to his. "I need to be with someone who is mine and mine alone. A person who wants me and only me."

Demetri was ready to defend himself and tell Remont that he would be faithful to him.

But could he?

He had always had lovers and thought nothing of it. But here Remont had been unfaithful once and Demetri wanted to kill the couple. He didn't want anyone sharing his lover's bed but him.

The sides of Remont's lips curved in a smile that did not reach his eyes. "And even now, Demetri, when faced with the truth, you still cannot tell me, even lie to me, and say that you will be true. And that is why I am leaving you . . . once I'm assured Gabrielle is out of trouble."

Demetri swiped a vase from a table in his fury, dashing it into a thousand bits against the wall. Footsteps sounded, and a servant bounded in a moment later, looking from Remont to Demetri, and then the broken glass. She left as quietly as she'd entered.

"If you do not want me, then get the hell out of my brother's home!" Demetri said, his voice full of rage. "Or I shall be forced to leave."

Twenty-Three

Darius dreamt of the sun.

He could even feel the heat of the rays against his face and body, the soft glow pulsing through him from the top of his head to the very soles of his feet.

And it felt wonderful.

Slowly, he opened his eyes, staring up at the sun that still had not made it fully over the hills in the distance. His eyes burned, unaccustomed to the intense light, and yet he kept staring, knowing too soon he would wake to the darkness.

Don't wake up, he thought to himself, and then felt someone resting against his shoulder.

He opened his eyes just as Gabrielle sat up on an elbow and looked down at him, a wide smile on her face. "Look Darius, the sun is rising above the hills."

He reached up and touched her, cupped her beautiful face. It seemed so real, this dream.

"Look Darius. Look!"

Sitting up, he looked down at the manor house, sitting amongst the trees. His heart jolted. This was the same spot he had brought Gabrielle to last night after finding her in the library. They had held each other, and watched the stars until they'd fallen asleep.

Merciful heavens . . . was this real?

The sun crept up over the hill, chasing the shade away.

Dear God, he would burn to death. The manor was too far away. Perhaps if he jumped—

"I will burn," he said, ready to start down the hill, but she caught his arm.

"Do you trust me, Darius?"

He stared at her, looked at the sun on the horizon. He could feel his heart pounding out of his chest. "Yes."

"Then stay with me now. You know I would never hurt you. Last night you told me how you loved to come here to think, and how you loved to wake up and see the sun as it made its appearance each new day." She kissed him gently. "I remembered a spell. You will not burn, Darius. You will not. I swear to you on my life."

The sun had always been his enemy. Always, he had gauged time by it, how many hours he had until sunrise or sunset.

Until now.

"Here it comes, Darius."

The sun rose in the sky, over the surrounding hills, casting the valley in a wonderful glow. He took it all in. The beautiful manor house. The lands where he had played as a child. His throat tightened with emotion as he looked at Gabrielle, who absolutely beamed. She lifted her face to the sky, and inhaled.

He had never seen anything so beautiful.

He did the same, lifted his face to the sky, and then held out his hands to the sun, palms up, half expecting them to burn.

But they did not burn.

For five hundred years he had lived in darkness. Five hundred long years. He had forgotten the beauty around him when cast under the sun's glow. All the colors that were so easy to forget, especially of the heather that graced the hills and valleys of his homeland.

"You are right, Darius. The manor is beautiful from here, as is all of it."

Overcome with emotion, he pulled her into his arms, held her tight to him as tears burned his eyes. The last time he had wept had been at Rose and their baby's burial. Now he let the tears slip down his cheeks unchecked.

He clung to her, wondering how he had been so lucky to receive her love twice in a lifetime, for he knew that Gabrielle and Rose were one and the same. She had returned to him somehow, and he would not question it ever again. He wanted only to savor this moment with this woman.

She had given him back his life in more ways than she would ever know.

"Thank ye, Gabrielle. Ye do not know what it means."

She looked up, tears shining in her eyes. "I think I do, Darius. You forget I can read your mind." She went up on the tips of her toes and kissed him gently on the lips, then on each cheek, his chin, and forehead. "You are welcome, Darius."

"How long do we have?"

"An hour, perhaps more. I do not know."

It would take at least a quarter of an hour to make it back down the hill to the castle, unless they jumped.

"I had forgotten the clouds," he said, looking up at the blue sky. "When you live in darkness ye do not see things as they are."

"I can only imagine. I wonder why it is that vampires can only exist at night?"

"It's a curse on our kind. We are known for having marks across our souls."

She remembered the black mark she'd seen on him in the mirror. "And that mark means you are cursed forever?"

He nodded. "Yes, as far as I know." Lifting her hand, he kissed it. "I shall never forget this gift, Gabrielle. Not for as long as I live."

She rested her head against his shoulder. "I know why you fell in love with this place. It's heaven on earth."

How pleased he was hearing those words from her sweet lips. He squeezed her tight.

He watched from a distance.

He could pull the trigger, end both their lives in a flash, but he could not bring himself to do that just yet. No, he yearned to look them both in the eye and squeeze the life out of the little bitch who'd made a fool of him.

And her lover who had spirited her away from London. Oh, he would take great pleasure in subjecting him to every kind of torture known to man. Darius MacLeod would suffer a slow, agonizing death that would make him think back on the day he had made a fool of him.

Oh yes, all of London whispered about Gabrielle, the beautiful young woman who had bested him. Disappeared without a trace. Her uncle even thought she might have been the infamous highwayman who had left as swiftly as he had appeared. One of her uncle's spies had followed Darius to an old woman's flat in Covent Garden and overheard a conversation between the two, where the gentleman highwayman had been discussed.

No doubt MacLeod had paid the old woman off for her silence, since she refused to speak to the spy after MacLeod's departure.

The whore. How long had she been fucking the Scot?

It didn't matter now. He would take her to Gretna Green, kicking and screaming if need be. At least she was already in Scotland, and Gretna Green wasn't more than a day's ride away, mayhap a bit more.

Some things still confused him about his fiancée. If Gabrielle had been able to save a boy from death on the streets of London, then why did she have to go so far as to steal from the rich? Could she not conjure up money with her powers?

Lord knows she owed him a good sum, especially since her uncle had spent every bit of the small fortune Sutherland had paid him.

But he had paid dearly. Even now Gilbert Fairmont lay dead in a ditch somewhere along the Scottish border. The man had insisted on traveling north with him, but had proven to be an obnoxious companion from the start. Fidgety, chatty, and sipping from one of many flasks he'd brought with him. After two days in the same carriage, the man reeked of liquor, making the interior stuffy and unpleasant. And his incessant chatter had been too much, always repeating the same question over and over again. Had Sutherland been able to ride on horseback, he would have done so. However, his size would not allow it, so he'd taken matters into his own hands.

When Gabrielle's uncle had fallen off to sleep, Sutherland had taken the pillow behind him, placed it ever so gently over the drunk's mouth, and pressed as hard as he could.

The struggle he put up had been downright pathetic.

His groom and driver had helped toss the body out shortly thereafter.

And now Gabrielle Fairmont would marry him or follow her uncle to hell.

He crouched down beside a fallen tree and watched the couple, who had their arms around each other. Indeed, MacLeod lifted Gabrielle's chin in his hand and kissed her.

Sutherland bit back a retort. How he would love to shoot them dead on the spot, but this was not the time or place. No, he wanted Gabrielle to suffer greatly, and he had plenty of time.

Darius pulled Gabrielle to the ground, pulling her on top of him. She feverishly unbuttoned his breeches, releasing his huge cock, her fingers moving over the thick length with surprising deftness.

The whore!

She leaned down and took the man's cock in her mouth.

Darius played with her large breasts, toying with the nipples through her gown.

He lifted her above his straining erection, and she went down on him, taking him inside her body slowly, her head falling back on her shoulders in ecstasy.

Darius lifted the gown, and Sutherland could see Gabrielle's creamy thighs and rounded bottom. Her mouth opened in ecstasy, her moans mocking him.

She rode him hard, her tits bouncing with the movement.

Sutherland's hand slipped past the band of his pants, and he touched himself, his fingers gripping his nub of a cock.

MacLeod flipped her onto her back and fucked her skillfully, his lean hips thrusting hard as Gabrielle lifted hers to meet MacLeod's rhythm. They moved fast now, the whore clinging to her lover, her nails grazing his back as she cried out his name over and over again.

Sutherland matched the same rhythm, sweat dripping off his forehead, his heart pounding.

Darius slowed the pace, making her lift her hips and nearly beg for it.

His strokes gained in tempo again, and he pounded into her, scooting her across the grass. Gabrielle cried out, nearly weeping.

You'll be that wet for me, too, Sutherland promised her as his balls lifted and he spewed his seed onto the ground.

His entire body still shaking from the force of his orgasm, he slipped his now limp cock back into his breeches, watching with fury as Gabrielle gasped and moaned in pleasure, arching her hips as she came along with her lover.

Demetri could feel the tension in the room.

Remont sat at the piano, his slender fingers pounding on the keys, no doubt letting out all the fury he felt toward Demetri. A young man who Remont had met in the village sat near the piano, gazing at Remont with open admiration.

The boy could not be twenty, with chestnut-colored hair and dark eyes.

Demetri hated the young man on sight. Had Remont invited the boy here to make him jealous? If so, it was working quite well. Too well, in fact.

Darius and Gabrielle sat on a settee, looking comfortable and very much in love.

He emptied his glass in one swallow, and instantly a servant came to fill it. A young woman with nice tits and a nicely rounded ass. Demetri smiled at her, and she trembled, managing to splatter wine on his sleeve. "Sir, I am sorry."

"Do not fret, lass. It will come out."

"Are you certain, sir? I can see to another shirt."

"Do not bother yourself. I think I shall retire shortly anyway."

She swallowed hard, her lips curving softly.

Remont pounded on the keys, and Demetri tried not to smile. So his lover did mind if he flirted with another, even if he had a neighbor boy nearly frothing at the mouth.

They had both become almost comical. Is this what happened to couples who had been together for so long?

Demetri winked at the girl, and walked away, toward the window, which proved to be a nice vantage point. At least he could look at Remont without seeming obvious.

If only they could go back to the way they'd been before. Back in Venice where life had been so simple. But instead Demetri had wanted to see the world, or more importantly, his brother.

He did not regret visiting Darius. Indeed, he had seen Gabrielle and knew in an instant why he had been so compelled to leave Venice.

Gabrielle was the reason he came to London. To reunite his brother with Rose. After all, he had lived with the guilt of having Remont turn his brother without his consent all those years ago. Just because Demetri could not imagine a life without Darius in it. He would never forget the torment in his twin's eyes when he told Demetri about Rose's death. Darius had mourned her greatly, his child too, wondering if ever again he would find that happiness.

Gabrielle obviously adored Darius, and now Remont detested him. He had not even looked up when Demetri entered the parlor.

Nervous, Demetri paced the room full of beautiful marble statues. He contemplated one, a naked man with sword in hand. The artist had captured the human body in its most perfect form. The model's high, firm buttocks flowed into long, muscled legs. Even his shoulders were wide and pleasing. He walked a full circle around it, frowning when he noted the model's genitalia had been covered by a fig leaf.

Disappointing.

Of course, the statue and Remont had a lot in common. Both beautiful. Nearly perfect.

For a moment he considered sitting next to his lover on the piano bench, but Remont might just push him off the end, so he refrained.

Ye are letting him get to ye, brother. Quit your pacing. He will know ye are jealous. Just now, when ye spoke to the woman, Remont watched the two of ye intently. He still loves ye.

I don't think so, Darius.

He does.

Has he told ye this?

In so many words, yes.

Demetri sighed heavily. *What am I to do, especially with the new admirer here, making doe eyes at my lover? Where is he from, anyway? Look at those clothes. They are practically threadbare.*

Do not make fun of those who have less than ye, Demetri.

You're beginning to sound like Mother now.

Be that as it may, Remont invited the boy personally. It is not right to take it out on him solely.

Do you think Remont invited him just to anger me?

I think ye already know the answer.

The guest suddenly burst into song, his voice surprisingly loud and booming for someone so slight of frame. He walked toward the piano, rested a hand on it as he gazed at Remont with obvious interest.

Demetri rolled his eyes. *For the love of God!*

Worse still, Remont grinned from ear to ear.

If he sits on the bench next to him, I will tear his head from his body.

Darius laughed then, the sound vibrating in Demetri's ears. Gabrielle elbowed him, and Darius covered with a cough.

And now the boy was on the prowl again, his steps taking him directly behind Remont.

He had better not . . .

The dark-eyed devil placed a hand on Remont's shoulder, and Demetri nearly came out of his skin.

Do not do it, Demetri. He wants ye to react, else he would not do it.

You think the boy knows Remont and I are lovers?

Darius shrugged. *I doubt he knows the truth, especially since Remont personally invited the boy here.*

Perhaps I should call an old lover to Scotland as well? Will that put me on more equal footing? Or no, I know. Let me send for Lord Whitcomb's whore, the very one Remont detests so much.

Did ye ever wonder if perhaps that is exactly what Remont wants? He yearns to be the only one in your life, brother. Ye have never been faithful, and he has accepted that, but now he grows weary.

Then why does he not leave me and give us both peace?

Because he does not know how to. That is what he is trying to do. Prove that he too is desirable. That he can have lovers, just as ye do.

He was with another couple not long before we left for Scotland.

Only because ye were with Whitcomb's mistress. And perhaps he wanted to see for himself why ye stray. Maybe he found the experience less than gratifying.

His heart skipped a beat. *Do you think that is the case?*

Lord, he hoped so.

I suppose ye should be asking yourself if ye can live with only one lover. If ye cannot, then I suggest ye let Remont go. He will survive, just as ye will survive.

I am with those others to feed, Darius. Just as you do.

Feeding and making love are two different beasts now, aren't they?

Yes and no.

Can you have one without the other?

Demetri shifted on his feet, glanced at the duo at the piano, who seemed so content. Remont grinned boyishly as he looked up at the younger man whose hand still rested on his shoulder.

Now that Darius brought up the subject about feeding and making love, perhaps that was exactly the problem. Making love was just a part of feeding. He had never thought much about it, save he could feed two desires at one time.

But love was never involved in the act, ever. Just sex and drinking blood.

Is Remont not enough for you?

I never thought about it before.

Well, I think ye had best start thinking about it, brother. Before it is too late. You have your answer, Demetri. Either be with Remont—and only Remont—or let him go.

I cannot imagine my life without him.

You might not be able to imagine your life without him, but what about imagining your life without your many lovers? Can you remain faithful to Remont?

He frowned. *I suppose I could.*

Then perhaps you need to tell him that. Tell him what is in your heart. If you don't, then there could come a time when someone else beats you to it.

He had never been attracted to another person the way he'd been attracted to Remont. His maker's beauty had taken his breath away from the moment he had spotted him at the loch.

Once Remont had made him, Demetri had embraced his many gifts. He loved everything about being a vampire. The hedonistic lifestyle, the power, the strength. It had been like an aphrodisiac. All his senses had heightened as well.

But perhaps the very things Demetri loved about the dark gift were the qualities Remont disliked.

TWENTY-FOUR

Gabrielle ran through the woods, her heart pounding hard against her ribs.

Daring a glance over her shoulder, she couldn't see her pursuer, but she could hear him.

The brush rustled, and she knew he drew closer by the second.

Run Gabrielle!

Her mother's voice called out to her over and over again. A tree branch scraped Gabrielle's face, but she refrained from crying out.

Sinister laughter echoed in her ears, taunting her. "I killed your uncle, and now I'll kill you!"

Sutherland!

Before she could scream, her feet left the ground and her back made contact with a tree. The fingers at her throat tightened, squeezing the breath from her.

She struggled against him, pushing at his heavy chest, but he was too strong. Gasping for breath, she knew he would kill her, just as he had killed his other wives.

Gabrielle awoke with a start and touched her throat as she fought for breath. When would the nightmares ever stop? If the dreams were not about Rose and Darius, then they were about her uncle and Sutherland.

Something bad was about to happen. She knew it, felt it with an intuition that had her on edge. She found it difficult to even eat.

Darius and Demetri had gone out for a ride. He had asked her to join them, but she had refrained, given Demetri's solemn mood, no doubt brought on by Remont's absence.

So she had gone to the bedchamber she shared with Darius to read. But her mind kept drifting, and she found reading impossible.

Hopefully Darius would return soon. Lighting the candle on her bedside table, she continued her task, lighting all the candles in the room, before walking to the window. Heavy shutters covered the windows, but at night they were opened. Gabrielle looked out, and saw very little beyond the manor's entrance, where torches flickered, casting shadows upon the manicured lawns.

From the corner of her eye, she saw a man standing near the garden, just out of range of the light.

Her heart jolted. Was it Darius or Demetri?

No, this person was not as tall, or as slender. Indeed, it did not look like the groom either.

The man turned, and she saw him in profile. Her mouth went dry. Merciful heavens, was that Sutherland?

She stepped back from the window, hoping he had not seen her. Perhaps her mind was playing tricks on her. Yes, that could be it, especially since she'd just dreamt about him.

It was probably just a servant. To her relief, a groom stepped out, and she released the breath she'd been holding.

The door opened behind her and she jumped.

Darius smiled. "Sorry, love. I didn't mean to startle ye."

She tried to smile, but failed.

"What is it?" She could see the concern in his blue eyes.

"Nothing, I just didn't expect you back so soon."

His brows furrowed. "Ye are disappointed I'm back early?"

"No, not at all," she said, reaching for his hand, enfolding it within her own. Already she felt a large weight lift from her shoulders.

"Did ye rest?"

"A little."

His thumb brushed against hers. "Ye look so tired, Gabrielle."

"It's only the nightmares."

"I wish I could take them away for ye."

"I know you would."

"What would ye like to do? Both Demetri and Remont are gone, so we have the entire place to ourselves."

"I prefer to stay here, in this room."

He stared at her so intently it made her nervous. "I have something I wish to discuss with ye."

Taking both her hands in his own, he kissed each and held her gaze. "Do you want to stay with me, Gabrielle?"

"Of course."

"Forever?"

Her pulse skittered. "Forever?"

"Yes."

"But is that possible with you being . . . what you are, and me being what I am?"

"We can have whatever life we choose."

If only it could be. A human and a vampire, living harmoniously.

But that was a fantasy. It could never be. Like her mother said, Gabrielle would grow old, but Darius would always remain the same age, never changing. She would go on to die, and he would continue to live.

What kind of life would that be?

As she looked at him she realized how pale he was, the purple beneath his eyes even more obvious. He had not fed, and she wondered if she was the reason he didn't. "Your skin is so pale, Darius. Are you well?"

"My skin is always pale."

"But it is even more so now."

"Do not concern yerself, lass."

"But I worry about you."

This seemed to please him. She sat and pulled him down onto the settee, and he laughed, the sound rolling over her like a warm blanket.

She loved the feel of his hard body against hers. In fact, everything about him excited her. Apparently he felt the same way, since his thick cock pressed hard against her belly.

He kissed her softly at first, but grew more urgent.

"Should we lock the door?"

"It doesn't lock," he said, matter-of-factly.

"Should we push a cabinet in front of the door?" she asked.

"Nay, I think not."

"I am willing to take the chance."

"If someone walks in, I assure ye that my servants are discreet. Your honor will never be questioned."

She lifted a brow.

He smiled then, and kissed her softly.

Her thighs fell open as he deepened the kiss, and she arched her hips, loving the feel of his hard cock pressed against her sensitive flesh.

He caught the hem of her gown and brought the skirt up, his long nails brushing against the tender skin there.

Unbuttoning his pants with one hand, he unleashed his cock and thrust home in one, smooth motion.

"So tight," he whispered against her ear. "So hot."

"So big," she replied, and he laughed, his breath hot against her neck, his teeth gently scraping there.

She went still, her nails digging into his broad shoulders. *Do it! Bite me and make me what you are. Let me live forever with you.* How she longed to say those words, but she found she couldn't say them aloud. Why could she not say them aloud?

He kissed her neck, at the pulse beating wildly, and then he moved lower to her chest, and lower still to the swell of her breasts. He placed kiss after kiss there.

"Make me what you are," she whispered, tears welling in her eyes.

His entire body went still, and he looked up at her, his blue eyes questioning. "Ye do not know what ye ask."

"Make me what you are, Darius."

He moved then, in and out of her, his long cock filling her so completely she could not possibly take any more, then withdrawing, leaving just the crown inside her, before impaling her again and again with even, fluid strokes.

"Darius."

"Hmm," he said, dipping his head for another kiss. "What is it, love?"

"If you will not make me what you are, then at least take my blood."

He stopped in midstroke, looking down at her. "I can't."

"Do it."

"I fear I will not be able to stop."

"I trust you."

He moved again, and she could see the indecision on his face.

As her body reached for orgasm, she cried out; at the same time she felt the sharp pinch at her neck, and the wonderful sensations she had experienced before rolled through her, but more intense and powerful, shooting her like an arrow up to the sky.

Remont hadn't seen Demetri for hours. He had been acting strange all evening, and Remont knew the cause. Duncan, the young man from the village who he'd ran into earlier in the day. He'd paid the boy to deliver items to the manor, and he had done so for one reason and one reason only.

So Demetri could see him.

Remont ran a hand through his hair. Why had he stooped so low in order to make his lover jealous? Knowing Demetri, he was at this moment fucking some random man or woman. Some things never changed, and Remont had finally come to the conclusion that Demetri would never be faithful.

Which meant Remont must move on. Once he was sure Gabrielle and Darius were safe from Sutherland's threat, he would return to

Venice and move his things out of the villa. Who knows, perhaps he might move back to his native Austria. Find a home in the Alps and hopefully find a mate who would not mind spending eternity with him . . . and only him.

If only Demetri didn't hold his heart and soul.

Damn him!

A friend of his had said she always fell in love with the one man who hurt her most. The quintessential alpha male, who had the ability to bring her to her knees.

Remont closed his eyes, concentrating on Demetri, hoping to find him. But nothing came. He walked the perimeter of the manor, and even the gardens, where Demetri often found solace, but he seemed to have disappeared.

After a thorough search of the surrounding area, he went back to the manor and to his room. To his surprise, lying there in the middle of the bed was Demetri.

Remont's heart gave a sharp tug. Relief rushed through him, followed by anger.

He stared at his lover who lay flat on his back, one hand resting on his naked stomach, several fingers reaching beyond the band of his breeches, the other hand flung out to his side.

How lovely he was in slumber, the sharp lines of his face relaxed. His long, thick eyelashes casting shadows on his high cheekbones. His perfectly formed lips were slightly open as he breathed, and he had a cleft in his strong, masculine chin.

Remont's heart constricted as his gaze shifted lower, over Demetri's wide chest that rose and fell with each breath. The defined ridges in his abdomen clenched with each inward breath. And his gaze moved lower still, to the defined bulge in his breeches.

Need swept through Remont. He had not fed for days now. True, he could have fed from Duncan, or any number of people in the village, but he had not felt so inclined.

Now he salivated for it, particularly the blood of his lover. The man he loved above all others.

Demetri let out a groan and said something Remont could not make out. He always talked in his sleep, but they were usually unintelligible words.

"I want him," Demetri said, or at least that's what it sounded like to Remont.

Remont's stomach tightened. Exactly *who* did he want? He inched closer to the bed, listening intently.

Demetri's hand slipped lower into his pants, cupping his cock, which swelled past the band of his pants. He shifted his hips.

Remont swallowed against the lump in his throat and turned toward the door.

He was one step from the door when Demetri said, "Come to bed, Remont."

He should have known he was awake. *Devious bastard.*

"No more devious than you," he said, his voice silky soft.

Remont bit into his bottom lip, one hand on the knob.

A second later, Demetri was there, standing behind him, his body heat emanating into Remont's back, even though their bodies did not touch.

Remont rested his forehead against the door. "I am not tired."

Demetri's long-fingered hand settled on Remont's shoulder. "I'm not either."

His head was screaming "don't do it," yet his body and soul were telling him something altogether different.

Demetri's other hand came to rest on Remont's hip, his long fingers ran up and down his side, sending delicious shivers throughout his body.

"I thought you left the manor."

"I can't leave Darius when he needs me. You know that."

"Is that the only reason you stay?"

His hands fell away. "No."

Typical Demetri. He would not make this easy. He never did. Well, Remont wouldn't either.

He turned, and Demetri's hand was suddenly at the back of his neck, pulling him closer, so close their lips nearly touched. "I want you, Remont. I burn with my need for you."

Remont's legs felt weak, but he would not give in so easily.

"Do you feel what you do to me?" Demetri asked, taking Remont's hand in his and pressing it against his hard cock. His blue eyes were darker than usual, and the lids heavy. His long dark hair was ruffled, as though he'd run his hands through it one too many times. He had never looked so sexy.

"Yes," Remont said, his voice sounding lower and huskier than usual.

Demetri kissed his neck.

Remont closed his eyes. "Demetri, not—"

Demetri's lips were inches from Remont's. "Do you want me to leave?"

"You do this only to torment me."

"Torment you? Who is the one bringing a young man from the village to your friend's home? Hell, I am surprised you did not make love on the piano while you were at it."

Remont opened his eyes and noticed Demetri actually trembled. Indeed, he had never seen Demetri so jealous . . . and oddly, it pleased him.

"He came to deliver items I had purchased at market."

"And those items fit into one bag. Are you so weak and frail you cannot lift a bag?"

"I enjoyed his companionship."

"You *enjoyed* his companionship?"

"Yes."

"In what ways?"

"In—"

Demetri's lips covered Remont's, his fingers weaving through his hair. A second later he pulled away, but only a fraction. "I want you, Remont. I've always wanted you, and I will not let anyone else take you from me. If you don't want me, tell me as much and I will walk out that door and you will never see me again."

His fierce eyes narrowed as he watched Remont, awaiting an answer.

Remont thought back over all the years they'd been together, and knew Demetri could not change. And he was just stubborn enough to walk out the door and never come back.

"You're wrong, Remont. I can change. I want you. I've told you that over and over. I love you. I've told you that, too, and Lord knows I've tried to show you. I'm guilty of not showing it enough, I know that."

"But that was never the issue, Demetri. I want you to love me enough so that you do not need another. But that is not possible, and I know that now."

"I love you, Remont." Demetri kissed him, his lips soft, but he sensed the urgency. "I want you, and only you. I'll not share another person's bed. I won't. I'm guilty of it, I know, but I want you to know that it was always about the feeding. Always, and never about the passion. No one can make me crazy with need the way you do . . . in and out of the bedchamber."

How Remont wanted to believe him.

"Give me a chance, Remont. If I do you wrong again, then you have every right to walk away and never look back." He brushed his thumbs along his cheeks. "Please give me this chance. I love you and only you. Let me prove myself to you."

Remont stared into the blue eyes that pleaded with him. The handsome face he had committed to memory the very night they met. He remembered Darius saying that he and Gabrielle belonged together—just as Remont and Demetri belonged together.

Remont leaned in and kissed his lover softly. He embraced him tightly, loving the feel of his hard body flush against his own. "I love you, too, Demetri. I love you, too."

TWENTY-FIVE

Gabrielle sat on the hill overlooking the manor and the village below. She had not gone to the very top where she and Darius had made love. It was a windy day, and even now her hair whipped about her, making her pull the hood of her cloak over her head.

The fear on Darius's face when he had awoken to the sun shining on him had made her angry with herself for not having warned him. After all, the sun was his enemy, and he had lived in fear of it for over five hundred years. But she had wanted to see the look on his face after living so long in the dark, and what a look it had been. One of exultation and immense joy. A look she would never forget for as long as she lived.

If only it had been possible to give him more time to savor the sun. To spend an entire day, now that would have been perfect; but her mother always reminded her that one must never become too greedy.

Plus, using her gifts, in whatever way, exhausted her. She had slept a few hours after making love to Darius, but she had awoken, unable to fall back asleep. She wanted Darius to turn her into what he was. It would be the only way she would ever have peace.

But he would not hear of it. No, he would bite her, and make her believe that perhaps he had turned her, but every time she raced to the nearest mirror, she found that the bite marks had disappeared and there was no mark across her soul.

Unable to sleep, she'd dressed and headed up the hill, but not too far. In fact, she'd best get back before Darius woke and found her gone.

"Well look who we have here."

Gabrielle's blood ran cold.

She knew that voice too well.

The tip of a blade pressed against her neck.

"You have been a bad little girl, have you not, Gabrielle?"

She swallowed, a difficult feat with cold steel pressing against her throat.

"You've become quite the whore since you've left me. I didn't pay for damaged goods, you slut."

She forced herself not to move, or to respond.

"Oh yes, I've watched you fuck him. Right here on this hillside. What, coming back to relive the event?"

He pressed against her, and bile rose in her throat. He reeked of sweat, ale, and stale body odor.

He began fumbling with his breeches, and Gabrielle knew he would rape her right here and now and then kill her.

"Will you sigh for me now, like you did for MacLeod?"

Despite the fact that the blade now cut into her throat, she pushed hard against him, surprising him enough that he lost his hold on her.

She stumbled, fell on her hands and knees, and managed to get to her feet, but not before Sutherland grabbed one of her ankles, his nails digging into her skin.

Looking over her shoulder, her stomach churned seeing the murderous gleam in his eyes. His pants had fallen down to his knees, his small cock peeking out from his drawers. She screamed.

He smiled lasciviously. "You want that, don't you, girl? Ah yes, once you get a bit of cock, you will never turn your back on it."

Repulsed, she managed to pull from his grasp again and lifting her skirts, ran for the manor, screaming as loud as she could.

The sun still shone and she knew she would have to make it inside in order for Darius, his brother, or Remont to help her. Plus, when they slept during the day, it was almost a trancelike sleep, one that was hard to wake from.

She dared a glance back and saw Sutherland right behind her, huffing and puffing.

"Get back here, whore!" he said, his voice slurred. "I will take what I am owed."

She rushed through the courtyard, up the manor steps, and just then the door flung open and Darius was there, his eyes wide. He winced as the sun hit his arm, burning his flesh.

"Sutherland is here," she cried out, rushing into the manor, pulling him back inside and shutting the door behind her. "I was sitting on the hill, and out of nowhere there he was. He has been watching us. He knew we'd made love on the hill."

She glanced down and saw the red burn mark across his hand and wrist. "You are hurt."

"It will heal. What of ye?" His gaze shifted to her neck, where he pushed her hair aside. "He cut you." He shook his head. "The son of a bitch will die."

"Open this fuckin' door, or I will blow a bloody hole through it," Sutherland said, his voice booming.

"The sun is setting, sir," Jacob said, coming from the study. "Shall I get your sword?"

Darius stepped outside and nodded. "Aye."

Minutes later Jacob appeared with sword in hand. "Wake my brother and Remont. Tell them to look after Gabrielle."

"I will not leave you."

He cupped her face in his hands. "I must do this, Gabrielle. I have to end this, here and now. I refuse to live the rest of our lives looking over our shoulders."

She kissed him, then backed up toward the staircase.

"Go to our room. I shall come after ye when I'm done." He would not open the door until she left, so she turned and walked up the stairs, terrified she'd never see him again.

The door opened, and she heard Sutherland. "Where is the whore?"

Darius stepped outside and closed the door firmly.

"She is no whore, and ye will do well to remember that."

"That whore is my betrothed, MacLeod, and I demand satisfaction."

"She will not be marrying ye, Sutherland, because she's marrying me."

"Over my dead body."

"I am happy to oblige."

Gabrielle felt rather than heard someone behind her, and glanced up to see Remont and Demetri. Remont put a finger to his lips, while Demetri kept walking down the stairs. He ripped a sword off the wall display and continued out the door to join his brother.

The sound of metal against metal resonated in the air as Demetri rushed outside.

"He will be fine," Remont said, pulling her into his embrace. "You forget he is a warrior. Sutherland has no idea what he's gotten himself into, or with whom."

"Sutherland has a bad reputation. He's killed many people, my uncle included."

"Are you sure?"

"I had a premonition earlier today, and then another when I saw Sutherland."

"As horrible as this might sound, your uncle had it coming. He sealed his fate when he took money from Sutherland."

"I cannot stand here and not know what's happening."

"Nor I," Remont said, taking her by the hand and opening the door.

For his age, Sutherland had more agility than Darius had expected.

Sutherland nodded toward Demetri. "Your brother is here. Will I have to fight the both of you?"

"Nay, I am merely here to make sure you fight fair, Sutherland."

Sutherland shook his head. "You worry that I will fight unfairly?"

"Aye, your dead wives can attest to your reputation."

Ignoring Demetri, Sutherland lunged again, missing Darius's side by a mere fraction.

It had been centuries since he'd taken up a sword, but it came back to him quickly enough.

Darius attacked, beating Sutherland down with each stroke. The older man fended him off well enough, but he grew weary, sweat pouring off his head, his breathing becoming labored.

Even better, he could see the fear in the older man's eyes. He knew he was going to die.

"Kill him!" Demetri yelled, looking like he wanted a go at Sutherland himself.

Sutherland stumbled, but caught himself before falling. He moved quickly; a second later his pistol was drawn and he pulled the trigger.

Darius heard the bullet make contact a moment later, heard Gabrielle's sharp cry.

"Oh God!"

"No!" Remont cried, his voice full of the same dread Darius felt all the way to the bone.

Darius could not bring himself to turn around, but he did see the satisfied smile on Sutherland's face, the triumph there a full second before Darius took him by the neck, his fingers squeezing his throat.

The smile soon faded as he struggled for breath, the sound of bones crushing in his ears. "Remember my face as ye burn in hell," Darius said between clenched teeth.

Blood flowed from Sutherland's mouth, nose, and eyes and he gasped for breath, his feet kicking, and then fell limp.

Darius released him, the man falling in a heap to the ground.

He turned to Gabrielle, who lay on the grass beside Remont. Demetri glanced up at him, concern in his eyes. "Brother, it is not good."

Darius went down beside him. Gabrielle's face had turned ashen, her lips a blue hue. Death was minutes, perhaps seconds, away.

The bullet had entered her body, just right of her heart. Blood covered the bodice of her gown and seeped into the ground beneath her.

"Darius, you can save her," Demetri urged.

"Make her one of us," Remont said, putting a hand on his shoulder. "If you don't, she will die."

"But she will be reborn as one of us."

Remont and Demetri shared a look, and Darius knew he only had seconds to decide. Could he lose the woman he loved more than life twice in one lifetime?

The answer was a resounding no.

"Forgive me," Darius said, biting Gabrielle's neck, her blood flowing into his mouth. It tasted so sweet, so pure.

Her body had already gone limp, and now her heartbeat faded fast. He had never changed anyone before, and he thought perhaps he'd been too late, until he felt a gentle hand on his shoulder.

"Darius, she sleeps for now," Remont said. "In a couple of days she will wake, wanting blood, and you must supply that blood."

Darius trembled from head to toe. He had done the one thing he swore he would never do. To the woman he swore he would never hurt.

"Some promises are made to be broken, Darius," Remont said, his voice gentle. "Just as I made you, and saved you from death, you have saved Gabrielle from death. She wanted this anyway."

"But what if she does not wish this life after she becomes one of us? What if she hates me for having made her into a creature of the night?"

"You learned to accept your gifts."

"Aye, but I lived with guilt for years."

Remont smiled softly. "As did I, my friend. I was made without giving consent, and I did the same to you."

"And I wanted Remont to make me into what he was," Demetri added, going down on his haunches across from Darius. "You had no choice, brother. Accept it. You may be surprised by Gabrielle's reaction."

TWENTY-SIX

Gabrielle had never been so cold in her life.

Even her teeth chattered.

Not only did she feel cold, but every muscle in her body ached. What in the world had caused such pain?

She opened her eyes slowly, recognizing the canopy above Darius's bed immediately. *Scotland.* At least she was still in Scotland.

Had she fallen ill?

She turned, expecting to see Darius, but it looked like the bed had not been slept in at all. She pulled the bed curtain aside, saw the shutters on the windows.

Something was different.

The room itself had not changed, but she saw so much more. The fine stitching in the tapestry on the wall, the textures. Sounds were more pronounced and even the sheets beneath her were softer.

She sniffed at the air. *Heather.* So rich and fragrant.

She glanced at the mirror for a moment, at the side table beside it, and then her gaze backtracked to the mirror.

Her heart missed a beat as she slid from the bed and approached the mirror.

She began trembling from deep within as she stared at her reflection. A black mark ran across her chest.

And it all came back to her.

Sutherland attacking her on the hillside. A blade at her throat, and her running for the castle, screaming Darius's name.

And Darius fighting Sutherland.

Sutherland had lost, but he had shot Gabrielle.

She had lay dying, thinking of all the years she would never have with the man she loved. A man she adored more than life itself.

A bright light had beckoned, and she'd had the sensation of rising higher and higher.

Until something sharp penetrated the soft skin of her neck.

Her heart missed a beat.

Darius had made her a vampire.

A creature of the night.

And that is why she was able to hear everything, see everything so differently, smell everything. Indeed, every sense had become amplified.

Feeling light-headed she sat down in the nearest chair. Where was Darius?

"Ye are finally awake."

She opened her eyes, and Darius stood looking down at her with those lovely ice blue eyes of his. Tall, dark, and so handsome, it made her heart ache.

"Yes."

"I could not bring myself to watch ye die, Gabrielle. I suppose I am too selfish. Having lost ye once, I had no desire to do so again. I hope ye can come to forgive me."

"I would have died had it not been for you."

"Yes, but what if ye do not want this life?"

"I wish to be with you."

He closed his eyes for a moment, smiled. "Thank ye."

"I would have done the same if the tables had been turned. I could not have allowed you to die if I could prevent it."

"Even if it meant living in darkness for all eternity?"

"Yes, even if it meant living in darkness for all eternity."

Relief shone in his fierce blue eyes.

"I love you, Darius. So very much."

Tears shone in his eyes. "I love ye, too, Gabrielle."

He pulled her up into his arms, and she could hear the fierce pounding of his heart.

She lifted her face to his and he kissed her with an intensity that left her breathless.

Along with the longing came a deeper ache. An ache she did not understand.

He put her at arm's length for a moment, looked into her eyes. "Ye must drink, Gabrielle. Ye are weak." He took off his shirt, tossed it aside.

Cutting his chest with a small dagger, he pulled her closer. "Drink."

The scent of his blood filled her nostrils, and she licked her lips as she leaned in and tasted him. Instantly the blood rushed through her veins. Her fingernails dug into the skin of his back as she continued to drink, and he moaned, his cock hard against her stomach.

She was shocked by the thrill that raced through her, the energy and exhilaration. And not just from the sustenance of his blood, but from the act itself.

He whispered to her, words she did not understand, in a language she could not quite grasp.

But perhaps one day she would.

"That is enough, Gabrielle," he said, cupping her face.

She noticed he looked paler than moments before, but he also looked pleased. He dipped his head, kissed her again.

How strange it was to taste his own blood on her lips. She had taken to drinking easily enough, and Darius hoped she meant what she'd said and that she did not blame him in the future.

Her hand brushed over his buttocks. The other splayed against his chest, and the cut there that she had kissed.

"I can't wait to spend the rest of eternity with you," she said, putting all his fears to rest.

"Marry me, Gabrielle. Say that ye will be my wife."

She grinned. "Again?"

"Aye, again."

She nodded. "Yes, my love. I'll be your wife . . . again."